IMPERFECT BLADES

A GRITTY URBAN FANTASY SERIES - BOOK 8 OF THE IMPERFECT CATHAR
C.N. ROWAN

CONTENTS

To Craig.

A true friend who has always believed in me and cheered me on.

Good souls are ever a blessing in this life.

CHAPTER ONE

AUCH, 29 OCTOBER, PRESENT DAY

This town is an appropriate place to start. The sentence "Auch shit, what a mess we are in" fits perfectly.

Honestly, I miss the distraction of dying.

Allow me to clarify. Dying is no fun. Hurts like fuck nine times out of ten. And you can guarantee the tenth time is the most inopportune one because it means someone's poisoned you or murdered you so efficiently, you don't have time to feel any of the usual agony that really should accompany a body's final moments. Which normally means they got the drop on you. And that almost certainly means you wish they hadn't and doubtless will now have to pull on your new body like your big boy pants and go hunt them down. Recover whatever they've stolen or avenge whoever they've killed. A victim who doesn't have the advantage of popping back up in a new body like I do.

Like I *did*.

Thing is, I may still have it. The...god? Higher vibrational being? Whatever the entity was I met a few times in that weird shack outside of life and who had the power to send me back to this plane of existence...they very deliberately chose not to tell me if I get a do-over if I kick the bucket this time or not.

So now I'm having to do something that does not come naturally to me in the slightest.

I'm having to be *careful*.

Although, by the number of dead bodies currently littered through the town of Auch, you might find that hard to believe.

The deaths have paid off though. Gil, our friend, the now non-magical kid who saved all our bacon in Lourdes by stabbing Melusine in the chest, is safe, and the demonic possession has been driven from his body.

Sadly, the deaths of the possessed standing between him and us weren't the only price to pay.

The Alp's hat. The headgear of a peculiar fae creature from Bavaria that we – well, that we just straight up robbed, if I'm being honest. Like the characters from the latest *Rockstar* console game, and I'm not feeling wonderful about that. Well, that hat burned up while fighting the demon essence coursing through Gil. It normally would have turned him into an alp as well, but with the two energies fighting for control, they cancelled each other out.

Problem is, that hat was also keeping demon energy from taking over Isaac, my mentor and father by all but blood.

And judging by the black mess crawling up Isaac's arm? The amount of time we have left before it swallows him whole is limited. Last time we had months. Months he wasted by hiding it from me, trying to find a solution on his own.

We don't have months till it reaches his head and his heart. We'll be lucky if we have days.

And that's why I miss the distraction of dying. It kept me on my toes. Bam, dead! Then popping back up in a new body. Where am I? What's going on? What physical shell am I dressed in this time? How long is it going to take for exercise combined with my magic to reshape this mass of previously dead fat and muscle and get it fighting fit again?

Questions. *Distractions.*

Instead of which, I have to be here, in the present, fully and totally. I can't take a quick breather by getting killed and worrying about simple things like making once-dead lungs remember how to suck in air.

Nope. Instead I'm stuck watching Isaac's life get eaten away before my eyes.

It's for the best. We don't have time to mess around. But I'd sure love something to distract me from all the pain and worry that's packing into my heart; it's going to burst if anything else gets added to it, good or bad. It just can't take any more than it's already weighted with.

Aicha, my sister soul, is missing in another dimension, and our mission to find her has completely stalled thanks to these fucking demons and their attacks on Isaac and the rest of us.

Why they seem so obsessed with Isaac, I've no idea. I can only assume it's the whole "he's sharing his body with an angel" thing. Everything we've learned so far has been a shock, to say the least. As far as either of us knew – as far as the angel 'Zac shares his body with chose to tell him – the angels' and demons' rivalry of the Abrahamic s was nonsense, an exaggeration. Now it's turning out to be far closer to the truth. A rivalry extending back over the millennia, a rift between a species divided. I only have to look at how those sort of divisions work in my own species to imagine what impact that could have. Plus, demons were supposed to be ineffective against angelic power, an irritating gnat's bite at worst.

The demon essence infecting Isaac, an oily goo creeping through his veins, consuming him slowly, working its way up his arm towards his heart, gives the lie to that one too.

Isaac rolls his sleeve down, tugging it tightly into place. His eyes flick to Gil, and he gives his head a sharp, tiny shake. The message is clear. *Leave it be. Don't worry him any more than he already is.*

Okay. He doesn't need to know about it for the moment. 'How are you feeling now, Gil? Any better?' He's regained his feet, but he's still looking more than a little thrown by the whole encounter. He's blinking, making occasional head movements, half-shakes like when you're trying to dislodge water from your ear after a plunge in a swimming pool. I'm not a hundred percent convinced he knows precisely where he is yet. I'm absolutely sure he doesn't remember what's going on.

'I think so, Paul, yeah.' His gaze drifts off towards the horizon. It's a spectacular view. Auch Cathedral holds a commanding position on top of the hill the town grew up around, but I think he has things other than the verdant scenery to worry about. Maybe he needs a distraction too. Understandable after the horror of being possessed.

Sadly, I don't have the luxury of time to allow him to process it all, to deal with what's happened and get his shit together. We've saved him. I'm extremely glad. Chalk a win up in the Team Bonhomme column on the blackboard. But my priority is sorting out Isaac.

'Can you remember anything? About what happened? Or...' I trail off.

I want to ask him if he can remember the demon's thoughts. That's what I'm really hoping for. Some kind of stroke of incredible fortune, where as a side effect of getting possessed, he got an unfiltered look into the demon's mind, seeing all the bastard's plans laid out. Ideally with carefully labelled diagrams and explicatory notes.

Of course, while that might happen in films, it doesn't tend to happen in real life. There'll be no equivalent of zooming in on some grainy group of pixels from a car park security camera and miraculously cleaning them up to give us a line for line treatise on the villain's evil plan.

Nope. They shared a connection, but no demon is stupid enough to allow unfiltered access. All we can hope for is that a little bit of *something* has leaked through.

'I remember the...whatever that is.' He gestures at the shaggy monstrosity lying in a pool of its own blood, its metal-like horns glinting in the sunlight.

'The Warabouc.' A nasty magical creature, supposedly unkillable. Turned out the trick was while we couldn't kill it, it could kill itself. There's always a get-out clause with magic.

'And...and I remember the worms...' His voice cracks, breaks as the words falter.

'Enough, Paul!' Isaac's by him in a moment, his arm around his shoulders. 'It's all right, lad. Just breathe. No need to go back there again.' He fixes me with a harsh glare. Bit unfair considering I'm doing it to save him, but I get the message. Stop haranguing the traumatised kid for answers he doesn't have.

Easier said than done, though, for one simple reason. I don't have anything else to go on. No other clue, no other lead. We've won a victory – got back Gil, killed the Warabouc, slew a load of poor possessed simiots, magical ape-like creatures who were forced to attack us. But none of that really helps us with the bigger game plan. With a lot of effort, we avoided killing all the simiots, but too many of them still died. We've no idea who this demon is, why they've come to our plane of existence, or what they want.

The startling vibration of my phone in my pocket breaks me from my frustrated reverie. It also makes me nearly leap out of my skin, but that's beside the point. Unless the point is "I'm so high-strung right now, you could pluck my nerves like a well-tuned harp". I look at the screen; it's the number of the Mother – witch-in-chief of the Sistren of Bordeaux coven and my new bestie since she made us go on a stupid fucking mission that got my magic eaten (thankfully, I got it back) and got us stabbed in the back by the Sistren's representative. Who happened to be my dead-for-centuries wife, come back to life as a fae. Because that's how my weird little headfuck of an existence works.

I hit call accept and get straight to the point. 'Did you manage to clean up the mess?' "The mess" in question is the simiots, living and dead, we left scattered in our wake as we battled our way to the cathedral. Somehow, the demon had got all the local inhabitants to clear out, setting us up for the showdown with the Warabouc. But we've no idea how long that's going to last nor what's going to happen now that particular plan didn't work out for him. The locals might come wandering back in, or governmental authorities might pour into the town. The latter would be spectacularly bad news considering the absolute fucking slaughterhouse we made of some of the streets, having filled them with barbecued flaming apes. And as they were already on fire by choice and magic prior to us frying them with a shitload of electricity, they're not something I particularly want the government to get their hands on.

'There has been a collection made. Living and dead, they're safely secured.' The Mother's voice is as serene and as unruffled as ever despite the whole "getting a call asking her to collect previously possessed fire apes". I guess her life has enough weird in it to stop that from fazing her too.

'Any idea what happened here to get rid of the locals?' I still don't know if they're even alive. The idea that the demon or the Warabouc might have slaughtered all the inhabitants of this medium-size town is crawling all over my brain like a drunken centipede.

'There was a government announcement. Possibly a gas leak or explosion risk. With that, there was a working, dark energy that, apparently, persuaded even the most contrary to follow the instructions.'

I don't even try to hide the sigh of relief. They're alive. That'll do for the moment. 'What are they saying now about it?'

A pause hangs between us for a moment, no less pregnant for the use of phones. 'They aren't. Nobody is mentioning it. There are no further announcements but also no questions. No demands for clarification.'

Good God damn it, that's a hell of a lot of influence the demon is wielding. Persuading authority figures to evacuate a town, getting all the inhabitants to follow along with such a massively disruptive order, then just cancelling it and not having anyone asking questions after? No inquisitive, pissed off locals demanding answers? No French civilians irritated by their government?

I look over at Isaac, who's listening in, grim-faced, to the conversation. 'This was all just a demonstration again, wasn't it?'

He nods, but it's the Mother who replies. 'There is...suggestion that this was the equivalent of a bicep flex. There are stories that need to be shared. Information needed for the coven to help both ourselves and you.'

Understandable. She wants to know exactly what the fuck is going on. Can't blame her. 'No question. I'll give you a ring on the way back to Toulouse, update you on everything. Right now, we need to get packed up and get the fuck out of Dodge before all the locals arrive and wonder why we've trashed their pretty little square.'

I'm about to hang up, but the Mother stops me. 'Wait, Good Man. There's one other thing.'

Of course there is. What are the odds it's good news? 'Go ahead.'

'The simiots. We found markings on them all, both alive and dead.'

Now I perk up. Fuck me. This sounds like that rarest of mythological beasts – a potential clue. The odds might have swung in our favour for once. 'Can you describe them for me?'

'There is a photo coming now, with a strong chance of recognition. There *will* be an explanatory call very shortly, Cathar.' The line goes dead.

Right. Don't forget to call her back unless you want a very *powerful*, very influential ally getting the hump. All jokes aside, our new alliance is massively beneficial, but I'm not stupid enough to believe we're really friends. Not pissing off the Mother is a very good policy indeed.

The phone buzzes in my hand, and I open up the image. Isaac and Gil crowd round, peering at the tiny screen. And I do know it. Though what I don't know is what the hell to make of it.

The symbol is a central diamond, with four compass point lines coming off it. At the end of each is a letter. R at the north point, S at the east, L at the south, and K at the west.

'Karolus,' Isaac mutters. He's right, as per usual.

'Karolus?' Gil's brow furrows. I guess it's not a symbol he's seen. Of course, signum magnus have disappeared these days, and I suspect he's not had much chance to study ancient French history. Isaac and I are just showing our age.

'It's a signature.' I trace my fingers across the centre point, K to the R, then down to the L before ending at the S. 'The diamond in the middle is an A, an O and a U, where they used the letter V for that vowel before. It says Karolus. Latin for Charles.'

Gil doesn't look any more enlightened. 'Who?'

Isaac answers this one. 'The father of Europe himself. Charles The Great. Better known as Charlemagne.'

The legendary King of the Franks, creator of France, arguably, and holy Roman Emperor. Over twelve hundred years ago.

Which doesn't explain why his signature just turned up burned into the skin of a group of possessed, fire-elemental simians who came looking for a rumble with us.

My hoped-for clue raises a whole lot more questions than it answers. Probably because it answers precisely none.

CHAPTER TWO
AUCH, 29 OCTOBER, PRESENT DAY

Charles the Great's signature on the flesh of the simiots? I suppose it's more likely than Charles the Average's or Charles the Rubbish's though.

On the drive back, I call the Mother because I have precisely zero wishes to piss her off. She still owes me for saving her daughter; cleaning up the simiots doesn't scratch the surface. There's nothing she can do to help me in the search for my best friend, Aicha, but I'm hoping this might be more in her wheelhouse. Unfortunately, she has no idea regarding the meaning of Charlemagne's signature but promises to give us a call if inspiration strikes.

We discuss it en route, Isaac and I, batting back possibilities ranging from them being part of some secret cult created to protect his secrets, like something straight out of Dan Brown's shittiest book of plot ideas, to them being a bunch of history buffs who are also into scarification. A hipster's wet dream. It's only after about half an hour that Isaac clocks something, his eyes flicking up to the tiny, little mirror in the sun-visor.

'Are you all right, lad?' I can hear the concern laced through his words. Of course. Gil. He's a quiet kid even at the best of times, but he's been through a heap of trauma, with him remembering enough details, I'm sure he wishes he didn't. I can't see his face, with him sitting behind me and my preference for not performing high-speed explosive crashes right out of *Grand Theft Auto V*, but based on Isaac's tone, he doesn't look well.

'I...' The hesitancy in his tone is clear, but it doesn't sound like trauma. It sounds like someone when they're trying to crack a particularly tricky puzzle, when the crossword solution is just on the tip of their tongue.

'What is it, Gil?' I really want to have a look at him, see what's going on, try to read his features instead of just his voice, especially off a single word. My job is simple though. Drive us home. Get us behind the wards. Worry about the rest after.

'I...I think I remember something. To do with the symbol.'

I avoid swerving wildly off the road and screeching to a halt only because I can hear Aicha's voice in my head, mocking me for being a twat and fucking up the manoeuvre entirely. Me, I might come back from dying if I'm lucky; I might even be able to pull up enough magic to stop me from turning to toast if the car transforms into a fireball. Nithael, the angel inside Isaac, will keep him safe, but Gil? Gil has nothing, no magic to help save him. Outside of the fact that killing your friends isn't the best way to express said friendship, turning him into Barbecued Gil won't help me get the answer he's trying to give me either. Hard to talk when your tongue's been turned to charcoal.

So despite my instincts, I concentrate on driving, gripping the steering wheel's rubber so tight I'm pretty sure I've left grooves in it. I leave it to Isaac to do the delicate questioning, to tease out what we need to know.

'Remember? Are we talking about you, Gil, or...' By the Good God, between all the doubt and careful words, there's an awful lot of conversation trailing off. It's like everyone's just developed an allergy to complete sentences or something. My lack of involvement in said conversation may be making me a tad grumpy.

'Not me. Not...not me.' Apparently, the surety of that fact is enough to get us to a complete sentence. I can understand Gil feeling very definite about that. Poor kid.

'What can you remember?' Isaac's voice is as calm and as gentle as ever, a soothing monotone that promises no pressure. No harm, no foul if you can't remember; just give us whatever you can. Which is exactly why I'm leaving this to him. Me screaming in high-pitched frustration for *all of the fucking answers right now* probably wouldn't work as well.

'The symbol...I seemed to know it. Been wracking my brains ever since.' As always, Gil's words are sparse, deliberate. All carefully chosen. I don't doubt that for someone like him, who prizes self-control so highly, the previous time period must have been an utter nightmare. Not that "demon possession complete with skin-burrowing worms" is ever going to be anyone's idea of a fun Friday night, but I can imagine it must have hit him doubly hard.

'What did you get?' I really don't know how Isaac does it. Actually, thinking about it, he's had to pry information from my over-excited brain for eight hundred years. He's only had two real options dealing with me – to learn to reach a zen-like state of calm at all times or get struck down by a coronary.

'Just...some senses.' The frustration is clear in his tone. 'The demon...it wanted something. A task it had set for the simiots. A task they'd failed, which resulted in them getting the tattoo?'

The question, the doubt is evident as well. I'm not surprised. Demons are on a different vibrational energy plane to us; they live in a dimension that's incomprehensible to our spatially limited understanding of reality.

The demon wasn't trying to communicate with Gil, just dominate him. I'm honestly amazed he got anything out of the connection at all.

Silence falls, and I know we're all ruminating on this fragment Gil pulled from the shit deal he found himself stuck in. Seems to be a specialty of his – getting one over on magical creatures well out of his league. Good on him.

'So what's the connection with Charlemagne then?' Isaac speaks up, breaking the silence. 'What could he be looking for?'

'I don't really know anything about him.' Gil's voice comes from the back.

Of course. He was raised in an abusive religious cult up in the north of France. They were more interested in praying the gay away – and failing that, resorting to extreme forms of torture to attempt the same – than giving him a good education in French history.

'Okay, big picture stuff.' I'm not about to go into all the ins and outs. 'Charlemagne was definitely a real person, although all sorts of legends and apocrypha have sprung up around him. Ruler of the Francs in the eighth century, he united a large swathe of western Europe for the first time since the Romans, earning him the name Father of Europe. Fought the Moors in Spain, I think the Saxons to the north too. Considered by many scholars as the origin of the Arthurian legends – although I think Arthur and Merlin might have something to say about that – but definitely a source of tales of chivalric derring-do and legends of heroism and wonders. Lots of medieval poetry filled with them, not least his adventures with his equivalent of Excalibur, Joyeuse...'

'That's it!' Gil sits up so suddenly, he bangs his knees into the back of my chair, nearly sending us careening into the central railing. 'That's what he was after!'

'Joyeuse?' I can hear the doubt in Isaac's voice. 'Why would he send the simiots after Joyeuse?'

Gil's voice falters. 'Because he felt they were best equipped to seek it out?'

'Really?' Now suddenly none of this is making sense again. 'They're about the last people I'd have chosen. They'd never stand a chance.'

'Why not?' There's a plaintive tone to his words. Of course he doesn't know any of this.

'Because we know where Joyeuse is.' I avoid saying, 'Everybody does,' because Gil's a smart kid. Smart enough and easily hurt enough to read that as meaning, 'So why don't you?' even if that's not exactly what I mean. 'It's in the Louvre, under lock and key.'

'And the simiots would have had even less success trying to penetrate through to the heart of Paris and stealing from the Lutin Prince than they did trying to block our path.'

Isaac's right. Which is why none of this makes sense.

'But...' Again the uncertainty in Gil's voice. Poor bastard. He's rummaging for snatches from a terrible, traumatic event, the little traces left inside his psyche. Precisely zero fun.

'But,' he starts again, 'they definitely weren't looking in Paris. I can't say where, but it was *wild*. Natural. Not the city. Definitely not.'

Okay. Weird. Still, there's an easy way to solve this. I hammer the prerequisite numbers onto the car's touch screen without piling into the lorry that suddenly brakes in front of us, the carried load piled on its bed weaving back and forth. The familiar sound of a calling phone fills the car.

'Hello?' Precise but warm. Understandably cautious. Amazing how much can be carried in a single word.

'Al-Ruhban? It's Paul.' I wince, bracing myself for what's going to come next.

'Paul! Is *Lalla* there too?' There's evident delight in his voice. Delight I'm going to have to destroy.

'No. Aicha's missing. I'll call you back, explain it all properly later.' Easiest thing to do. We need to get moving, get this solved so I can get back to finding a way to rescue her. 'I'll get her back, but we've other problems standing in our way before we can. There's information I need. Can you get hold of Leandre?'

I could ring him myself, of course. I got his number from Al-Ruhban when we were playing at gathering our Infinity Crisis crossover team-up, thinking we'd bring all the combined powers of French Talented to bear on De Montfort before he could destroy the world. If you think I didn't lock those particular digits down safely in my Memory Palace, you're out of your mind, but I'd rather save ringing the Lutin Prince directly for real emergencies. Not least because my ability to savagely mock his mannerisms is limited, whereas his *talented* ability to savagely make my brains explode isn't. For a tidbit of information like this? Better to take a few seconds delay and go through Al-Ruhban. I can always ring him myself afterwards if I don't get the details I need.

'Absolutely!' He's burning with concern and curiosity. I can tell that even without him saying anything else, but the Good God bless him, he sticks to what I've asked him. 'He's been most pleased with me since the whole Scarbo fiasco. Sees how trustworthy I am.'

'Can you give him a call, please? I just need to know something. Is Joyeuse still at the Louvre, and is it safe and guarded?'

'Peculiar.' He muses, obviously lost to the thought for a moment, but then he snaps back. 'Of course, anyhow, anything for you, *saabi*. I'll call him right now, then ring you back.'

He hangs up, and I risk a glance across at Isaac. 'The chances they've managed to get in there?'

'Almost infinitesimally small, lad, but those won't be the only agents the sod can put in play. First, make sure it's there...'

'Second, make sure it's well guarded.' Considering last time we contacted Leandre to tell him to guard something, it was stolen immediately afterwards, hopefully this time he'll be willing to listen properly.

If he has any sense, after our escapade, where Aicha and I evaded capture across the capital, he'll have rethought his security measures entirely. He might have been mistaken about us, having been fed phoney information painting us as the villains of the piece, but we still penetrated all the layers of security supposedly protecting his domain. I'd be amazed if he hasn't spent the past few months redesigning it, beefing it up, and patching up any flaws.

The car speakers start chirping at me, letting me know there's an incoming call.

'Hello?' Al-Ruhban. No surprises there.

'What did you find out?' I don't want to be rude, but I do want to know what the hell is going on, so my patience for small talk and social niceties is significantly diminished. Call it a tribute to my missing best friend.

'Well, the Joyeuse at the Louvre is still there, and Leandre is happy that it's safe and sound.'

And just like that, alarm bells start going off in my head so loudly, it's surprising I even hear myself speak. 'What do you mean, the Joyeuse at the Louvre? I thought there was only one Joyeuse?'

'Ah, well. Yes.' I want to yell at him to stop stalling, but he's obviously not looking forward to relaying whatever it is he has to tell us. 'According to the Prince, that's not the original sword. It's certainly the one that the nobles and names of France have owned for hundreds of years. The ceremonial symbol of power they've taken great delight in adding flourishes to, repairing and replacing bits as needed. But he said, as he owes you, he'll tell you the truth for free.'

Considering the fact that the Prince speaks like a throwback to the eighties trader mania, I bet he said something about 'being solution-orientated and circling back round to a synergistic collective market strategy when he touched base with us' or something equally brain-meltingly appalling. I appreciate Al-Ruhban translating it for us into understandable English.

That still leaves a burning question that needs answering. 'If that's not the real Joyeuse, then where is the original?'

'He has no idea. That's the problem.'

Of course he doesn't. Otherwise, there's no way he'd rest till it was under his auspices

'What does he know?' Worth asking, though I suspect the answer is "diddly squat".

'Only that it's been missing for a thousand years at least. Possibly since the time of Charlemagne himself.'

Otherwise known as diddly squat. Thanks a lot, Leandre.

CHAPTER THREE

TOULOUSE, 29 OCTOBER, PRESENT DAY

Percy Bysshe Shelley said, 'Joy once lost is pain.' Whereas, Joyeuse once lost is a pain. In the backside.

It's only another twenty minutes, give or take, before we make it back to mine. Maybe it's unnecessary paranoia on my part, but ever since the wards came down the first time Isaac succumbed to the demon essence, I'm less happy about being out at his. Not to mention, Isaac's house is within spitting distance of the edge of our boundaries. If they start shrinking again, we could find ourselves outside of the protective circle really, really quickly. Plus, one of their big advantages is that they act as early warning systems. It's not much use them screaming about being penetrated like an eighties porn star, only for the moustache-twirling villain to be at our front door ten seconds later.

My house has been mine for a long time. Since it was built, in fact. I've interwoven my essence into every single brick, every inch of cement. Even if everything else crumbles into ruin around us, this one spot will remain a stronghold. There's no safer place to retreat to and regroup

Or at least, that would be the case if the fucking wards would let us in.

'I don't understand.' I'm standing just inside the hallway. My lounge, with comfy sofas and poofs and pillows that mould themselves instantaneously to the shape of my overly weary noggin are just through *that* door. The kitchen, with real food and even realer whisky is just through *that* entry point. But I can't go. Because Isaac's standing just outside, Gil's arm slung round his shoulders, ready to half-carry him the rest of the way, only to find he can't get through.

'Sorry, lad.' I'd be pleased about the colour in Isaac's face –the embarrassment turning him a lovely shade of pink– if it didn't only highlight how wan and pale he looks when not glowing like a battery-powered beetroot. 'It's this blasted demonic energy.

Oh, fuck. Of course. It's only because I'm so tired, I haven't clocked it. The dark otherworldly poison pulsating through Isaac's arm is hardly going to be welcomed by my wards. No doubt Gil probably has some traces of it clinging to him too, so between the two of them, it's no wonder my personal barriers are giving them both the metaphysical middle finger.

Good God damn it. Which means this isn't the best place to have come to at all. But I'm far too tired — and far too close to a ready supply of decent alcohol – to go traipsing back across to Isaac's right now. So with a little bit of muttering (not actually needed to get the wards down, just me being a grumpy old man), I take down the protections across the doorway temporarily and get them both inside. Then I have to delay getting to drink some booze for even longer while I put them back up

Delay. Drinking. To say I'm not a happy bunny is an understatement. I'm a fucking *Watership Down* bunny, right now. One of the ones with torn ears, missing an eye, working in the bunny gulag. Such a cheery work of children's literature. And let's not mention the film, shall we? Still, it's done. We're here. Of course, as I turn around, my phone goes off, the vibration in my pocket sending shivers down my leg. Pulling it out, I sigh. It's Faust.

I'm not sighing because I don't want to talk to him. Quite the opposite. I desperately want to have a chat with him, fill him and Mephy in on what's going on. I just don't want to do it *now*. In twenty minutes, once I've got a decent swig of whisky into my gullet? Absolutely. Only right now I don't want anything to delay me getting that golden nectar into a glass and from there into my mouth. Once that's done, a conversation can have my full, undivided attention.

I do really need to talk to them both though. And Isaac is even more important to me than alcohol. Truly, a statement to make the hardest of hearts melt. I click accept on the phone.

'Paul?' One of those mind-numbingly stupid questions that even the cleverest of people can ask. It's not like we're back in the days of a dial phone, where a slip of the digit could lead to you talking to some weirdo for half an hour, trying to extricate yourself from their inane ramblings by explaining that they really weren't who you meant to call, and you genuinely don't need to know about either their bunions or why their next-door neighbour's budgerigar is possessed by an Incan demon. I know Huamancantac, by the way. He's a lovely fellow for a demon-slash-god of shit. Literally, the God of Guano for a load of the river people. He was normally happy to oblige, with whatever avian form he picked up along the way. But there's no way he'd hassle some old dear, however much of a nosey parker she was. Plus he's more of a condor kind of a chap than one who would possess a lowly budgie.

'Yes, amazingly, Johannes, by opening your telephone and pressing the number next to the name "Paul Bonhomme", by the modern wonders of elec-trickery, you've been connected to me rather than the Sarcastic Magic User Hotline. Truly, it's a miracle.'

Look, I know I might be laying it on a bit thick, but it's been a hell of a few days, and this is eating into my drinking time. Which is even more irritating than it drinking into my eating time, albeit only just.

I can hear a kerfuffle on the other end. 'Sorry, Paul, Mephy wants me to tell you that you're a twat and to knock it off. It's making his hackles rise outside of his control.' Faust sounds vaguely apologetic about his demon-possessed dog best friend telling me to shut my pie-hole. It's fine. I'm not offended. Honestly, I'm amazed I can manage more than a few words ever without someone telling me to close my gob, or they'll do it for me.

'Fair enough. Right, glad you rang. We've got a problem.'

'An additional problem?' It's a fair qualifier. We already had enough problems last time we spoke, what with the "demons invading our plane when they shouldn't be able to do so under any circumstances ever".

'Yep. The alp's hat's been destroyed.'

'*Schitze.*' It's unusual hearing Johannes swear. Not that he's a prude like Isaac. I think it's just that, when we're together, between Mephy and I, he probably feels like we use the whole allocated quota for the group.

I give them both a quick rundown of what's happened – our encounter with the demon at the airport, his kidnapping of Gil, the fights with the simiots and the Warabouc, as well as the particularly creepy manipulation of a whole city's populous to turn Auch into our own private ghost town for the showdown. By the end of it, I can practically hear the tension, like we're talking with two tin cans down a piece of string, and their voices are as taut as that piece of rope between us.

There's a moment of indistinct mumbling, then Faust's back on the line. 'We're on our way to Toulouse.'

'What, literally now? That's amazing. Personally, I'd have to pack and get my shoes on and stuff, but damn, you both move fast.' One day, I'll be capable of responding to statements without sarcasm. Today is not that day

Faust wisely ignores me, though I can hear Mephy muttering about me being a wanker in the background. 'We'll be there as quickly as we can. As soon as I've got flight details, time of arrival, et cetera, I'll let you know. Keep an eye out for a text, will you?'

'Will do, dude. And thank you both.' I know they'll make exceptions for my snarky, snappy behaviour – I've spent months worried out of my mind about Aicha, and now I'm dealing with all this bullshit with Isaac getting demonised, literally. Still, it doesn't hurt to acknowledge that I appreciate them being there for me. They don't have to jump on a plane and come help save the day. The fact that they don't hesitate to do so shows what good friends they are.

We say our goodbyes and hang up. And I have precisely long enough to get an ice cube into my tumbler and the bottle of Nikka coffee grain out of the cupboard before I have to bite back a high-pitched scream and then narrowly avoid hurling my glass directly at the nearest wall because I am not going to get to have a fucking drink however much I bloody well want one, apparently.

Why? Because we're going to have to leave. Right now.

Someone or something, out to the west of the city, is testing the wards. Repeatedly.

Chapter Four

TOULOUSE, 29 OCTOBER, PRESENT DAY

Unless this turns out to be the Dalwhinnie Distillery being run by talented beings and them coming to make a drop-off delivery of several barrels of their finest single malt? I'm going to be very put out.

A few minutes later, we're back in the Tesla. Thank fuck Isaac has the larger battery pack and a fastidious obsession with keeping it topped up. Leaving Gil at the house is an easy decision. He's dazed still, utterly wiped out by his possession and the effects of losing control of his body and possibly his mind. Half the time, he just seems zoned out. I'm hoping it's sheer exhaustion. We'll see how he is after a good night's sleep.

Meanwhile, we're motoring towards Leguevin, a pretty little town just after Pibrac – now the limits of our western boundaries since they shrank; Isaac's own demonic infection saw to that. It's only about a twenty-minute drive, but it's far from comfortable, mainly because every few seconds feels like someone's playing double bass on my spinal cord. Thrums of interfering power wash up and down my nervous system as whoever or whatever it is keeps prodding at the barriers. As they're hooked up to me, that's how my body chooses to translate their testing. It's not good for my resting heartbeat rate or my stress levels. By the time we pull into the town, I'm ready to kill someone just to alleviate the tension from having my nerves plucked at like a ham-fisted, pissed-up troubadour's lyre. I'm constantly tensed up in anticipation of the next thrum, and it'd be fair to say it's doing my head in now.

The road drops away, then climbs again, like the terrain has rollercoaster envy and has decided to do its best to imitate a big dipper before we pull into the centre. Pretty off-pink brickwork marks the modernity of much of the place. It's really a spill over for Pibrac, a tiny village that's expanded at rapid rates, mirroring the explosive growth of Toulouse itself.

There's a huge central market square, an open expanse packed with stands and trucks on a Sunday morning. There's a lovely Irish couple who do a mean soda farl that I get with egg and Aicha always liked with bacon and sausage. Right now, though, it's practically deserted. And to those with the *sight*, it's almost perfectly bifurcated by my barrier.

Once I see what's on the other side of it, I stop looking and keep my eyes carefully fixed on the ground. I'm giving these cobblestones a thorough inspection, checking in between the cracks like I've lost a contact lens. Though I don't want to see clearly, anyhow, right at this particular moment. I run my eyes over the cracked ground, keeping my attention firmly locked on the cobbles, studying their irregular pattern. Anything other than making eye contact with the creature on the other side of my wards

After all, the gaze of the Karnabo puts a basilisk's to shame.

And by the Good God, it's hard not to have a look. Actually, it's hard not to just outright stare because the Karnabo's a peculiar-looking chap to put it mildly. I know that, both from the quick glance I stole before realising who it was and from the pictures I've seen in rare books at Isaac's, which are stacked like the world's most expensive game of Priceless Esoteric Texts Jenga. This is another one of those occasions where all the studying he made me do is going to turn out saving my life. Not that I'm going to tell him that, of course. He'd expect me to do something terrible like act grateful. Not going to bloody happen.

The creature standing just a few yards from us is tall and broad. Somewhere around two metres in height at a guess and with a build that speaks of natural strength, although not the toned form of a professional athlete. More that kind of Andre the Giant build – huge by birth rather than effort. The eyes, the ones I'm avoiding looking at so as to not drop dead instantly, are glistening slate, gleaming and sparkling because the fucker wants you to look at him. I've no idea if that magic will work on us when we're in *here* and he's out *there*, but I'm not in any hurry to find out.

It takes all my willpower not to leap a couple of centimetres off the ground when the crackle of the wards runs up and down my spine again, and I hear him snort with glee

Because the fucker's just banged on them *again*, with his trunk.

That's the most obviously inhuman aspect of the Karnabo. He has an enormous proboscis, elephant-like, hanging off the front of his face. I don't know his real origins. By legend, he's the offspring of a devil and a sorceress, although I don't buy a demon backstory. More likely he's either part-fae, or else he's a seriously powerful magic user who fucked himself up searching for ever greater magic.

The one sure thing we know about him is he's a nasty piece of work. And that elephant trunk of his is the magical equivalent of a machine gun. He can fire off *talent*-based workings like live rounds with a simple thought.

The good news is he's on the other side of the barrier. For as long as it holds anyhow. He's not someone I'm looking to rumble with if I can avoid it. Plus, I don't want Isaac fighting anyone at all under any circumstances. We've already seen categorically that Nithael using his *talent* allows the demon essence to spread through my mentor's system. He has to just be the brains from here on in and leave all the grunt work to me whether he likes it or not. Luckily, those are roles we're both born to fill. Him think, me act. Together we'll be unstoppable. Ultimate tag team partners.

That's the theory anyhow.

First, though, we need to find out what the magical Joseph Merrick-looking motherfucker in front of us wants. Apart from our attention, clearly. What he's been doing is the equivalent of knocking on the door. Repeatedly. Every two seconds. While leaning on the doorbell with the other finger. And constantly kicking at the hinges. Just to emphasise the point. The point being that he's an impatient fuckknuckle and rude to boot.

'Enough!' I don't need to look at him, not properly, to see his trunk recoil, ready to tap again. 'We're here. What do you want?'

'Messages, that's what I'm bringing. Yes. Deliveries, not of my own though. No.' There's a strange back hiss to his words, like the static of a poor phone connection or like talking through a half-tuned walkie-talkie.

'Okay, so you're just a messenger boy. Got it.' I probably shouldn't poke the incredibly powerful magical being that can kill with a glance, but boy, has he been pissing me off with the continuous prodding of my protections. Not to mention stopping me from getting a drink.

'Messenger? Of sorts. Yes.' Still that sibilance is unchanged. I've not annoyed him with that dig. More's the pity. 'Trade-offs, there's the way of working. Yes. There's trades to be made, though I doubt you'll like them. No.'

'Trades? Like, information?' Whether I trust the Karnabo or not, if he's going to give us something useful, I'll need to consider a trade. Even if it's one I don't like.

Except, it doesn't look like that's what he means at all. At least, I guess that's what him erupting into laughter that sounds like a medieval bugler playing his toot stick with his arsehole signifies. His trunk shakes, swelling and constricting, and it's all about as musical as a five year old hopped up on sugary treats and luminous "juices" the colour of plutonium, running riot in a room full of instruments. I have no idea how one creature with a single proboscis can sound so cacophonous.

'Me, give you information? Yes. Of sorts.' The amusement hasn't disappeared. It drips from the Karnabo's words. 'But not my trade. No.'

Ah, okay. Now I get it. 'So why don't you tell us who the trades are on behalf of?'

'Tell you *what* he is? Yes. A demon. You know that. Tell you *who* he is? No. Not what's being offered, Good Man.'

So he's working for the bastard who's poisoned Isaac and grabbed Gil. I surreptitiously *look* at the creature. Not surprisingly, he's swirling with *talent*, a yellow miasma of power that clings to his skin. There's no evidence of possession. He's obviously working willingly with the demon. Either the Karnabo ranks higher up in his confidence, or else the Warabouc was involved in controlling Gil's body-jacking because there's no sign of the dark demonic essence we saw streaking around the ram's-skull-faced creature in Auch.

'So what is he offering? Is it a funky wiggly black veined arm? Because if so, we've already got one, thanks, and it's rubbish. We're going to return it to the manufacturer...by shoving it down his throat and ringing his tonsils like a doorbell.'

Again, the creature makes the discordant trumpeting laugh. At least I amuse him. Sadly, I think it's more in a "funny like a clown" than a Tommy DeVito way.

'You think you'll be able to beat him? Yes. But will it actually happen? No.'

Okay, definitely that he finds our confidence misplaced. I'm a bit worried he might be right. Doesn't mean I'm going to show that to this Lotsa Heart Elephant Care Bear reject.

'So what is on offer behind door number two then, Dumbo?'

He ignores the jibe, looking entirely at ease still, at least as far as I can tell by his visible body language. There's no way I'm looking up at his face if I can help it. Nope, studious study of the cement between the slabs at his feet is my plan of action.

'The trade is very simple. The Rabbi and the angel come with us. Yes.'

My heart sinks, but I hide it. 'Okay, someone needs to explain to you the basics of an exchange system. You don't just say, "I want this," and then call it a trade. Not that there's any way you're getting your grubby mitts on 'Zac or Nith, but you're supposed to offer something in return.'

'Oh, you didn't understand. No.' The heaving wheezes behind the voice are still present, like old bellows pumped in front of a half-dead fire. 'The offered trade is simple. Yes. If they come with us, then the humans will not tear the world apart. No.'

Shit. If what they were after didn't sound good, this sounds even worse. 'What do you mean?'

I can feel the creature's gaze boring into me, drilling a hole in my soul. It takes all my willpower to keep myself from raising my own to meet it, to keep my eyes fixed on the ground. 'Humans are so very easy to influence. Yes. And can they protect themselves from a demon's suggestions? No. If the one who sent me decides, his mood will spread across the land and beyond, tickling and twisting those dark little desires that sit like dormant seeds in every heart and mind. Yes. Anger, hate, spite, jealousy all combined, one on top of the other, and will they resist? No. Would the war that came after ever end again?'

The creature bugles in soul-dirtyingly sordid amusement again, the fucking arsehole. 'No.'

The Good God damn it, it makes sense. We've already seen that the demon can possess multiple people in a sitting; he took over a few hundred on the aircraft without breaking a sweat. And his showing off, his muscle flexing at the airport combined with evacuating Auch, showed just how easy he finds it to manipulate the population and authorities. The threat? To send the population mad till they tear themselves apart. And letting it spread wider and wider, a spiral of violence and hatred until the whole species wipes itself out or destroys the planet in the process. We've come close enough sufficient times in the past, and the risk is clear and present for all to see. The threat is frighteningly plausible.

And all this to get their hands on Isaac and/or Nithael. Considering the whole, "demons and angels don't really have this great enmity" spiel I've heard so far, it's pretty weird that the bastard fucking with us is prepared to threaten to destroy the whole world to get his hands on Isaac...

Shit. I shoot my hand out just in time, wrapping it in the folds of my mentor's jacket, jerking him to a stop so hard, I panic for a moment, thinking I'll tear a section away, and he'll keep going. Luckily, it checks him to a halt and still holds. A good thing. He's already going to be upset enough. Don't need to ruin his favourite professor-style jacket at the same time. Although I want to slap him round the back of the head, then do the same to myself afterwards. Him for doing it and me for not realising sooner what he'd try to do. Of course he wants to go and hand himself straight over as a willing sacrifice. Fucking hell. Thankfully, I clocked it before he got out of arm's reach.

'Chill, 'Zac,' I hiss through my teeth. The Karnabo's amusement radiates from over the barrier. 'Not going to happen.'

'Let me go, lad.' His voice is low but strong. He's so damn sure of himself. 'There's no way we can let what he said occur. Better I go with him, and we bring an end to all this.'

"Zac, I love you, but you're a fucking idiot.' I need to get this through to him hard and fast. 'This is a Ben situation all over again but multiplied by a million. If the demon's so ready to threaten humanity as a whole, hell, possibly even the world itself, then there's every chance that *he's got something even worse planned if he gets his hands on you two*.'

My oldest friend freezes, stops trying to pull his way loose. Looks like that hit home, at least. 'Then what do we do, lad?'

'Same thing as we always do in a situation like this. Stall for time. Try to get a grip on what's going on. Learn the rules of the game, then stack the deck in our favour.'

'Gotcha.' He takes a step back, and I relax. Immediate crisis over. Now back to the one looming just on the other side of our wards.

'The Rabbi was coming. Yes. And now you think to not allow him. No.' The menace to the words isn't even concealed. It's clear and hostile in every syllable.

'Look, there's no way we're going to just make a decision like that, and you knew it when you came. We need some time to discuss it, to come to a consensus.'

'I can wait for a few minutes. Yes. Not too long though. No.'

Fuck. Not the sort of timescale I was working on. 'Minutes aren't going to cut it. We've...' I search for an excuse. 'We've got other team members involved. There needs to be time for us all to regroup, to discuss it, and come to a united decision. We need days, not minutes.'

The creature falls silent apart from the asthmatic sounds of its breathing. Finally, it speaks up again. 'There is some leeway. Yes. But not much. No.'

'How much?' Looks like it's already been pre-briefed. Time to see what the wiggle room is and if we can push it out any further.

The creature hisses like a half-cracked kettle, and by the Good God, it's hard not to look up; the whistling screech is pulling at my attention. Which, I suspect, is exactly the idea. 'Longer than hours, yes. As long as a week? No.'

Oh, good. So we're limited to a few days, and apparently, he wants us to play a yes/no guessing game to find out how many he's going to benevolently give us. Let's start high. 'Six days then?'

'He's so full of hope isn't he? Yes. But is he right? No.'

God, this guy is fucking irritating. 'Five?'

'Still too high, yes.'

'Four?'

'No.'

That was almost a direct answer. I'm getting desperate now. 'Three days?'

'Is that acceptable? Yes.'

I have to hand it to the Karnabo; his negotiation tactic is effective. The panic was building as I counted down the days, and now I have to work hard to resist a huge sigh of relief that we've stopped at three instead of counting down further to two. It's like he's done us a favour instead of imposing an almost impossible limit on us. Clever work. I need to try and do some wiggling now, make some more room.

'It's going to be tight.' I rub my chin doubtfully. 'We've got to get all our people together, bring them all up to scratch...'

'Do we care? No.' The last "oh" sound is stretched out, fading away after a few seconds. He's definitely going for some creepy kind of Elephant Nazgul vibe. Emphasis on the creepy.

So three days. Three days to find out why the demon wants Isaac, come up with a way to turn the tables, and to ideally send the fucker screaming back off to the lower dimensions. Otherwise, humanity's going to start tearing itself apart and probably the planet along with it.

No pressure then.

CHAPTER FIVE
LEGUEVIN, 29 OCTOBER, PRESENT DAY
Three days to save the world from an evil Heffalump. Where's Piglet when you need him?

The Karnabo's still just standing there, doing his weird "deranged stalker breathing through a trombone" impression.

There's one thing I'm not following. 'Why are you here, Karnabo? What's in it for you?' It doesn't make any sense to me. The creature holds the forests of the Ardennes, has sway and dominion over huge swathes of land. 'Why would you throw your lot in with someone threatening to destroy the whole world? Last time I looked, you live here too.'

'Live here? Yes. But am I content? No.' Out of the corner of my eye, I see his trunk rise, mirroring my earlier chin scratch. 'You want answers for free. Yes. But that can't be. No.'

Of course there's no such thing as a free lunch in a negotiation with a Talented creature. 'So what do you want in exchange for answering the question?'

I can almost hear the creature thinking, or I would be able to if it wasn't drowned out by its rasping breaths. 'They want to make a deal, yes. How about this – if you can come up with what the demon wants and can tell us when our paths cross again, then I won't refuse your question. No.'

Brilliant. So if we can solve the whole fucking mystery, then the bastard will tell us why he's playing the part he's chosen to. Not exactly what I consider helpful, but there we go.

Apparently, that's all we're getting though. There's a noise like the swell of a storm over the distant mountains, a rumbling that promises to grow until it rains down darkness on the land. With it, the sky does seem to respond, the light dimming, shadows stretching across the greyed-out concrete, and it's so damn hard not to look up and see what the Karnabo's doing. But again, this matches with everything we've seen about him so far. Plenty of attention-grabbing dramatics in terms of noise and effects. All things to make you want to crack, to raise your eyes and look at him.

Without giving in to temptation and lifting my gaze, I can still see that the darkening is happening around where he is, can still spot when he steps back into it. It swallows him up, wrapping around him like an ominous crevice swallowing a dropped stone. Then the daylight seems to regain its strength, rallying to spread across the square once more, and I don't need to reach out with my *talent*, to test just beyond the barrier, to search and probe to know that the Karnabo is gone.

But you'd better believe I do it anyway. Just to be sure.

Now that we're able to raise our eyes without risk of insta-death, I look at Isaac. The same level of worry is reflected back at me from his own expression.

'Three days, lad?' The question is clear. How the hell are we going to manage it?

I sigh. 'I've no idea, but *it's better than just handing yourself over, for fuck's sake.*' Okay, I might have got a little shouty on the end bit, but he deserves it. I mash my eyelid with the palm of my hand, trying to rub some of the exhaustion and tension from that talk away.

'Well, we can't let the demon do what he's threatening to.' I can hear the attempt to persuade me, and it's seriously worrying. He's still ready to hand himself over if needs be. Right, I need to get this nipped in the bud right now.

'You're right. Absolutely. But what we also can't do is give him exactly what he wants. Which is apparently you or Nithael or both. Whatever he's got planned is bad news, and you need to promise me right now that whatever happens, you won't go and give yourself to him. Not unless we've both agreed that it's the only possible course of action left.'

I can't write off the chance that might arise, although if it does, I hope it'll only be as part of a double bluff – getting us close enough that I can throw some clever spanner in his works. Or just smash it to pieces with a sledgehammer. Ideally along with his stupid trunk-rocking face. Either is acceptable.

Isaac hesitates on a half-drawn breath, and I can see he wants to argue or refuse the request. The Good God love him, though, he doesn't. Instead, he nods. 'Aye. All right, lad. I won't go unless you agree. But you'd better believe if we don't get somewhere with this by the end of the three days, I'll be badgering you to let me go until you're begging the bastard to take me just to give you a rest.'

I snort, one of those instinctive half-laughs when you're entirely not in the mood to laugh, when desperation is tugging at your heart and mind and panic's flitting around your system, but still someone says something that is so unexpectedly funny, it's a moment's peace in the madness all around. Of course, it's only funny because the idea that I'd ever get fed up of Isaac, no matter what he did, is utterly ridiculous.

My phone buzzes in my pocket, so I fish it out and check the text I've received. Good. Progress. 'Right, come on.' I give Isaac a half-slap on the shoulder, a mixture of reassurance and motivation. 'Time to head over to Blagnac Airport. Faust and Mephy have just landed.'

We slope back over to the car and roll out towards Pibrac to pick up the dual carriageway to the airport. Isaac's driving, and it's obvious just how concerned he is. His knuckles are half-white, he's gripping the wheel so tight, and every steering movement's a sharp tug that makes the drive about as comfortable as the mood is.

'What is it?' It's a stupid question in many ways. There're enough things wrong between the demonic energy infecting him, the threat of World War III, and an impossible time-limit imposed on us. But I know Isaac. He's not just stressed out by the pressure. He's identified a puzzle, and now, whatever that conundrum is, he's wrestling with it.

He takes a moment before answering, 'You already put your finger on it, lad, and I'm bothered by the same thing. Why is the Karnabo working with the demon? Why was the Warabouc?'

'Are we sure the Warabouc wasn't possessed?'

I'm clutching at straws, and Isaac knows it. He shakes his head. 'He absolutely wasn't. The energy was a gift, a tool to use, not all consuming. We've seen what possession looks like.'

He gives a tiny shudder, and I know he's thinking of Gil lying on the bench, the worms diving in and out of his flesh. Or perhaps of the passengers on the plane, their eyes oil-slicked with demon energy, ready to tear us to pieces with their bare hands. He's right of course. The Warabouc wasn't like that. Hell, we beat it by using its own magic against it. I'm not even sure that would have worked if it was fully possessed. Although, I've no idea.

None of us do because we've never run into anything like this. We're flying blind, and it's making an already impossible job even more impossibler. Or something along those grammatically incorrect lines.

'Plus, the Karnabo didn't have any demonic energy on him, lad.' And again, he's right. There wasn't any sign of him being under the dark influence of the demon. 'He made a choice. He's chosen to work with them.'

'You're right, 'Zac. So what's bothering you about it?'

'The same thing that bothered you. Why? Why would they be working for the bugger? What can they possibly stand to gain if he destroys the world?'

Ah. So that's what's bothering him. And now that he's brought it back up, it's what's bothering me too. He's right. It doesn't make sense. We lapse into silence, both of us wrestling with the issue, trying to make sense of it.

'What it means,' I say slowly after a while, 'is that the demon is promising them something. Something that either is worth the world being destroyed...'

'Or that means the world won't be destroyed at all.' Isaac grins sharply for a moment, though it fades almost instantly. 'I think you're right, my lad. They think he won't do it, or else they believe he's going to get them out of here if he does, taking them with him to the lower dimensions or whatever. And my money's on the former. There's something he's offering them that means they think he's going to come through for them. But what?'

'Power?' It's the first thing that comes to mind. Isaac nods gravely.

'Makes sense. Neither of them are exactly after money or fame or the things humans would be influenced by. Both the Karnabo and the Warabouc prefer the wilds to the city, and both are *Talented* creatures capable of working magic alongside their own innate abilities.'

It's a lovely theoretical discussion, but it's not getting us any closer to the real issue. 'Well, the Karnabo's made it easy for us anyhow.'

Isaac shoots a glance across at me, and I instinctively grab at the little handle above the car door as if this piece of plastic is going to provide me with salvation from the sheer terror I feel as we lurch sideways in synchrony to said glance. 'In what way, lad?' Isaac asks, entirely oblivious to the heart attack he's just come within inches of giving me. Inches from that – and the tree. In the field. Three fields back from the side of the road.

I take a minute to get my breathing back under control, to talk my overly stimulated heartbeat down from the heights of sheer panic it's teetering on the edge of, back to the familiar plateau of normal mild terror that Isaac's driving causes.

'In the way,' I say once I'm able to speak again, 'that all we have to do is work out what the fuck the demon is up to and then the Karnabo will tell us the rest. Remember the offer he made us?'

'Oh, right you are, lad.' Isaac's attention goes back to the road, thankfully, and we lapse back into silence. Because that, of course, is the real issue here. We might have slowed down the possession of Isaac temporarily. We might have saved Gil against all the odds. But we still have no idea what the demon wants or what he's after by being on our plane of existence.

As we drive along the road towards Blagnac, with the snowy peaks of the mountains confusable with distant clouds on our right, I can only hope that Johannes and Mephy have some ideas.

Because the Good God knows I'm fresh out of them.

CHAPTER SIX

TOULOUSE, 29 OCTOBER, PRESENT DAY

I wonder what Johannes thinks when he hears people talking about a "Faustian bargain". Probably, "It worked out pretty well for me, thanks."

The airport remains the same monstrosity, constructed out of concrete and glass and the feverish terror and confusion of too much humanity collected and shoved together into a single building. It's painful to be here because my first instinctive thought is, *Thank the Good God Aicha isn't here this time*, and then, of course, I remember why Aicha isn't here this time. And my heart hurts. It feels like I've betrayed her even thinking that, and the whole fucking saga with this demon is a bullshit distraction from going and finding her and bringing her home. Sure, the world might be at risk. But Aicha's missing, and part of me just wants to say fuck the world until I know she's safe.

I can't do that though. Not while Isaac's possessed anyhow. After that, well. Let's get past that first.

By the time we get into the main building, having managed to weave our way around the various cars that decided two lanes going to two different short-stay car parks meant they could just stop their vehicles in those lanes while they waited, the duo are already out with their luggage, striding to meet us. I wonder how they got Mephy on board, if they used a *don't look here* or whether Faust registered him as an emotional support animal or something again. Honestly, I find it hard to believe any airline in the world is going to buy that the enormous black Doberman, all bunched muscle under the sheen of his coat, is providing anything except bodyguard duties. The glowing red eyes probably don't help with that either.

Faust himself looks the same as ever. He's wearing jeans and a T-shirt, as well as a thrown-on jacket that manages to look both stylish and slept in simultaneously. He's taller than me, barrel-chested, with his beard bristling out like a red chin halo. His arms are thrown wide open, and he sweeps me up into a chest-crushing hug that doesn't leave me much room to do anything like breathe.

'Paul, it's good to see you!' Considering it's only been a couple of days, it's a bit over the top, but Johannes has always had a flare for the dramatic. He turns his attention to Isaac, and the concern is clear on his face. '*Herr* Isaac. I'm sorry to hear about your loss of the hat. From what Paul told me, it speaks great volumes to your character how it was lost though.'

'Yep, he was a spectacular idiot; you're quite right.' I don't mean it, of course. Not really. I'd like to think I'd have done the same for Gil in his place, but either way, there's no way I can condemn Isaac for it. If I didn't do the same, it'd be my failing, not his.

We start back towards the car, Johannes waving away my attempts to take his suitcase off him.

'So...the pair of you look like someone's announced a death at a strip club. What's going on?' There's a number of reasons why I'm glad Johannes is here, but that's one of them. He's razor sharp, observant as hell. Plus, he knows how to party. Hopefully we can resolve this all quick time and get to celebrating. Then once I'm past my hangover, I can get back to finding Aicha.

'We had a visitor.' The grim tone of my voice matches exactly how I feel. 'Just before you arrived. There was a...'

I break off. Stop. Turn around and lower my gaze. 'Mephy. Please take your nose out of my arse. It's weird and freaking uncomfortable, and every time I feel the cold through my jeans, I think my heart's going to tear through my chest like a fucking baby alien. I've already had to put up with Isaac's driving, and I'm mentally gearing myself up for the return trip. Keep your nose to yourself.'

Mephistopheles doesn't look even slightly abashed. 'Not my fault your bum smells good. Just my way of saying hello, isn't it? Bloody prudish humans.'

'What's wrong with my driving, lad?' The outrage in Isaac's tone isn't even slightly forced, only highlighting once more how such an incredibly intelligent individual can be entirely blinkered about certain things.

'Mephy, keep your greetings to yourself. A simple hello will suffice. 'Zac, I haven't got time to count all the ways. We can break it down with flow charts and Venn diagrams later on if you want, when I've got enough whisky to make the conversation bearable.' We're almost at the car, and I've completely lost my train of thought. 'What the hell were we talking about before that?'

'The visitor?' Johannes' focus hasn't been distracted, at least. I guess he's more used to Mephy's shenanigans.

'Oh, right, yes. The Karnabo came calling.'

'Who?' The growled question from knee height seems way too close to my legs. Mephy better not be sizing them up for a sexy time clinch again.

'Talented creature from the north of France. Wields magic. Kills with a gaze if you look into his eyes. Poisonous breath. Nasty piece of work. Holds a big swathe of territory in the Ardennes and for some bloody reason is working with the demon. Who we've had precisely bugger all luck identifying. Anything on your end?'

I can see by their expressions, the answer's no. Damn it.

We get in the car and back en route. After a quick detour to mine to pick up Gil, resulting in an interesting discussion as to who is going to sit in the passenger seat out of him and Mephy and who is going in the middle, which is then won by Mephy plonking himself down on Gil's lap, leaving him a choice between moving and having his pelvis crushed, we head towards Isaac's. There're two reasons. First, I can't be taking down my wards to let all those tinged by demonic energy through each time. It's going to weaken them, and however crazy everything else is, however messed up the dangers we're facing, I need to know there's one place that's mine, that's truly, properly safe. Second, I'm with two hardcore scholars, and we're no closer to an answer. If we're going to find one, it's going to be through us brainstorming or through research. There're more answers likely to be found in Isaac's clutter than in my comparatively neat home. I don't tend to consider priceless grimoires scattered randomly across every available surface as maximalist home deco.

It's good to get back into Isaac's even if it does feel weird, seeing all the new brickwork and repairs wrought. There's still marks of the damage done by the attack of the Grail-hunter zombies, which is, incidentally, definitely a B Movie title that would pique my interest, and I know it hurts 'Zac. He never imagined that his sanctuary could be violated, never dreamed that anything could get past the defences he created with Nithael. Now, not only has that been proven untrue with his home but with his very body as well.

We sit down around the light-wood kitchen table. It's the most comfortable space for the five of us and relatively clear. Only three leather-bound tomes are spread across it, and Isaac quickly but reverently closes them, then shuffles them onto the sideboard.

I get right to the point. 'Johannes, Meph, any ideas on how to slow down or stop the infection spreading?'

Again, hang-dog expressions –literally in Mephy's case– confirm my fears. 'Nothing at all. Don't use any *talent* is the best I've got.' Johannes' tone is depressingly down beat, strange sounding on such a positive person.

'Okay.' I wasn't expecting anything else, but it still knocks my mood. And I wasn't exactly feeling like a perky nineties Valley Girl to start with. 'So what do we have?'

There's a moment of silence as we all ruminate on what we know, searching for a clue.

'Well, there's the mark on the simiots,' Isaac starts the conversation off.

Of course. With all the excitement of the Karnabo's visit, I almost forgot about that. 'That is weird.'

'Could it be just a trend? Like a tribal marking? Or a fashion statement?' Johannes asks.

'What, like tattoos of the signatures of ancient Frankish kings are suddenly all the rage among fire-elemental apes?' I shake my head. 'The simiots aren't like that. They're societal, intelligent even, but the evolutionary trait that gave them fire magic also means they skipped the whole stage most apes go through of getting into using tools. I guess when you can fry your prey with a thought and have barbecue food on tap, it's less essential.'

Gil sighs. 'I loved the stories of Charlemagne as a kid.'

Surprised, I look over at him. 'I thought you didn't know who he was. Plus, I'm amazed you were allowed to read them.' Gil grew up in a hardcore

Christian cult in the north of France until the attempts to torture his homosexuality out of him drove him into making his escape.

He shrugs. 'Not the real history. Just stories. I found a book, *Vie de Charlemagne*, on a bus to town once, when I was meeting the rest of the Church for a conversion mission, trying to recruit new members. I managed to hide it, get it home, and stash it in the attic. Then when they locked me up there to consider my sins, I found a form of escape in the pages. The battles and adventures, the chivalry, the magical powers of Joyeuse itself...' Gil looks up, his eyes alight. 'Hey, what if the simiots are the guardians of Joyeuse? You know, like the sacred keepers assigned by Charlemagne himself generations before?'

It's a valiant attempt by the young lad to be helpful, but he knows so little about the Talented world. It's a nice idea but doesn't work. 'Nah. The simiots and humans don't get on.' And if they were these special caretakers, they'd hardly have come rampaging out into the Languedoc to kick the shit out of all the people and boot them off the land, as they did hundreds of years ago. Isaac and I managed to turn them back then, send them back to the mountains. It wasn't easy though. 'Plus, I hope it's not the case.'

'Why?' I can see Gil's disappointed with my answer. Guess the dreams of chivalry and derring-do die hard even for someone who's lived as much misery as Gil has.

'Because if they were the guardians, then that means the demon has Joyeuse. And he's already powerful enough. I don't want him having any super-charged magical items to help him out.'

'Wait.' Isaac flaps a hand at me, telling me to stop doing the same thing with my gums. 'Go back, lad.'

'It'd mean the demon has Joyeuse?' I'm confused, trying to work out what Isaac's heard that I've missed.

'No, no, no.' Again with the hand waving. 'Not you, the other lad. Gil, what did you say about Joyeuse?'

'Umm.' The kid looks blank for a minute, no doubt trying to replay the conversation in his head. 'That it has magical powers?'

'Of course!' Isaac slams his hand so hard on the table that I almost jump. From the disapproving squawk overhead, Hubert, the eagle who roosts in the rafters, is equally surprised. 'That's the answer!'

I can feel my own excitement mounting. 'To what the demon wants?' Fuck me, we might have solved this and with two and a half days still to spare.

'No, not quite.'

Damn it. Yeah, that would have been too simple. What he says next, though, more than makes up for it.

'Not what he wants, but how to get his bloody mark off me.'

Now my heart leaps. Because it sounds like Isaac's found a way to get rid of the demon essence threatening to destroy him and Nithael.

CHAPTER SEVEN

TOULOUSE, 29 OCTOBER, PRESENT DAY

Demon Essence. Sounds like the latest fragrance from Paco Rabanne. Or the Beast Rabban perhaps.

I manage to restrain myself from leaping over the table and shaking Isaac until he tells me what he's come up with but only just. Clearly Faust feels the same.

'What? How?' For a moment, I think the German scholar's going to go , when, where, and why just to complete the set, but apparently he's happy to settle for two of the six.

'What Gil just said!' Isaac's on his feet, pacing now, and I am still astounded by my self-control to not scream at him in frustration because *obviously what Gil said*. The fact he's had his eureka moment after getting Gil to repeat himself makes it fucking categorically clear that it's because of what Gil said.

'Yes. Obviously.' Johannes is keeping his patience far better than I am, but it's wearing thin. I think he recognises the delight in cracking a conundrum that his fellow scholar's exhibiting, but he wants that answer too, same as me.

'Right, yes, sorry.' Isaac calms himself a little, but his eyes are still bright, and he's working hard to keep the quirk of his mouth from breaking into a full-on grin. 'Well, you know the legend of Joyeuse, right?'

Urgh. I love Isaac so much, but sometimes he does forget his audience. Does Johannes, a Talented scholar, know the story of the most famous magical sword of all time after Excalibur? To Faust's enormous credit, he manages to just reply with a simple, "Yes," rather than the weapons-grade sarcasm I'd have responded with.

Isaac carries on, entirely oblivious, 'Right, so what are the magical properties Joyeuse has?'

Ooh. Good question actually. I'm wracking my brains because honestly, it's all a bit vague from what I can remember. Again, a bit like Excalibur. Everyone agrees it's a magical sword, but what does it actually *do*? "Makes you the rightful King of Albion" isn't magic; it's feudalism. I have no idea with Joyeuse either.

Gil knows though. 'It could light up as bright as the sun...'

'But only if enemies are around? Are you trying to tell me we're searching for Bilbo's Sting?'

Gil shakes his head. 'No, it was whenever Charlemagne wanted. He used it to blind his enemies during battle.'

Okay, so the medieval equivalent of a flash-bang grenade. 'Useful, but I don't see how that helps 'Zac.'

'That's because it's not the only magical trait it has, lad, according to legend.' I can see how excited Isaac is. This is the big reveal, the moment he's been building up to. 'There was another power it gave to Charlemagne.'

'Poison!' Gil butts in. Now he's looking just as excited, his eyes gleaming, no doubt remembering those forbidden stories of his childhood. 'The sword made Charlemagne immune to poison!'

'Exactly!' Isaac claps his hands together, not bothered in the slightest by Gil stealing his thunder. 'And not just "immune to poison", lad. Legend said no dark infection could take hold of the wielder.'

'Dark infection.' Now I can feel my own excitement rising. 'That sounds like a pretty good description of what you've got going on right now, 'Zac.'

'So if we get hold of the sword, and Isaac holds it...' Faust muses, scratching his enormous beard.

'Then he'll be the rightful King of the Francs!' Mephy barks from his feet. 'No, sorry. Wrong magical sword. It'll perhaps drive back this demonic energy. Because now, apparently, we're a "dark energy" and an "infection" to be "driven out".'

Oops. Perhaps we have been a touch insensitive. 'Sorry, Meph. You know we're not talking about you here.'

Mephistopheles chuffs, shaking his head back and forth. 'Of course I know, you blithering idiot. I'm only fucking with you, mano. His arm's literally infected with demon energy. Less being polite, more saving your friend.'

Oh. Yeah. 'Right you are.'

Gil raises his hand like the polite young man he is. 'There's something that's been bothering me. Slightly off subject.'

I give him a gun finger. 'Go for gold, dude.'

'How did the simiots stay undetected for all that time in the mountains? Like, I'd have thought human-hating, fire-covered apes might have ended up getting stumbled across sooner or later? Perhaps when they set some fell walkers on fire or something?'

'Well, there're two reasons why not,' Isaac starts, and I visibly watch him relax as he settles into the role of lecturer. 'Most importantly, they're covered by a natural protection, a sort of *don't look here* so that they're basically invisible unless they decide to attack you.'

'I'd have thought being unseen until they bring down fiery death would make them more dangerous, not less.' It's a good point from Gil.

'Well, yes, but when we sent them back to the mountains, it was with an oath to leave humans be on their *power*. Not easy, as they don't use verbal language like we do, but we managed it with a little help from Nith.'

Gil nods, satisfied. 'Okay, that makes sense. Thanks. I guess you checked in on them from time to time after?'

Isaac waves a hand carelessly. 'Ah, not so much, to be fair. We weren't their favourite people. But I did ask Dunixi to keep an eye on them when our paths crossed. I believe they've adopted them and have looked after them from thereon in.'

For a moment it feels as if the world stops and tunnels as my head swings slowly towards Isaac like it has a massive magnet strapped to it and he's made of pure steel. I had precisely zero knowledge of this. Gil beats me to it.

'Who's Dunixi?'

'Ah, the leader of the jentilaks.' Isaac looks across at me, clocking my open mouth and look of agape disbelief. 'What, lad?'

I massage my temples with both hands. 'What you're telling us is that the fiery apes who attacked us, the ones who have mysterious tattoos on them, tattoos that have led us to searching for the legendary sword Joyeuse, which might *save your life* –' I can hear my voice rising, and I take a breath, forcing myself to calm back down. 'You're saying that those creatures were being looked after by another group of Talented beings?'

Isaac, of course, demonstrates once again that it's possible to be a certified genius and still be unable to see the woods for the trees even when you can label each of their different genus and explain how the process of photosynthesis works. 'Yes. What's your point?'

I move from my temples to rub at my eyes, half in disbelief –as if when I open them again, Isaac will stop being obtuse and missing the point– and half to wipe away some of the grains of tiredness that have accumulated there, like the Sandman keeps blowing the grit for de-icing the roads straight into my peepholes when I turn my back. 'Isaac. I love you, but you're a bloody idiot sometimes. Do you not think that if the jentilaks are looking after the simiots, that it might be a good idea to go and have a chat with them? Find out how the simiots got possessed? Perhaps ask them if they happen to have stumbled across any magical swords recently?

'Oh. Oh!' At long last, understanding lights up in Isaac's eyes. 'That's a bloody good point, lad. I'd not thought of that.'

Nope, Isaac. You hadn't. That much was categorically clear to everyone.

The excitement's palpable in the room afterwards. Of course, Gil has no idea who the jentilaks are, so we give him a crash course on the little we know. Big hairy mountain giant men, they're the Basque equivalent of the Sasquatch and live over on the Spanish side of the Pyrenees. Gentle giants who keep themselves well away from modern humanity. And that's where our knowledge starts running out.

'...I mean, I've met Dunixi a couple of times during my travels. The jentilaks are supposedly incredibly long-lived with a fabulous tradition of oral history, and I wanted to ask him some questions about the development of civilisation in the region.' Isaac sighs and takes a drink from the glass of water he's just fetched himself. 'Sadly, he wasn't very talkative. Friendly enough but very reserved and kept his answers to a minimum. Left as soon as he could and gave me as little actual information as possible, all while staying terribly nice about it. Once I knew the simiots needed an eye keeping on them, I tracked him down again and asked if he'd be so kind as to do the job. He was very happy to take it on, and once again a charming fellow, but I got nowt else from him apart from that.'

'So can you find him again?' That's the key question. Time is against us, of course. Through the window, the light is fading, the gloaming starting to seize hold as day turns to dusk. We've already used most of one day. I can't be sure if the Karnabo meant three days as in seventy-two hours from our conversation or three days as in sunup to sundown, but we'll have to operate on the latter as the worst-case scenario.

Isaac nods. 'Oh, yes. There's a way to get him to join me for a conversation. After the chat about the simiots, and it took me some time to track him down, I can tell you, our paths crossed one more time. I did him a favour, and he was kind enough to give me a gift. Hang on a minute...'

He dashes off, back into his laboratory. I don't even think about following. There's precisely nothing I'll be able to do to help. Somewhere in there is whatever Isaac is looking for, but it'll be hidden under a bog witch's spell jar or crammed behind a priceless thirty-volume tome of medieval street graffiti. Isaac would insist it's filed, stored logically. I suspect he's just relying on Nithael remembering where everything is for him.

Sure enough, after a few minutes and a huge amount of banging and clattering, he reappears, wielding a small silver whistle. It's one of those that looks like a bird call – a thin metal tube only about twenty centimetres long and only designed for making a single noise. There're no holes to cover to produce a tune.

'Dunixi said if I ever needed to talk to him, simply to take this and head up into the Basque side of the mountains, then give it a blow.'

I give him another of my strongest looks, the ones I've stolen off Aicha. The ones she always used to give me every time I said something a bit stupid. So the ones she gave me most of the time. And by the Good God, I'm not going to think of that in the past tense. The looks she'll give me again soon, when I find her and bring her home

'Are you saying you can just blow that anywhere in a section of the Pyrenees, covering hundreds of square kilometres, and he'll find you?'

Isaac shrugs. 'It's his terrain, lad. Hardly less likely than the Nain Rouge coming anywhere in the mountains as long as you burnt that finger of his he bit off and gave you, is it?'

I open my mouth, then close it again. He's right of course. The jentilaks are a mysterious group of Talented, and that's their terrain. No reason why the whistle wouldn't work at bringing us to their attention.

Of course, there's one more thing that needs to be mentioned. 'What if they're also possessed?'

Isaac looks up sharply. 'What?'

'I said what if they're also possessed? The simiots were. And you said they were under the stewardship of the jentilaks.'

'Ah.' Isaac's clearly not thought of that. He stops, rubs his chin, and I can see the cogs whirring in his brain as he thinks through what this added dynamic might mean in terms of the problem. 'Then they'll probably tear us limb from limb, my lad.'

Oh. Brilliant. That wasn't really the answer I was hoping for. Bollocks.

CHAPTER EIGHT

TOULOUSE, 29 OCTOBER, PRESENT DAY

Jentilaks. Better than Ruffswords, I guess. Although as they can dismember us without any need of weapons, perhaps not.

I want to set out straight away, of course. The pressure of the time limit imposed by the Karnabo is like a ticking clock implanted directly into the back of my cranium, the constant sound of passing seconds clunking away as the hand clicks its way around the dial. It's like Captain Hook having his crocodile strapped to his cerebellum. The others aren't so sure though.

Faust lays a caring hand on my shoulder. 'Paul, have you ever met yourself?'

I try to wrap my head around the question. 'Like, in terms of running into a doppelganger or an evil twin? Not yet, although considering how shit my luck is, it's only a matter of time. Or do you mean more as in "going on a spirit journey and finding the true essence of who you are"? Because in which case, yes, and he told me that the thing I need to do to be happy is stop going on stupid adventures and instead to chill out in front of the telly with a big glass of whisky and several tubs of ice cream.'

Faust shakes his head. 'I meant more in the sense of how easily you go blundering off into trouble, dragging everyone around with you.'

Ouch. I can't help but wince at that one even if there's a lot of truth in it. 'Thanks, Johannes.'

He pats my shoulder, letting me go. 'I just mean that if we go hammering off into the mountains now, by the time we get there, it'll be midnight. Next thing, you'll probably fall into a blasted crevice and then we'll have to rescue you, at which point, no doubt, it'll end up being the roosting spot of a cockatrice or some such nonsense, and then before you know it, we've lost more time than if we just got a decent night's sleep first.'

'But I'm not going to sleep!' There. That's a solid tactic. When faced by logic you can't argue with, you should whine petulantly. Always guaranteed to work. 'I'm just going to stress out, turning it over and over in my head, and then next thing, it'll be morning, I'll be just as tired, and we'll be no closer to getting the problem solved.'

'You should do what I do when I can't rest.' Mephy pops his head up from under the table, resting his snout on Johannes' lap. 'Find yourself a good tree or leg. Give it a good seeing to.' He lifts his head, his tongue lolling out of his doggy grin. 'Johannes packed me a spare leg. Do you want me to lend it to you? The sexy little minx.'

Okay, what? 'You've packed him a *leg*, Johannes?' For a moment, I'm worried my old friend has plunged off the deep end and gone all Jeffrey Dahmer to please his demon companion.

Faust tuts, frustration and affection warring in his expression. 'Not an actual human leg, Paul, relax. You know those dolls that people get sometimes? The ones for sex? I found a factory that produces them. Negotiated a good rate for their cast-offs. Purchased a few of their faulty legs.'

'There's nothing faulty about them!' Mephy says indignantly. 'They're perfect. Long and lithe and soft and hard in the right places...'

'Mephy!' I put my hand down to stop my mug of tea from vibrating. The dog demon has started rubbing himself up against the table leg, lifting his massive paws onto the top of the surface and bouncing himself back and forth enthusiastically, threatening to send everything positioned on top crashing off onto the floor below

'Oh, right. Sorry!' He pulls away and looks up at Faust. 'The case is open, right?'

Johannes nods, amused. 'It is.'

'Right. I'm heading back to the room. I'll bid you all adieu. Knock before you come in, Faust!'

He drops down onto all fours and lopes quickly off towards the stairs and his date with some synthetic flesh.

'And now I have a whole new source of nightmare fuel. Thanks, Meph!' I shout after him. A bark of, 'Welcome, now fuck off, mano,' comes reverberating back down the stairs seconds before I hear the slam of a door.

Well, it seems like I'm out-voted. Looking round, I can understand it. Faust's rushed here from another country and looks like he's been burning the candle at both ends, no doubt trying to find out anything he can about our demon problem. Isaac's skin is drawn. He looks stretched thin, like Frodo after popping on the ring too many times, and I can't help wondering if the dark energy pulsing away in his arm might not be having a similar effect. And Gil?

Gil's eyes are closed, and he's already drifted off to sleep. His skin still hasn't recovered its normal colour. He's grey and worn out. At least there's not demonic worms doing their best *Tremors* impression through his flesh anymore. No wonder he's exhausted. Full on demonic possession is going to take it out of anybody.

I lean forward and lower my voice. 'He stays here.' I nod my head over to the young sleeping lad.

The other two nod. 'He's done in,' Isaac says, worry clear on his face.

'Plus, if he can be possessed once...' Faust leaves the sentence unfinished, but he doesn't need to say any more. We all understand what he's saying. If Gil can get taken over by the demon once, it could happen again, and this time, we don't have a handy Alp hat to drive the creature's influence back out of his body.

Next time, we might lose him altogether.

We've got as far as discussion is going to take us for the night, so I give the kid a gentle shake, rouse him, and send him to a spare bedroom. Then I help myself to a generous measure of Balvenie single malt. It's not quite a bedtime story, but it might just help me to actually drift off.

It doesn't. Or at least not noticeably.

Instead, I toss and turn, grappling with my sheets like an American high school wrestler, throwing myself physically around the bed, searching for that magic position where I'm suddenly going to just relax and instantly fall asleep. I don't find it, but at some point, exhaustion forces stress and worry to tap out, and I drift off into an uneasy sleep, broken by moments of waking. Those strange instances where sleep and the real world seem to merge, and neither is real or both are equally so.

It's fair to say that when I get up in the morning, I'm ready for a coffee.

I feel like I've been battling a fever all night, like I should be soaked to the bone with that uncomfortable dampness that carries a sense of relief still, like you've passed a key point, like the worst might be behind you.

Sadly, I don't think that's true in my case.

For a moment, I consider whipping together pancakes. Then I remember the last time we sat for a breakfast of crepes in my kitchen. Aicha was there. Jakob, too, so excited to be tasting pancakes again after hundreds of years of disembodied imprisonment. And Susane...

Susane made them for us. A moment of peace. Of possibility. Before it all went to hell in a handbasket. A handbasket filled with hand grenades and middle finger hand gestures.

I shake my head, trying to forcibly propel the dark thoughts out of my mind, like a dog drying himself after a plunge into an icy river. Then I settle for stealing Isaac's car keys and driving over to the nearest bakery. A selection of croissants and chocolatines seems like a less portentous selection than tempting fate by cooking.

By the time I'm back, the rest of the house is stirring, if not fully awake. Isaac's already downstairs, wrapped in a dark-navy flannel bathrobe that looks almost as old as he is. Silk pokes through the holes; light-blue pyjamas, which look remarkably comfortable and surprisingly recent. I guess even Isaac has to replace worn-out possessions every now and then. Burning through bodies at a rate of knots over the past few centuries has left me without much connection to material possessions. If even the body you're possessing doesn't stand a chance of surviving much past lunchtime, your clothes or watches or whatever certainly don't.

While he fusses about, making up an oversized cafetière with enough caffeine to give everyone their first necessary hit of the day at least, I set the table and pile the patisseries in the middle. I'm no less anxious to get on our way, but at some point during the night, I came to peace with the fact that having everyone else in good form increases the chances of us getting the mission achieved. A few minutes sacrificed on the altar of food and caffeine now might save us hours later on.

Faust comes stumbling downstairs, rubbing at his eyes, with Mephy just behind him. 'Morning, all.' He sounds relatively breezy. Isaac's guest beds are comfortable. The Good God knows Aicha and I have crashed out here often enough to be sure of that.

I've set a plate for Mephistopheles at the table, and he springs up onto the kitchen stool I've provided, squatting on his haunches while crossing his paws in front of him to lean on the table. He looks longingly at the pastries in front of him.

'Help a brother out, will you?' He gives me a toss of his snout, to show the idea of the breakfast food hopping from *over there* to *over here* as quickly as possible. I start to slide a couple across and then nearly headbutt Hubert up in the rafters when Mephy barks so loudly at me that I leap what feels like twice my own body height into the air.

'Dude! What the hell?' Christ, I've no idea how long I'm going to keep this body. As long as possible is the hope with no guarantee I'm coming back afterwards. The level of stress shit like that puts on my heart isn't exactly helping the cause.

'Do you hate me, Paul? "Fuck all demons." Is that the vibe now? Are you trying to kill me?' It's amazing just how much sorrow-ladened guilt he can put into a canine expression. If I could film it and then give it a witty caption, it'd go viral on social media tomorrow.

'While I appreciate a little melodrama in the morning, what in the Good God and all of fuckery are you talking about?' I'm no closer to understanding what I've done wrong.

Faust sighs and leans over, swapping one of the pastries on his plate with one of the demon dog's. 'You gave him a chocolatine, my man. Chocolate and doggie digestive systems don't mix. Don't expect to hear the end of this for the next few weeks. I once offered him a Ferrero Rocher, and he was still complaining about it next Christmas.'

'Poison! Assassins! Murderers for friends!' Mephy gives a small howl that's packed with disappointment at a world so full of injustice and betrayal before burying his face into the pastry layers of a croissant to comfort his wounded soul.

Faust gives me an eye roll and then thanks Isaac as he places a big bowl of steaming black coffee in front of the demon dog.

'What time are we leaving then?' The voice from behind me might have made me start had the scare from Mephistopheles not effectively overloaded my fight-or-flight responses for the next few minutes. Looking over my shoulder, I see Gil is dressed. He still doesn't look well – not that he's ever looked in incredible form in all the time I've known him, between life on the streets and getting his magic eaten by his patron, Franc – but there's a set to his jaw, a glint to his eye that says what I have to tell him next is going to go down as well as Marilyn Manson performing a set at an old school Church revival meeting.

'Gil...' I start, but Isaac cuts me off.

'We need you here, lad. To guard the fort. Make sure those demon bastards don't get in, okay? There's stuff here we can't let them get their hands on.'

Oh, clever old Isaac. There are times when he's so oblivious that I forget just how smart he is. Of course, he's always there to try to help people, to make them feel better. He's spotted Gil's resolve as well. This is a good way to give him an out.

Not that Gil wants to take it, of course. 'I want to come with you! That bastard took me over.' He looks at me with a certain scrunching of his eyebrows that seems to say *and that's your fault*. In a way, he's right. If Franc were still alive, the demon probably wouldn't have been able to possess him. There's only room for one evil shitstain joyriding your soul at a time. He looks away quickly though. Gil might still have some mixed feelings about Franc, but he found his storehouse in the mountains with Aicha. Filled with salted and preserved body parts of those "lovely lads and lasses" who'd tried to leave Franc's service. I'm glad he's dead. My only regret is that I didn't kill him myself. As ever, Aicha did the necessary dirty deed when I found myself hesitating.

Isaac pushes down on the air with his hands, a calming gesture. 'Now, lad, I understand that. But that's the problem. He's already grabbed hold of you once. I'm infected, but Nithael's keeping me in the game, and he won't be able to seize me. Faust's protected by Mephy, and Paul's got enough magic to hopefully keep any attempt at bay. Here, you can be a major help, ready to call us if the demons attempt to break in. Out there...'

He leaves the sentence open, but it doesn't need to be said. Gil knows what he means. Out there, he's a liability, a potential hostage or worse, turned against us, a violent extension of the demon bastard's evil will. It'd break my heart to kill the kid, but I'd do it without hesitation if he threatened any of the other three. I like him; he saved my life, and I owe him. But the others are family, pretty much, and that pips my debt to him every time. Better he's not out there with us, and I'm not put in that situation.

I have to bite my lip when I see the minute wince at Isaac's line, but his jawline softens, and I know it's worked. There's a bit of half-arsed arguing from him for a little, but his heart isn't in it. Eventually he nods, albeit morosely, and we leave him with Hubert for company. I'd prefer he was further from the edges of the wards but not enough to drop the ones at my house again. At least here, he can come and go. Isaac's wards are more flexible than mine, so the kid can get out and go for a walk if he wants without being under threat. I show him on the map the limits of the protections, and Isaac shows him the pantry and the food stocks available. He's not about to run out of supplies anytime soon, and we shouldn't be gone long enough for it to be a concern.

With Gil mollified and all the basic admin tasks of letting someone know all the things needing doing in an unfamiliar house they've been left in charge of done, the rest of us pile into the Tesla and belt up.

Let's go see what secrets the Pyrenees hold for us this time.

CHAPTER NINE

TOULOUSE, 30 OCTOBER, PRESENT DAY

If the jentilaks think they can mess with us, they'd better sasq-watch out.

I t's just over three hours, the drive. I'm confused by the route at first as we head out towards the west rather than straight south into the mountains, but Isaac's insistent. Apparently, this is where he met the chief of the jentilaks last time, so he feels it offers the best chance of the whistle working.

The direction makes me feel more than a little morose. The previous few runs we did this way were to see Lou Carcoilh, the giant snail-dragon who doubled up as a magical vault for us, storing any treasures too powerful to leave unguarded. Simon De Montfort robbed us and murdered Lou at the same time.

I try to think on happier times from the past. Today is the anniversary of mine and Aicha's trip to Nice, when we investigated dead kids washing up on the beaches of the Cote D'Azur. That this is what my mind considers happier times shows just how fucked up I am. That because I had Aicha with me, it really was better only goes to underline that further.

So I plug Isaac with questions, seeking a distraction outside of the rolling green and the far off mountainous grey tips. 'What are they like, these jentilaks?' It's amazing, really. I've been in the Pyrenees on and off for most of my lives, and I've never run into them.

'Shy. Noble. Not interested in the trappings of the modern world at all. They're much more *natural*, really connected to the world around them.' Isaac's enthusing with all the delight of an anthropology professor who got the chance to have a sit-down chinwag with an early human. 'You know about all the caves around these areas? The Neolithic ones?'

'Sure.' They're quite the tourist draw to the area. 'The earliest cave paintings in Europe, right?'

'Not quite. That's the Chauvet Cave over in the Ardeche, but close. Anyhow, personally, I'm not convinced it was Neanderthals that made them. I suspect it might have been the jentilaks. Legend has it they taught the early Basque people how to farm and cultivate crops, as well as how to use tools. From what I can glean, they've never moved away from that simpler lifestyle. Just away from us and all our noise and pollution. And who can blame them, really, eh?'

There's a wistful tone to his voice, and it makes me snort with laughter. 'Sorry, Isaac, are you pining for a "simpler life" working out in the fields, toiling from dawn till dusk? A world without technology like the Gutenberg Press or the universe of information at our fingertips? You've done it. Finally. After more than eight hundred years, you've finally become an old codger, looking back on the past with rose-tinted spectacles.'

'Bloody cheek!' Isaac flushes, the red creeping down his face, spreading to his neck. 'I'm just saying I admire their honesty, their satisfaction with the basics, the real necessities outside of the world that we complicate.'

'Okay.' Faust leans forward, one hand on each of our seats. 'I'm with you to a degree. I appreciate the simple lifestyle aspect, but do they have *distilleries?*' He grins, the expression of a debate team champion who's just single-handedly shut down the competition.

I hear Mephistopheles mutter, 'Too bloody right,' and what sounds like the distinctive smack of a paw giving a hand a high five. Isaac mutters something about philistines and goes back to concentrating on the road. I notice the colour he's taken on doesn't disappear for quite some time. That keeps me entertained for a good bit of the rest of the drive.

It's getting on for lunchtime when we pull into Saint-Jean-Pied-Du-Port, a complicated name for a simple little town. I can remember it as a village still – wealthy land-owner properties overlooking the river, the stone bridge pulling together the two halves of the settlement and providing a steady flow of footfall through that brings money and trade to enrich the local populous. Or at least those already comfortably off enough to be able to take advantage.

Now it's dying. The number of houses shut up is staggering. Some will be second homes, holiday properties for people from Toulouse or farther afield to use during the summer months. But judging by the permanently closed down retailers, with all but the very last remaining basics out of business for good, the town's not healthy. The elderly remain, the ones who've lived here all their lives or came here in search of an idyllic retirement. The youngsters all head out, seeking employment opportunities no longer available in the rural setting. Although, I do hold on to one spark of hope for gorgeous little idylls like this. Remote working might change that, might bring people back to these once vibrant communities, inject a little much-needed life back in. Keep it from keeling over once and for all.

We don't stop for a meal. I've already gone above and beyond, allowing time for breakfast and coffee. Instead, we find a fast-food establishment and grab some supplies. Faust and Mephy get introduced to the delights of the French "taco". Nothing to do with the Mexican food; it's a wrap filled with meat, melted cheese, and chips, folded up in a square brick of a heart attack. Faust's a little dubious, but Meph sets about his with utter relish. Isaac settles for a chicken shish kebab, and I just go for a box of chips with some falafel. Honestly, the chips on their own are probably enough. My stomach feels too tight with stress and tension to accommodate more than a little food, especially the grease-laden options on offer.

Fortified with food and supplies, including some bottles of water and some off-colour warm dishwater that's apparently supposed to be coffee, we get back in the car and pick our way into the mountains proper. The roads, already narrow, start to constrict further –no doubt like our arteries after the food we've just consumed– and the bends become less curving, more hairpin as we go higher up.

After about half an hour, Isaac pulls onto a side road. There's a tiny green space set aside and a panel that indicates we're at the start of a walk.

'Here's as good a place as any.' Isaac's right. The panel means we're somewhere with public right of way, which reduces the chances of us catching a buttload of shotgun shrapnel from some irate farmer due to us short-cutting across his field. 'Let's get a bit of distance from the road and then we'll see if the whistle works.'

There's a small stile, nothing more than a half-plank of wood wedged between the fence and balanced on two supporting struts that brings us onto the main path. Trees to our left shadow the path, which wends up, coiling between two foothills, deceptively manageable compared to the true mountains it's going to lead us up into. Meph is ecstatic, racing off ahead a few metres before skid-turning and haring back towards us, swerving aside at the last moment before collision. He obviously thinks it's hilarious. I'm more concerned about him fucking up his timing and making contact. Seems like a recipe for two snapped leg bones to me.

After a short walk, we reach a plateau. The ground naturally flattens out, forming a meadow cosseted by the hillocks on either side. We have a good view in either direction up and down the path and can make sure no innocent hiker or dog walker gets to stand witness to our hopeful rendezvous with the jentilak leader. Of course, their natural camouflage magic should keep them safe, but I throw up a *don't look here* spell just to be sure as Isaac blows on the whistle.

It's a strange effect. There's no audible sound, but I feel all the hairs on my arms, of which there are plenty, stand up suddenly. It's like someone is giving tap-dancing lessons to an army of ghost mice wearing clogs on top of one of my many graves. Eerie, unsettling. Mephy's ears flatten back against the sides of his head, and he raises a whining ululation that echoes back off the flanking hillside, only adding to the disturbing feeling.

'Bloody hell, mano, that was horrible.' Mephy's lip stays peeled back, his incisors displayed, though I'm not convinced he's even aware of it. I have to agree, and my hearing's nowhere near as sensitive as his is.

I stand there for a few moments, my head swinging around from side to side, waiting for the chief of the jentilaks to appear. Then realisation sets in that, actually, he could be anywhere in the mountain range, and unless he has the power of teleportation, it's probably going to take him a while to make an appearance. There's an old severed tree trunk just this side of the fence. I'm guessing it got felled for daring to not follow the man-made restrictions laid down by the barriers in place, but either way, it makes a handy seat. I ease myself down with a sigh, settling in for a long wait.

'What want?' Apparently, today's the day for people aiming to make me shit my pants every time I relax. The voice comes from behind me, and I'm pretty sure I wedge several considerable wood splinters into my posterior as I skirt my arse forward, shooting back up to my feet to look around. And I get my first sight ever of a jentilak.

The first impression I get is *big*. The second is *hairy*. My first thought is how very similar the jentilak is to the North American myth of Bigfoot, of how closely that matches to the yeti. My mind –being as it's mine– starts whirring off into all sorts of questions about previous migratory habits of the jentilaks and ancient civilisations of giant hairy creatures. Do they still have lines of contact? Are there twinning programs between different mountains in the Himalayas, the Pyrenees, and the Appalachians? Do they organise cultural exchanges? A hundred and one irrelevant questions that I'll probably never get the answer to flood my brain as I stare up at one of the shaggy, wild mountain men of Basque legend.

The creature is seriously tall. Well over two metres. I'm craning my neck back to look at him, and I can feel a crick developing. If we get into any extended conversation, we're either going to need to sit down, or I'm going to spend the whole time talking to his overly developed pectorals. He looks like Cousin It if he'd started training for the World's Strongest Man competition. It certainly doesn't look like he'd have any problems tossing a tractor tyre. Probably not even a tractor. His hair is that sort of reddish brown that some black-haired men's beards turn out to be, causing this weird top-head/bottom-head colour juxtaposition. Of course, that's not an issue for him as his curtains definitely match his drapes, so to speak, from tip to toe. Luckily, said drapes are very long and luxuriant, so as to hide whatever he has behind them from sight. Which is a good thing as if they're even vaguely in proportion to the rest of his oversized physique, I'd end up suffering a sense of comparative inadequacy for however much life or lives still lie ahead of me. He's completely naked apart from a headband with what looks like an eagle feather poking out the back of it, but then I would be too, if I basically spent the whole time swathed in the equivalent of a shag carpet straight from a seventies love den.

Of course, with that, I'm basing his masculinity off the deep voice and the impressive chest musculature without the defining mammalian breasts. Possibly an error on my part, but hey, if there's one thing humans are good at, it's forming snap judgments and sticking with them. So until I find out differently, my brain's fixed on male and isn't going to vary from that, no way, no how.

Isaac bows his head respectfully, placing a closed fist over his breast where his heart is. 'Dunixi, it is an honour to see you again.'

The creature grunts, nods stiffly. 'Honour mine. Why here?'

Isaac keeps his head low. 'We have come to seek your wisdom and guidance, great leader of the jentilaks. My friends and I have travelled in our metal carriage to discuss goings on affecting us all.'

The jentilak looks us over one by one, scouring us with his glance. 'These pale-faces not all local. Flew in metal bird?'

'Indeed, great chief of the noble jentilaks –' Isaac starts, but he's cut off by a loud chuffing noise.

I look down to see Mephy, who's sat back on his haunches, shaking with doggy chortles. I've never seen a dog cry with laughter before, but life is full of firsts. One of the reasons I'm so keen to keep having another go at it when the 1 UP symbol starts flashing

Isaac looks less than amused. 'What's funny about that, demon?' Ooh. He's really pissed off. It's not often I've heard that sort of tone from him, but it's been turned on me a time or two. 'Zac feels like we're being rude, especially to someone he admires.

Mephistopheles is gasping for breath at this point. He's actually rolled onto his back, and he's kicking his legs feebly in the air, like he's getting a ghostly belly rub that's tickling him at the same time. It takes him a few goes to calm down. Each time he starts getting himself back under control, he cracks up again. Faust gives us all an apologetic look and shrugs.

I understand. It's a look my friends have had to give people because of me plenty of times before.

Eventually, Mephy calms down enough to manage to wheeze out a syllable. 'Bull... bullshit...' he gasps out.

'I beg your pardon? What did you say?' Goodness me, if I thought Isaac was unhappy before, now he has a face like thunder, if Thunder had just found Lightning in bed with his wife and both his daughters.

'I said bullshit.' Mephy's rolled back into a sitting position and raises a paw to wipe delicately at his eyes. 'Seriously, you've spoken to this guy before' –he jerks his snout at the jentilak– 'and you bought all this ""' bullshit? Are you a fucking idiot? What did you do for them that got you that little whistle?'

Isaac's looking like he's struggling to know how to breathe, and his skin seems equally confused as to if he's upset or embarrassed, flushing a mixture between pink and purple as he tries to find his words. 'I...I found one of their children,' he manages eventually. 'While walking through the mountains, I came across one of their youngsters. They'd got their leg trapped by a rockslide. I freed them with Nithael's help and got them back to the tribe.'

'How long did you spend with them afterwards?' Mephistopheles is still grinning, his tongue hanging out, looking delighted with the whole situation.

'Two days.' Isaac flushes again when the jentilak holds up his fingers to correct the count. 'Three, maybe.'

'At their homes?'

'Not...precisely. They were camped. There were some shelters they'd thrown together. We stayed and talked. It took me a little while to teach them some rudimentary English. Plus they were often absent, going hunting, with only a mute old fellow who kept me company. But I still found out a little bit about their fascinating culture.'

'And did part of this teaching them to speak English, mano, involve educating them to speak like a poor knock-off of a Native American from an old western movie? Because if it did, you're a terrible racist.'

Poor Isaac is spluttering at this point, practically apoplectic. Mephy starts chuckling at this again. 'Oh, bloody manos. Even those of you with an open heart can have a pretty closed mind sometimes. I can't believe you bought this total act he fed you. Clever work though. A mind like yours is a bugger to dissuade from investigating once it sinks its teeth into a puzzle. Trust me – I live with another one who's just the same. Bloody genius of these jentilaks to persuade you they are a bunch of basic bitches to keep you from digging any further.'

The demon dog swivels his head away from Isaac, who's incapable of forming any words right now anyhow, and looks at the enormous mountain man. The shaggy creature has watched all of this impassively. Personally, I'm in no hurry to piss him off, considering he looks like he could pop my head off my shoulders like a cap off a beer bottle and without needing a bottle opener, but Meph doesn't seem in the least bit bothered.

'Right, matey. Any chance you'll stop fucking with the manos now and drop the whole schtick?'

The jentilak stares down at him, straight-backed, his arms ramrod by his sides, and for a moment, I think Mephy's fucked it all up for us, that the creature's going to take offence and disappear as suddenly as he popped up, and we'll be back at square one with no way to find out more about what the fuck is going on. Then suddenly, he sighs, sags, and nods.

'Demons. Incorrigible fiends by all accountings. Never crossed your type before personally, but it would seem that rumour and reality correlate with a certain exactitude.'

Well, blow me down with a feather and paint me in tar. It really was an act. And judging by Isaac's impression of a Crazy Golf obstacle – his mouth opening and closing with a mechanical regularity – he had absolutely no idea

It really is a pleasure that someone other than me gets to look like a bit of a dopey bastard for once.

CHAPTER TEN

THE PYRENEES, 30 OCTOBER, PRESENT DAY

I guess it goes to show that even the most open-hearted of us carry some prejudices tucked away deep inside. Also, you can guarantee I'm going to be teasing Isaac about this for the rest of existence, however long that may be.

'B...But how?' Isaac's regained his voice – and his sense of outrage, going off the rising pitch and tone of his voice. 'Why? I helped you!' There's a plaintive whine to the last phrase. I feel for him. Isaac doesn't help people to get anything in return. But getting made a fool out of after doing so is enough to upset anyone.

The jentilak sighs and crouches down, bringing himself towards our level, a half-smile on his face that suggests he either feels a bit embarrassed or he has bad gas he's trying to keep in. It's always the problem of trying to read cryptid expressions; we humanise those who aren't human. Or else we go the other way and treat them as animals rather than people just because they're a different species. Basically, we tend to fuck it up whichever way we go.

'Look.' The giant furry creature stares Isaac in the eye. 'You're an inordinately intelligent individual. Plus, your erstwhile colleague was entirely astute in his observations. One hardly needed to be a master of the psychological arts to determine your innate curiosity and endless drive to decipher each and every enigma that should stumble into your path.'

He lays a hand gently onto Isaac's shoulder. Good thing he does it with such care and attention. His arms are as thick as a telegraph pole, and his hands have that sort of cracked leather padding that large apes often have, which seems purposely designed to allow a perfect grip as they tear the limbs off anyone who irritates them like they're perforated cardboard.

'You seem like a genuinely splendid chap, and your saving of our little girl was a wondrous and endlessly appreciated act of largesse. But we've learnt long ago what comes of interacting with you lesser simians. Simple of thought leads quick to anger, and it's always such a blasted mess. It's why we've withdrawn up here. Stay well away from all your constant bickerings and so much endless noise.'

Damn. That doesn't sound good. 'You said you don't have anything to do with lesser simians?' I suppose I should take offence at the description, but, well, we don't exactly do much as a species to put ourselves on a higher pedestal than the other hominoids if I'm honest. Rape, greed, murder. Not exactly shining characteristics to hold up as defining achievements of your race.

The jentilak looks over at me. 'That is correct, my good fellow.'

'So you haven't been looking after the simiots since they retreated up here?'

The giant hairy humanoid blinks at me, an expression that looks very human indeed. 'The simiots, you say? Well, absolutely, we have assisted in their accommodating in these rocky climes since they, too, withdrew from the larger world. I did specify *lesser* simians, chap.'

This time, it's not just Isaac looking like a goldfish having a stroke. it's all of us, punctuated by the wheezing chuffs of an endlessly amused Mephistopheles.

While those of us who are actually human recover from the unintentionally savage burn from the jentilak leader, Dunixi raises a finger, looking at me.

'You wanted to ask about the simiots. Why? They've gone missing. We've not seen sight nor sound of them for more than a Gregorian month. A most mysterious disappearance.'

So I tell him. I update him about their usage by the demon and explain how we killed as few as we could but incapacitated them, passing them over to the Sistren to look after until we could find a safe home for them.

'... so we'll organise getting them back here in whatever manner suits you so you can pick them up.' A thought strikes me. 'Can you keep them safe from possession again?'

The giant ape-man sighs. He squatted down while I told him our tale, sitting back on his haunches in a way that makes my own calves burn in sympathy after about thirty seconds, and there he still remains. 'The simiots have always been wanderers by nature. We shall have to encourage them to repose at our home for the time being. There they'll be safe until such time as you can notify us as to the passing of all threats and dangers. Assuming you will be so considerate as to provide such illumination?'

I nod. 'Of course. The least I can do.' This is looking like a bust. The jentilaks know nothing about the simiots' disappearance. 'What about the tattoo they all have?'

The creature freezes, every muscle locking into place, and his head swings slowly back in my direction. 'What tattoo?'

Oh. This is news apparently. 'The one that's Charlemagne's signature. The signum magnus.'

The jentilak watches me for a moment, studying my face. I'm not sure if he's searching for a lie, judging my individual worthiness, or calculating how much work he'd need to do with a lathe to plane my skull into a smooth enough shape to use as a bowling ball. After an uncomfortable silence that seems to drag on for about five years, he blinks again, twice. Long and slow, and it seems as though that's the indication of him having reached a decision. Although whether that decision is that I'm an okay sort or that he's going to book a lane for him and his pals to knock some pins down on Thursday night, I've no idea.

'Well then. My goodness.' He smooths down his long orangutan-like hair as he stretches back up to his full, enormous height. 'I think you should all accompany me back to Home.'

He puts an emphasis on the first letter that makes it clear it's a title. Sounds like a terrible store that's likely to sell "Live, Laugh, Love" wooden signs and garden gnomes making rude finger gestures, but I decide not to tell him that. Mainly on the grounds of him looking capable of beating me to death with my own arm in a single swing after popping it off my shoulder.

We start along the path once more, making our way farther up into the mountains. Our guide, if that's his role, has fallen silent once again, and I get the feeling he doesn't actually speak too much.

The silence means we can hardly discuss what's going on, so there's a lot of poor attempts at sublingual communication. Eyebrows waggle furiously; eyes pop, darting from the jentilak and back to us, although what that's supposed to mean other than, "he's him, and we're us", I'm not sure. As I'm performing the same face-dance, I'm sure the rest are equally confused by my weird gurning attempts to express my confusion and suspicions about what Dunixi's intentions are.

Eventually, he stops and sighs, turning to look at us all. 'I'm terribly sorry, but all this bizarre facial gesticulating is a bit unsettling.'

Oops. Apparently, jentilaks have excellent peripheral vision. He carries on, 'Was there something that you wished to express or clarify?'

Oh, bugger it. 'Yes, absolutely. Does mentioning the simiots' tattoos mean we've discovered some terrible ancient conspiracy, and you're now leading us away to be sealed below the earth, never to be heard from again?'

That's one of the problems of too much quiet and an over-active imagination. My brain's mapped out several detailed stories about what these giant muscle-bound ape-people might do to us to protect their mysteries. Especially now their whole "simple wild creatures" schtick has fallen flat, thanks to Mephy's powers of observation.

Dunixi shakes his head and chuckles. 'No, fear is entirely unnecessary in that regard. We mean you no harm.' He speaks the last few words slowly and loudly, annunciating as clearly as possible, like he's talking to a particularly dense child. He studies me carefully, doubtless looking to see if he's managed to calm me down. Satisfied, he carries on, 'No, what I'm doing is the greatest honour we can offer. Something no human has ever received. I'm accompanying you into the heart of our society. There we can discuss your tribulations more efficaciously.'

Ooh. Nice. Looks like we're taking a trip to the jentilaks' homeland as honoured guests. I can't help looking at the arriving forest. We're still low enough down on the slopes for the trees to cling on in enough numbers as to provide solid shelter, and I wonder if they've built villages up in their tops like the Ewoks in *Return of The Jedi*.

The jentilak sees my gaze and perhaps reads my mind – or at least my expression – effectively enough to understand what I'm thinking.

'Not up,' he says with a shake of his massive shaggy head and points one of those leathered fingers at the ground. 'Down.'

Interesting. So the jentilaks live under the mountains. And by interesting, I mean "deeply triggering and causing bucketloads of sweat to suddenly gush from every pore on my body". I don't have good recent memories of caves under mountains. My period trapped in one during my trip to Faerie, dying of thirst in the dark over and over again, still stains my psyche. And this time, there's no Aicha Kandicha around to ride to the rescue.

What there is, is Isaac. I feel a steadying hand on the small of my back. The Good God bless him, he's clocked my reaction to the news. There's no one in the world who knows me better.

'It'll be all right, lad,' he murmurs just for my ears. 'I don't think it'll be down into some dingy hole. Only a bloody idiot would believe these fellas are primitives, right?'

I can't control the snort that comes out nor the accompanying grin that spreads over my face. It might not have completely eliminated the cold sweats, but it's helped me get a grip on myself again.

We walk on, up the winding path for what feels like an hour or so. I could take my phone out, check the time, but that's only going to increase the sense of pressure. We're making progress; we've found the jentilaks, and they're prepared to talk to us. Now the ball is in their court. Putting any more pressure on either them or ourselves isn't going to help matters. It's just likely to lead to a mistake. Nope. For now I just need to go with the flow and concentrate on not having some sort of massive freak out screaming fit when we head underground.

'There.' The huge creature points one of those fur-covered digits that looks as muscly as my arm towards what I think is just a few rocks in the middle of a field. It's only as we close the distance that I realise it's a henge. Two smaller rocks on the side support a flattened top stone that's been placed horizontally over them, although not cleanly done. No, it rests on them and slopes back to the ground, forming a grotto of sorts, an entrance clearly placed between the two menhirs. There's a roll of barbed wire leaning against the wall and some old wooden beams that suggest a local farmer's been using it as a storage shed. There's also a major problem I can see with it...

It's about four feet high. If that. Like, I can squeeze inside, sure, with my head down. But one, I can see that I'd be scraping my back on the overhead stone when I do so, and two, I reckon if our host put his knee in there, he's going to end up knocking the whole structure over. There's literally no way he's getting in.

Isaac breathes a sigh. It's a soft breath, not shocked, but he sounds surprised. 'The dolmens of the Pyrenees, of course. I think this is the Dolmen of Gasteynia.'

'So you've been here before?' I shouldn't be surprised. Isaac loves wandering these mountains. Hell, that's how he met the jentilaks the first time.

'Oh, yes.' He smiles, though whether at the memory or me for asking a pretty stupid question considering the information he just shared, I've no idea. 'There're plenty of these scattered around the peaks in this part of the mountain. Prehistoric burial sites for the Neanderthals, perhaps their leaders or priests, dating back millions of years.' His eyes narrow, looking suspiciously at the huge jentilak. 'Supposedly anyhow.'

'They're ours,' Dunixi speaks, looking at each of us with a fierce expression. 'And I'll have an oath on your *power* not to reveal them to anyone else before we lead on in.'

I'm still not seeing how we're going to manage that, but at the same time, it's not my problem. We're definitely in the jentilak's hands, and, let's face it, physics tends to need to have a nice long lie down in a cool, dark room after magic gets involved.

We all agree readily. Oaths on our *power* aren't small promises to make; they're liable to lead to your magic malfunctioning or diminishing if you break them, but this is an easy one. Dunixi is protecting his people, and there's not one of us who underestimates how much good faith he's showing by taking us to their home. They've kept this place secret for unknown centuries. Hell, they didn't even trust Isaac with the information after he saved one of their kids, and he's *Isaac*. People fall over themselves to give him their most intimate details, down to their mother's maiden name and their bank account number. If the jentilak's being straight up, then we'd never want to betray the trust he's showing us. If he's setting us up, either the combined magical might of the four of us will be enough to resolve the problem, or else we're never going to be telling the secrets of it to anyone anyway. Or of anything else. Ever.

He nods gravely, taking a last moment to look us up and down. 'Good. I can see you all comprehend the exact magnitude of this. Whilst my preference would be to proceed in advance and give just notification of this arrival, my people will respect my decision. Still, they are not used to outsiders, especially not humans and' –he waves a hand at Mephy– 'a demon.'

'Demon dog.' Mephy yaps the words out. 'I embrace both sides of my heritage. Best of both worlds, baby.'

Dunixi looks at him hard. I think he's wondering if Mephy's taking the piss out of him. It's quite a common reaction every time he talks to anyone. I often squint at the Doberman demon. I can't help trying to do an Aicha-style contraction of the title. Deberman? Dobermon? No, the last one sounds like you'd try to collect him in a little ball and throw him at other people to make him battle. Try that, and Mephy would tear your face off. Your balls too, probably, little or otherwise.

'Fine,' the jentilak says after a pause. 'Demon dog. My point is that my people are not rambunctious or prone to great turns of dialogue. Please don't try to engage them in extended conversation. They're shy, quiet beings. Not subjects of curious examination.'

As he says the last part, he fixes both Isaac and Johannes with a particularly hard stare. Both of them blush simultaneously. Looks like he has their measure. Academics. Give them a world-ending machine, and they'll be prodding and pushing at various parts trying to work out exactly how much of the world would end if they theoretically pushed *this* button.

Dunixi turns away from us and starts to walk towards the henge, and we follow. As we do so, perspective distorts. It's a strange feeling, like being incredibly drunk. Each blink seems to distort the world, and distances stretch and contract with every step. Whilst we're definitely walking at a measured pace, one foot in front of the other, each time we move forward, the opening grows dramatically, as though we'd been a mile away instead of a few metres and we're wearing Seven-League Boots. By the time we've closed the short distance, the opening looks as large as the gates of the Mines of Moria, as huge as one of those entrances that Lou Carcoilh made in his cavernous prison under the hill of Hastingues.

'Welcome to Home,' Dunixi says and steps forward into the welcoming, enveloping darkness.

At least, it looks like that's how it feels for him. For me, it looks ready to swallow me whole and take me back into the endless night.

I feel Isaac's hand on my shoulder once more and draw the strength I can from it. Then I muster my courage and step into the unknown dark.

CHAPTER ELEVEN
HOME, 30 OCTOBER, PRESENT DAY

If I click my heels together three times and scream, 'There's no place like home,' will somebody please turn the fucking lights on?

There's that moment when I can't see anything, when pitch black wraps around me like a blanket, like a blindfold forced over my vision, where I almost can't take it. I can feel the breeze still at my back, and it's like it's calling to me, telling me to just turn and run, and the sky will be there, the open spaces without walls, without rock overhead crushing down on me without ever having to touch me, pressing on my mind until I'm sure it'll break. It whispers in my ear and tells me that if I go down again, I'll never come back up, never make my way back to the sun's caress on my cheeks. That I'll be lost to the dark forever.

But Isaac's hand is still there, and I'll not fail. Not falter. So I walk forward and hope my heart isn't about to explode. It certainly feels like it's beating hard enough to.

Then a everything changes. Because we're not walking in the dark anymore, no. The whole world is illuminated like someone stole the sun and brought it underground. Which I'm pretty sure hasn't happened as even I would probably have noticed that.

We've only been in darkness for a few seconds, those first few steps forward, but it's still enough to make me blink and shield my eyes. The tunnel we're in is no narrow passageway, and there's no need for torches, either in hand or on the walls. Because the walls themselves are aglow.

It's a strange effect because it's not like they're manufactured. This isn't some sort of human passageway. There're no electric lights stuck into neat-cut plasterboard. It's rock, smoothed and worked but natural nonetheless. Nor is it some sort of fantasy novel involving dwarves, where they've worked glowing crystals into the rock face, however much that gaping doorway put me in mind of Moria. It's more like the stone itself has been bespelled, granted a luminescence that one doesn't associate with the granite-like substance we're walking through. The glow is orange tinged, totally unlike the harsh halogen realities we're so acclimatised to with our strip lights and LEDs. It gives everything a rich warmth, makes the stone seem inviting, accommodating. And it takes me a moment before I realise that warmth isn't only visual. It's actual. There's a heat coming from them that fights off any chills that linger from the outside mountain air. Amazing.

The passage is large as well. I couldn't touch both walls even with my hands fully outstretched. There's space for two jentilaks to walk side by side and for a third to pass them without discomfort. And as I think that, I realise that's probably exactly the mathematical problem whoever built this had in mind. We're in a world that's built for the comfort of the giant simians. It makes me feel a little like a Liliputian who's snuck back to our world in Gulliver's pocket. This isn't a place made for humans.

The tunnel slopes down, and we follow our host deeper into the bowels. It's a veritable maze. Other passages spring off as we go down, in all directions, so that within what I'd take to be about half an hour, I'm completely lost. Luckily, the place is expansive enough and well-lit enough that my newfound claustrophobia isn't rearing up too badly, even with not knowing how to get the fuck out of Dodge should the need arise.

What I don't see are many jentilaks. Not really any, actually. Just flashes of fur as we turn this way, a glimpse of a hairy back as we round that corner. Looks like they're keeping well away from us. Can't blame them. There's a reason most Talented creatures avoid humanity like the plague. Because we've been more ravenous than the Black Death ever was. Whole species have been wiped out, normally for making the mistake of trusting people not to just kill them on sight and steal whatever valuables they had up to – and including, in some cases – their back teeth. Honestly, I'm not sure how we got away with them not exterminating us earlier on in our species' existence. I suspect they didn't recognise what a threat we were until it was too late. I'm also sure there's more than one of them who's regretted that lack of foresight.

There's some interesting *talent* at work in the way this particular honey-comb of tunnels operates as well. Effects similar to the one we had with the way in. Sometimes we'll be heading down a branching path towards what looks like a solid wall. Then as we approach, a mouse-hole sized opening that's impossible even to see at a distance grows up, enlarging with each arriving step until it's an archway hewn out of the rock and patterned with wonderfully detailed carvings, more intricate than any of the gothic spires littered throughout the French countryside. Much of it seems to be whirls and glyphs, crossing patterns that might be letters, might be hieroglyphics, might even be rune work. Perhaps it's these that create this strange spatial distortion effect. I wonder if I'd find the same engravings on the three stones overhead

Also, sometimes the entrances seem almost to appear from our flanks unexpectedly, cave-like mouths yawning open out of nowhere, and for a minute, I see a flash of fur, mistrustful eyes in an unnatural dark. Then when I put my foot down, it shrinks away, closing up. I look over at Isaac, see him rubbing his chin, studying where one of these apertures just appeared, then disappeared equally quickly.

He feels my eyes on him, looks over at me. 'Doors, I think.' He's musing, enjoying the intellectual exercise. 'At a guess, the stone responds to them. So they can set up a private dwelling and then open or close it at will. Perhaps they can even lock them, except to family members. My guess? They're jentilaks about to leave their abode –'

'Then seeing us,' Mephy interrupts, 'and noping the fuck back inside.'

Isaac winces. 'Exactly this. Only less crude had I explained it.'

'More bloody flowery and endlessly unnecessarily descriptive, you mean, mano.' Mephy snorts and shakes his head. 'Get it said. A fuck is a fuck, same as a leg is a sex machine. Honestly, no idea why you humans bother with porn. I watched some once. It was all the boring bits. Arses and tits and cocks. None of the good stuff. None of that hardcore knob-on-leg action at all.'

'And that's a deviation that none of us saw coming or wished to take.' I shake my head, trying to dislodge that particular mental image, which has sunk its claws in and is riding my brain like a mechanical bull in a theme park bar.

'Of course, I found some eventually. Did you know –'

'We're here,' Dunixi interrupts and wins my eternal gratitude for it. I've no idea where here is, any more than I know what Mephy was about to tell us. Only that, whatever it was, I can happily go through the rest of existence without ever having it taking up residence in my neurones.

Another arch lies ahead of us, but it's on a whole other scale of grandeur. The luminescence of the walls strengthens until it forms a surrounding band of sun-like radiance, encapsulating the entrance. It's as if someone created the world's best panel lighting and then melded it with the rock face. And cutting through that orange light is cool-blue script and shapes – lines and whorls, possible glyphs and almost recognisable images that seem to flicker and move, giving a sense of momentum to the archway. It's at least twice as high as Dunixi and wide enough for five of the jentilaks to walk through without bumping shoulders.

'Through here is the heart of Home,' the jentilak says, clasping his hands together, his head bowed almost as though in prayer. 'If you should bring any disrespect, then know it shall be the last place you ever see.'

'Threats?' Mephy's voice rumbles at the back of his throat, half-way to a snarl.

'Promises.' Dunixi wears an almost apologetic look, that same sort of expression when a waiter says that no, he's checked three times and you're definitely not on the reservation list and still won't be if he goes and checks for a fourth. 'You're walking into the heart of our power, and even demons and angels won't walk away if they turn against us.'

Interesting. That's the first time he's mentioned Nithael, and I see from the way that Isaac's eyebrow cocks up that he's caught it too. 'Zac's not mentioned him. I wonder if he told him about his Bene Elohim companion the first time they met, or if the jentilak's even sharper than I've given him credit for. When he's not got his guard up, when he's on home territory, Nith stretches out above him in the ether, a literal guardian angel. But when in among the unknown, the angel tucks away, out of sight, not exposing his hand, invisible to anyone Isaac doesn't trust implicitly. Isaac's radiant when *looked* at, of course, absolutely packed full of *talent*, but not everyone is going to link that to a being from the higher dimensions no one alive on Earth has ever seen before. Or, at least, no one that we've ever known of. These jentilaks continue to be more and more mysterious.

The jentilak waves us in through the enormous entry, and we step into an equally huge cavern. It'd be enough to make Michaelangelo start ordering up the whole of Italy's supplies of paint and tiles while ly sketching out painting plans. The space is vast – at least forty metres high and much wider, with the same luminescent smooth stone walls. And the patterning that we saw around the doorways is present too. Everywhere. But this time...

This time it's alive. And it's not marked or carved into the rocks. It's *talent*, pure and raw, and it writhes and dances across the walls. It's like someone took the Bayeux Tapestry and mixed it up with the designs on the walls of the Great Pyramid and the letter art from the *Book of Kells* and then translated it into animated pure neon. Glyphs and characters move constantly, shifting and changing, and I am utterly transfixed. There are stories here but not just stories. Questions and answers, neither of which I knew, both of which now must be known. There're secrets and solutions to every puzzle that ever tormented me, and it's all here if I just watch it long enough, study it hard enough. It's that feeling like when a realisation is budding on your branching thoughts, when you know that if you just feed it a little more, it'll blossom into a life-changing understanding. I'm turning with the movements, twirling to follow it, to take it all in simultaneously...

When I feel a hand, larger than my head, check me, and pull me to a stop. 'Calm yourself, human.' The jentilak's words are soft, understanding but determined. 'Don't get lost in here. The answers you seek won't be found on the walls. These are stories for my people.'

He's turned me, so I look him directly in his orb-like eyes, black on white. I focus on those, fighting the itching drag of the walls demanding my attention. Slowly, I calm and get myself back under control. He's right. Whatever the magic is saying is fascinating, deeply intriguing, and if we had nothing to do, no time pressures, I'd be delighted to spend a lifetime or two here studying them. A thought strikes me. My goodness, after eight hundred years plus of Isaac trying, have I finally become scholarly?

Thinking of which, I flick my eyes over to the two actual academics in our group. Isaac and Faust are both standing there like guilty schoolkids, their shoulders slumped. Johannes is scratching at the back of his calf with his right foot, and 'Zac's worrying his lip. Their eyes are downcast at the light-grey floor, like marbleised granite. Mephy, on the other hand, is simply sitting there. He meets my gaze with bored impatience.

'What?' He huffs. 'It's only bloody stories. Heard them all before.'

Heard them *all* before? This place feels like a treasure trove of the unknown, of fables that will weave together understandings that could advance a civilisation or crumble it to dust, and Mephy already holds them all in his head? There are times I forget he's from a different dimension, one that looks on our petty existence with something akin to pity or perhaps disdain. Or both. Not for the first time, I wonder why he stays. Perhaps some form of entanglement of souls, like 'Zac and Nith? But if we're so far down the evolutionary ladder, surely killing Johannes to get free wouldn't be such an ask? Instead, he's spent centuries trapped in our poor excuse of a reality. Meph distracts from it regularly with his leg-bothering antics, but he remains an enigma, and I'd do well to hold on to that. Somehow, it seems to slip away from me when I'm not concentrating on it, and I fall back into underestimating the demon dog

I've calmed down now, got myself back under control, and it's like the light of the living *talent* has dimmed slightly. It's still there, and if I let myself, I'll be completely enraptured in it a moment later, but as long as I concentrate on *not* watching it, I can look around.

The cavern's not empty. Now that I've pulled my attention from the walls and ceiling, I can see that. It has a natural curve to it, forming a bell-like shape. And throughout the room, on stands, are books. They're held on pillars of stone that look like the world's most perfectly formed stalagmites sprouting out of the ground, fingers of smoothed rock that finish in a slanted surface, like a lectern. The books themselves...

'Are...are they made of stone?' I almost can't believe it. They're the same light grey as the rest of the room, but they're not carvings. I'm almost sure of it. I look over at Dunixi to see his lips quirk, amused.

'May I?' Maybe I'm overstepping my welcome, but I want to see if they're how they look. He nods his acquiescence, and I step to the nearest one. Sure enough, it's the same smooth rock as all the tunnels have been. But I can open it, and inside are pages. Pages of malleable stone as thin as paper that I can turn, which I do with great reverence. The only thing is...

'They're all blank!' I can't quite keep the disappointment from my voice. Considering what's swirling around our heads, I expected them to be tomes packed full of secret esoteric knowledge. Instead, while each is an improbability, a work of art to have created *pages out of stone*, to somehow make them usable, flexible enough to bind and turn without them cracking, they're blank, plain sheets. Remarkable but not *magical*.

'They are. Now.' The huge, hairy mountain man takes up that same haunch-busting squat, bringing himself down to my level. 'We could fill them again if the need arises. The magic that swirls in the walls, the power that courses through these mountains? It once poured into these pages, filling them with knowledge and stories beyond the humanity of that time's ken. We shared some, passing on information that allowed you to grow, telling you parables and guidances half-hidden in codes and prophesies, ways to help you to advance. We were a more engaged species back then, more outgoing and exuberant, ready to get involved in the world.'

'What happened?' The question comes from Faust, but I don't doubt we're all wondering the same thing. Except Mephy, who's decided that licking his own arsehole is more interesting. The jentilak doesn't look offended. Apparently, he understands the fascinations of canines. Or demons. I really don't know how much is dog and how much is Mephy.

'What always happens eventually. The world disappointed us.' Dunixi wears a sad smile as he says it, trying to take the sting out of the words. 'Humans decided we weren't giving them *enough*, that we obviously had secret troves. Which, of course, we did, but not of what their rapacious hunger desired. They assumed we must have the same things they lusted for – gold, jewels. Wealth and riches. When we told them knowledge was our treasure, they assumed us liars. And then...'

A shadow passes over his face. 'Then they came to our homes. To entrances we'd shown them, with steel we'd helped them forge. With fire and fury and jealous hatred. And they made us kill them.'

Now tears are running down the jentilak's cheeks, leaving wet traces in the red-brown fur, sticking it down. 'They hurt us. And our children. And we, who wanted nothing more than to live in peace had no choice but to soak our halls with their blood and stain our minds with death wrought and brought.'

Dunixi wipes at his damp cheeks. 'I saw them. Saw the story of our people. Felt their inconsolable pain at the decision forced upon them. Nothing but terrible options.' He sighs. 'All we've ever wanted is peace. Peace in the world. Peace and quiet. A calm space for us to enjoy all the stories we've gathered to us. That's how we used our *talent* before. This working, you see? It's the collective power of all of our people, all of us who've ever lived. It gathers all the writings of every people, every species, of every plane. Think of it like the National Library, only on a far grander scale. An Intergalactic Library, if you will.'

I can't resist casting a glance across at Isaac and Johannes. Sure enough, they have that same wide-eyed look of Charlie Bucket walking into the Chocolate Factory for the very first time. This, this is their dream. All the knowledge in all the worlds gathered and placed at their fingertips. I'm not entirely sure I'll ever get them back out of this room. Not without a crowbar and dousing them in Vaseline.

But they've missed one important aspect, one distinct difference. 'Why are they all blank?'

Dunixi smiles, nodding at me. I think he's clocked the look on my friends' faces, sees they've not picked up on this vital point. 'That magic, it took all we had as a people. It forced us to go out into the world, to risk life on the topside, cultivating crops, putting ourselves at risk. Situations where our children might be harmed. And the stories still abound out there, of the jentilaks and their riches. We don't want to have to kill more humans just to control their greed.'

There's a heavy truth there. Sometimes, there's no other option. We'll get consumed by greed, possessed by it just as effectively as any demonic intervention. And when a human's lost to that madness, there's little short of death that'll dissuade them.

This sounds utterly tragic, and my heart breaks for the jentilaks. 'So you stopped using it?' I guess. 'Gave up on your knowledge, on your reading, to keep your people safe?'

Dunixi rears backwards, staggering to his feet. The look of shock and horror on his face is as if I just asked him if his mother was single and whether she accepted credit card payments. 'Stop reading?' He literally clutches at his heart or where I assume his heart to be, assuming the jentilaks follow most simian anatomy. 'Never, good sir!'

I definitely get the impression I've insulted his honour, that of his ancestors, and all of his progeny ever to come. 'I'm so sorry.' The words seem totally insufficient, so I look at the magic swirling in the walls. 'Um, sorry to you as well?'

Dunixi quits hyperventilating; he closes his eyes and calms himself. 'It's fine. It's fine. Just. Urgh. The very idea. The mana from which nightmares are manufactured, in my opinion.' He gets himself back under control, breathing more easily. 'No, of course we didn't stop *reading*.'

He shudders involuntarily again. 'Stories are the very source of life. They're what makes existence have any value or meaning. What separates it from paltry actuality. No. But for once, you humans came up with something that made our lives easier rather than the other way round.'

He rummages inside the long hair strands around his belly and sinks his hands in. Amazing. They must have something like a marsupial pouch there. Inbuilt pockets. No wonder they don't bother with clothing.

'Ah ha!' He stops and withdraws his hands, waving around a small black oblong. It's absolutely tiny in his hand, looking like some ridiculous, overly miniaturised telephone, maybe a joke toy or something. It takes me a minute to work out what it is. Just as I get there, so does Johannes.

'*Mein Goht*, it's an e-reader!' He slaps his thigh in excitement. I think, with all this wonder and mystery, he's delighted to have solved something, even just a "what the hell is that?" question, popping into our heads.

'Exactly!' Dunixi grins, his sharp curved teeth glinting in the light of the dancing *talent* sigils and shapes. 'What a brilliant idea. It took a little time, but we managed to create a sympathetic connection between our magic and the device. Then it was easy to persuade the human databases to fill them to the brim. The collective power of the jentilaks keeps them fully charged, and we have access to so many wondrous stories and sagas, all contained in a tiny device. More reading material than even we could ever devour in a lifetime.'

My mind is, officially, blown. The jentilaks aren't some noble savages. They're magical hackers who've created a pirate link to human book databases, allowing them to nick every book in existence.

Dunixi doesn't seem to have noticed how flabbergasted I am. 'In the meantime, now that we don't have to use our *talent* to allow us to read, we can use it to provide all our other needs. Food and drink, safety and security. If we want to go out, to walk and breathe the air of the mountains, we can. But most of the time, we're happy here. Safe at Home, with an unlimited collection of books and no need ever to vacate the premises.'

By the Good God. The jentilaks are the distilled essence of the bookworm introvert. They've achieved what most serious readers would consider perfection. *Here, have unlimited books, everything you need in terms of sustenance, and no requirement to ever leave the house again.* I'm not going to lie; I'm more than a little jealous. No wonder they call this place Home. It's definitely where my heart is right now.

'That's a lovely little story,' Mephy cuts in as he lifts his head, a bored expression on his face. 'But is there a particular reason why you've decided to share your most intimate special secrets with us all?'

Oh. My little heart, previously singing at the idea of all this hoarded knowledge, suddenly sinks again.

That's right. There's a well-known precedent of people monologuing all their intimate secrets to me.

It's usually right before they kill me.

CHAPTER TWELVE

HOME, 30 OCTOBER, PRESENT DAY

Killed by giant, introverted hairy book-lovers? Well, it wouldn't be the first time.

Dunixi sees the change in my expression, I think. Hell, for all I know he can hear it – the change in my heartbeat, the speeding up of my pulse. Perhaps he can smell the change in my pheromones as my body starts switching into fight-or-flight mode. We've allowed this creature to bring us to the heart of their domain, all confident in the image he's presented us of this wise, gentle giant. Except, he started off the relationship with a lie, deceiving Isaac from the get-go. And on top of that, he's not shown any concern about bringing us to the very heart of their community. Maybe it's because he's absolutely certain we're never going to leave again.

He lifts his hands up in an "I surrender" style gesture. Although, considering that will just add momentum to his huge paws if he decides to bring them sweeping down, making it even easier for him to tear our heads off our shoulders, I don't find that as reassuring as he perhaps intends.

'Peace, my friends.' His voice is low, calm, soothing. 'There's no harm meant to you. Yes, you're the first humans we've allowed in here since we sealed off Home hundreds of years ago and withdrew into our own little slice of paradise. But we mourned for the deaths we had to facilitate then, and we would do everything in our considerable largesse to avoid more deaths now. The tale you regaled me with of what happened to our simiot friends means we needed to talk further. And there are things you need to see, things I can only illustrate for you here.'

Dunixi sighs, looks at each of us, and lowers his hands, although he keeps them splayed, open, that old non-verbal communication we learned eons ago as a people. *Look, no weapons. I come in peace.*

'The simiots were given free rein in Home. Allowed to travel where they pleased. Home made them places that suited them, extended deeper under the mountain to allow them the space to roam without needing to go into the dangerous outside. They went out still, of course. We all need to lay vision upon the sun sometimes. It never occurred to us that might be a vulnerability, a way in for those who might pursue what we protect.'

My ears prick up. 'What you protect? Which is...'

Dunixi smiles and waves a calming hand. 'I told you no human has ever come here. That's true. But we met with one outside. He'd fought great battles across the lands in our purview, and his man Roland sought us out, seeking for ways to bring enlightenment to the lands to the north. He performed a great service for us. Brought magic that allowed us to stabilise the heart of Home. In exchange, we gave him a little assistance, pointed him towards weapons once forged by our people, gifted to the fae when they were less cold, less cruel. When their playful nature had a tinge of joy rather than only being spiked with malice.'

Now I'm lost. There's no time in humanity's past, in any stories I've heard tell of, where the fae were ever anything but cruel monsters, only seeing men as sport or sex toys, nothing more. Which suggests the jentilaks must have been working steel for millennia before we discovered the secret.

And that they were around as a civilisation long before we even dreamed of moving beyond our hunter-gatherer habits.

Isaac's obviously trying to decipher it all as well. 'Are you saying...' He sounds the thoughts out slowly. 'That the jentilaks forged the swords of Charlemagne and Roland? Thousands of years ago as fae weapons? And then gave them to the Frankish king?'

'Oh, no. Not gave. *Lent.*' Dunixi smiles that gentle smile again. 'Roland did us a huge favour – a tale not for telling, at least not now, and this was the price he asked in return. We told him how to find them, where we'd hidden them long before, when the Fae had fled the land. We'd woven the metal from the iron of the mountains, the material that runs through Home itself. So we knew where they were. And when Charlemagne came towards his ending, his lungs filling with fluid, each cough a step towards drowning, he came back to us.'

I'm engrossed. There's a musical tonality to the big creature's voice, soft and lulling but perfect in his delivery. It's a voice made for telling stories.

'He had a touch of the *sight*, of course,' Dunixi continues. 'More humans did back then, although Talented creatures were harder to avoid back then too. Perhaps it was a form of defence that became less necessary as the fae came less and less often to this realm.' He smiles, an apologetic look on his hairy face. 'But I digress. Excuse me.

'Anyhow, he said he was returning the sword as promised, but that a prophesy had been made, that the swords would be needed again. He asked if we would allow them back out into the world when that time came, and if we could arrange their protection together. We agreed, and the swords were hidden in the heart of Home.'

Now the story telling flow falters, and Dunixi gets up, starts pacing back and forth, a stilted quickness to his rhythm. 'Any who came and asked could attempt access to the sword. Once. Of course, no human knows where they are, so it's never been an issue we've had to deal with. But Home helped Charlemagne to weave a protection, to allow only a sole attempt –'

'And it gave them a tattoo afterwards, as a marker!' Of course. The idea, now that Faust has said it, is obvious. It's like it's been there, just behind my eyes, forming in a little corner of my brain, and Johannes has just shone a torch straight on it.

Dunixi nods sadly. 'Exactly so.'

'So the tattoo on the simiots...' I start.

'Means they attempted the trials or test or whatever is needed to get the sword!' Isaac finishes, leaping to his feet.

Damn. I hate to pour a damper on the excitement, but I need to. 'Which means the demon knows that Joyeuse is here. And knew about the relationship between the simiots and the jentilak. Knew enough to know they could just stroll in here, one by one, and attempt to get the sword without setting off alarm bells with Dunixi's people.'

I can see the worry on each of their faces, Dunixi's included. That's a huge amount of top-secret information for someone who's not been in our dimension very long to have. Is there a leak? An agent for the demon among the jentilaks? I'm pretty sure the same thought is running through everyone else's thoughts too.

Mephy picks up on it and shakes his head with a huff. 'Relax, manos,' he says. 'Your dimension is easy to watch from ours. We can peer across the barriers and entertain ourselves with your strife and struggles. May well be that the demon watched Charlemagne's last days and then the simiots' arrival here.'

'Are you saying,' I ask slowly, thinking it through, 'that we're like a soap opera or a reality TV show for demons?'

Mephy looks at me, his eyes full with something I think is sympathy. 'More like an ant farm in a kid's bedroom. We watch you from time to time until we get bored. Some people are more fascinated by you than others, of course. But you're not our prime-time entertainment, not for most anyhow.'

Oof. Burn for the human race there. 'Okay,' I say, 'so we know now why the demon grabbed the simiots. To have a crack at getting Joyeuse. When they all failed, they were of no use to him in Home anymore.'

'So he used them as cannon fodder against us,' Isaac says, grim-faced. I know how much the very idea of that sort of callousness goes against his very being.

'Right.' I nod. It doesn't shock me in the same way, doesn't surprise me in the least. I've seen humans do far worse time after time. Why would I expect any different of demons?

Which helps to solve a mystery, of course, but doesn't get us any closer to retrieving the sword and saving Isaac. 'How do we get to have a crack at whatever we need to do to retrieve Joyeuse then?' I ask the giant ape cryptid in front of me. He's calmed down as the conversation's gone on, has stopped pacing and settled in to listen. I think now that he has a reason for how the demon might have planned all this that doesn't involve treachery and betrayal within his own people, he's more relaxed again.

'Well, that's why I shepherded you hither,' he says and lopes over to the centre of the room. As he approaches, a small hole I couldn't even see in the floor expands, opening, yawning wider till it's more like a chasm. He beckons us over, and we follow his lead, approaching the edge and peering in.

Down below is something I can't quite figure out at first. It looks like a glowing rock, like Mothra's egg maybe or a radioactive menhir. The thing is at least ten metres down, and even with the illuminating walls –the surfaces leading to the bottom are radiant, like the rest of the stone walls of Home– it's almost impossible to accurately judge the depth.

It's the colour that helps me work it out in the end. The orange glow of the rock haloes it but deepens as it gets closer to the object, turning a darker almost-red that matches, I realise, the colour of the thing itself. It's a deep-rust colour, that orange-red sheen that old metal objects take on when they've been out in the elements, exposed to nature's weather until they're weathered and aged. It's iron.

'The heart of Home,' Dunixi murmurs, a reverent tone in his voice. And then I understand.

The Pyrenees are known as the Iron Mountains, and the stories abound about the fallen meteorites that have shaped them, giving them their strange properties, distorting compasses, interfering with delicate scientific equipment brought into their bosom. That's what this is.

'It's a meteor,' I say.

And at the exact same time, Johannes says, 'The Crown of Lucifer.'

Silence reigns. Oh fuck. I didn't understand apparently.

CHAPTER THIRTEEN
HOME, 30 OCTOBER, PRESENT DAY
Lucifer's Crown? Based on the shape, looks more like Lucifer's crown jewels.

I risk a look over at Mephy, trying to judge anything in his expression. Desire or anger or greed. I've no idea if Lucifer really exists, but if this is somehow connected to the demons, then maybe he's going to want it back. But the demon dog looks inscrutable, staring down at the glowing meteorite below.

I decide to prod him a bit. 'Could this be what the demons are after, Mephy?' It's the first thought that's popped into my mind. Perhaps that's why they've come here, why they struck the original bargain with De Montfort. Maybe they want to get this back.

Mephistopheles raises his head and stares at me silently for several seconds. Then he chuffs loudly. 'Seriously, mano?' His tongue lolls out as he grins that doggy smile at me. 'Are you actually being serious? It's a nice old chunk of power, don't get me wrong, but that's just not how things work down below, so to speak. We don't need objects like that to give us what we want. Reality itself shapes to us. You crave things like this to perform the simple tasks that we take for granted.'

I sigh, although I'm not a hundred percent sure if it's with relief or disappointment. On the one hand, I'm glad it's not actually Lucifer's Crown, that the jentilaks aren't about to suffer an influx of angry demons demanding their property back, like a more militant version of previously colonised countries knocking at the door of the British Museum. On the other, we're still no closer to understanding what in the good name of fuckery the bastard wants.

I push the thought away. Worry about that later. Right now, the main thing is getting Isaac safe, healed up. Then, with our powers combined like Voltron – and without worrying that if Nithael steps up to the plate because of faced threats, that the dark curse crawling through Isaac's veins will consume them both – we'll go and kick the shit out of the demon arsehole threatening not only us but the world as a whole.

Lifting my head, I look over at the jentilak chief. 'So what now then? How do we go to the...' I pause. 'What is it we're going to face anyhow?'

'A series of Trials,' he says, and I don't miss the vocal capitalisation of the word. 'Which, if you pass, you will be judged worthy and gain Joyeuse.'

'And if we fail?'

'Then you'll all gain a rather fetching tattoo, and you'll never be allowed to try again.'

Well that makes a nice change. At least it's not a "then agonising death" scenario like it is normally.

'If you make it back alive, of course,' he adds.

Oh, okay. Apparently it is. Me and my big internal mouth.

Still, nothing new. Getting into a staring contest with Death is a standard Monday morning for me, and normally, it's like I have conjunctivitis and he's just blown itching powder straight into my face. If the simiots survived, even though they failed, surely we have better than normal odds of surviving?

That's a very different thing from succeeding, of course.

'So,' I start again, having answered the most pressing question, 'how do we get to the Trials then, Dunixi?'

'Oh, that's simple. Just ask the heart.'

'Oh, right.' There's a moment of awkward shuffling of feet. It feels weird, asking an inanimate object for help, which is utterly fucking ridiculous because every time we use an item or a relic to help us, that's exactly what we're doing. And this is seriously powerful considering all the reality-bending it allows the jentilaks to do. Doesn't stop us all scuffing the ground and looking at one another though. I think part of it is trying to work out what the correct, polite form of address is for a magical meteorite.

'Excuse me.' Isaac breaks the awkward silence. 'But would you be so good as to take us to the Trials? For regaining the sword Joyeuse,' he adds because apparently he thinks there's a whole different set of trials that the meteorite might take us to. Perhaps the trials for who gets to control the telly remote on Saturday night. Or the trial for who gets to choose the takeaway for tonight, and no I'm not having pizza again; we had that the last two times for God's sake.

Still, regardless of his slightly ridiculous wording, he's actually got on with it and done something. And it works. That orange tinged glow expands, reddens as it reaches out, deepens, brightens, grows until it's the same shade as staring through your eyelids at a naked lightbulb and with the same effect because I can't see anything else.

And then the cavern, the heart, Dunixi himself... They've all gone.

Or we have.

I guess the latter is more probable. Moving the four of us is presumably less effort than shifting the whole mountain and everyone in it. Although, seeing as how Home seems to enjoy fucking with perspective and playing Alice Liddell-style games with shrinking and growing doors, I can't be entirely sure.

We're all here, but I've no idea where "here" is. It doesn't look like the inside of the jentilaks'...burrow? Warren? Hyper-designed modular living space? I've no idea what the correct term for it is, but whatever the choice of words, we're not *there*.

Where we are doesn't look like it's made of stone unless it's black marble. The walls look cold and smooth, solid slabs of a dark material that absorbs the light.

Because there is light. But it's not coming from the walls like in Home. Nor is it coming from the sort of light sources we're used to – strip lighting overhead, light-fittings nestled into the walls, light wells fixed into the ceiling. No. The room is box-like, perhaps fifteen metres wide, and the same height, and all the surfaces are the same smooth, bare marble-like material.

No, the light comes from the trees.

At even spaces, like a nursery, trunks push out from the floor, impossibly. There's no cracking or swell as it's lifted the material, no rippling breaks where the roots stretch underneath. No, they just emerge out of the floor as if the marble (if that's what it is) has somehow been laid like cement, poured and smoothed right to the base.

But that's not the most remarkable thing about them. Not by a long shot. No, that title goes to the fact they're all luminescent. The bark glows like it's charged with pure *talent* but without needing to *look* at it. Following up, each branch splits off, smaller interweaving offshoots that all glow, so as the effect is like seeing Yggdrasil, the tree of life, picked out on the air in neon. And when it reaches out into smaller twigs, and they sprout their prickles, the light intensifies, so it looks like some over-enthusiastic

Christmas lover has covered every single inch of bark, every individual needle with LEDs, and then Griffin, the Invisible Man, came and spilled his formula all over its branches, leaving only the lights hanging in the air. And there's not just one. There're four rows stretching from wall to wall, glowing branches stroking against the marble-like limits, casting shade on a sliding scale, shadow points crossing from different illumination points, scattering light and shadows across the dark surface that pulls at the mind, leaving me feeling slightly off-balance.

And there, in the middle, is a set of scales.

It's not just hanging in mid-air, although honestly, it wouldn't feel too out of place if it was. No, the same material as the walls and floor pushes up into a rectangular pedestal, perfectly formed, so I have no idea if it was grown or just cut and placed so perfectly as to make a joint impossible to see. And on it sits old-school balance scales, looking like they're made of bronze, flat wide plates hanging from link chains on each side, a balance needle in the middle. One side is flat to the floor; one is up in the air.

I don't quite break out in a cold sweat, but it's close. I've seen a setup like this not that long ago. I was caught in an escape room by that shithead bastard the Nain Rouge. He came into my territory, wanting to make a bet. If I couldn't escape his room, then I would have to give him free rein in my city. It took me a hot second, but I got out, and then Aicha burned his house down. Which made it a really hot second for him, the shiny red wankpuffin.

But it's not thinking about the Nain Rouge that's making me feel so close to unwell. No, it's thinking about the trap he set for me, the solution I had to find to get back out.

A solution that involved pulling all the bones out of my arm and leg, one at a time, and piling them up on the balance pan.

Except then, I was inside his magic home, which provided instant healing. And with reincarnating if I died as a backup.

This time, if I have to do that again, I have no ace in the hole. And it might have been fine for the Black Knight, but I'm really not keen on gaining any more flesh wounds.

CHAPTER FOURTEEN
HOME, 30 OCTOBER, PRESENT DAY

Hell, I think I'd prefer dragon
scales than balance scales. Even
if they were still attached to
the fucking Tarrasque. Actually,
that may be stretching it a touch.

I saac's been staring with fascination at the trees, no doubt trying to work out what material they're made of or what they feed on considering there's no natural light in the room or, indeed, any light apart from the trees themselves. Or, I don't know, something equally academic and irrelevant to the problem at hand. But I think he must register my discomfort because he follows my gaze and spots the weighing scales.

He knows the story, of course, and he's the smartest man I've ever met even if he doesn't always show it. A moment later, I feel his steadying hand on my left bicep.

'Relax, Paul,' he says. 'This isn't there. We're not dealing with a psychotic fae this time. We're dealing with the jentilaks.'

I look askance at him. 'Are we? Because I seem to remember Dunixi saying that this was made at Charlemagne's insistence and that the swords were originally made for fae nobility to wield. And in case you've not noticed, we appear to have been transported into the Arboretum of fucking Lothlórien. So excuse me if the scales conjure up an "all shall look upon me in wonder and despair" vibe, will you?'

I'm aware my words are getting a touch snappy when all he's trying to do is reassure me, but I've had my fair share of traumatic torture and death over our recent adventures. Enough to last me at least this lifetime, however long it lasts. So I'm not exactly jumping for joy and clapping my hands at the idea of mutilation.

Isaac just smiles, that endless kindness as clear as ever, and shakes his head. 'We don't have to get the sword, lad. No way I'm letting you put yourself through anything like that again.'

And just like that, I'm ready. Chop an arm off? No problem. Rip my fingernails out with a pair of rusty pliers? Bring it on. Because I love this man in front of me, who's been there for me every single time I've ever needed it, and I'll be damned if I'll do any less for him. He's ready to walk away from what might be the only thing that'd save his life, save Nithael's life just to spare me a little emotional and physical discomfort. No way am I letting that happen.

Faust and Mephistopheles have ignored our little discussion. Johannes is doing his scholarly routine, same as Isaac is no doubt itching to do – walking around, studying the strange glowing flora, trying to scratch at the bark with a fingernail, seeing if it's something underneath that's glowing, if it's hot. All that scientific investigation neither of them can help themselves but do when they run into an oddity like these trees.

Mephy has his head down, sniffing at one of the bases. He walks around it, then he turns. It looks like he has a scent. My excitement rises as he lopes over to another of the trees, then passes it, onto the next, his nose stuck to the ground like a bloodhound, tracking down the answer to a mystery. I'm about to pump my fist in glee when he circles a tree and stops, sure he's found the solution to the problem...

When he raises his leg against it.

'Ah, that's better, mano.' He saw me watching and gives me that wolfy grin of his. 'Been holding that for far too long. Oh, yeah, can I get all your attention? *All of you*? Listening? Good. This is my tree now, okay? Go and piss on your own if you want. Don't let me catch you pissing on this one though. Got it?'

I rub my eyes, trying to clear away the disbelief dust that the fuck-me-sideways fairy has obviously just sprinkled into them. 'That's what you're going for right now, Mephy? When faced with a mysterious, miraculous indoor grove ripped straight out of fucking Lothlórien, your instinctive reaction is to start marking territory?'

'Yes.' The demon dog looks at me unblinkingly, as though trying to peer through to my tiny, little underdeveloped human brain in desperate hopes of understanding me. 'That's what instinctive means, mano. Following your instincts. You could do with aping a little more, ape-boy. You might die less regularly.'

Ouch. Touché, Mephistopheles. Touché.

Isaac has walked over to the scales and is now examining them. It makes me realise just how much I've learned, how many habits I've adopted from him. He inspects them in an almost identical manner to how I did in the Nain Rouge's little trap – running his hand over and under them, checking for mechanisms keeping them in place. He pushes on the elevated plate to see if he can move it. I can see him casting his eyes around for a solution. No luck.

We regroup in the middle, gathering around him, and as we do so, I almost shriek and leap out of my skin because words appear, scrawling themselves across the air like some invisible Charlotte spider hopped up on amphetamines. You'd think after hundreds of years of experiencing random things happening due only to magic, I'd be used to it. Apparently not. I do manage to bite my tongue to stop my high-pitched alarums from escaping, but now I've a rapidly swelling damaged tongue to add to my list of woes.

Isaac is unfazed, of course. He would set himself on fire just to work out the average melting point of human flesh, so when air writing appears out of nowhere, he's more intrigued by what it says and the delivery mechanism that led to the apparition. It's the intrinsic difference between an academic and someone who has pointy things and magic – and often magical pointy things – thrown at them unexpectedly far too regularly.

'*When losses are rooted so soundly*
And branch through our hearts to begin
When we offer up the blossoming bounty
We can start to advance on the limb'

I look around suspiciously. 'Is this where we find out Scarbo survived and this is his incredibly intricate revenge?'

Isaac gives a half-hearted chuckle while Faust and Mephy just look blank. I guess you had to be there to appreciate just how truly dreadful Scarbo's supposed "poetry" really was. Ruler of the Thirteenth district of Paris – and treacherous, back-stabbing bastard – he'd been cursed so he could only speak in rhyme. And dreadful doggerel at that too. Aicha forced him to speak in plain English, which caused him to literally burst. I think she was disappointed because she was hoping to do it herself, possibly by hooking him up to an air compressor and flicking on the switch. That thought gets pushed away though because it just reminds me of how much I miss Aicha. Not helpful right now.

So not quite riddles in the dark. Riddles in the peculiar glowing tree light. Luckily, I have two certified geniuses with me. Or certifiable geniuses. One or the other. Possibly both.

Faust is stroking his bushy facial hair, smoothing it down – an act it immediately rebels against, springing back to protrude out in all directions the moment he lets go. This is not facial hair easily calmed and coifed. This is the stuff that's only one small step up from bristles, and it's not about to be cowed by a simple hand gesture. The amount of wax and brushing you'd need to get it into a tameable state is unimaginable. Probably enough to prep California's annual allocation of surfboards for the next few centuries.

'It seems to me like the puzzle must be connected between these trees and the scales, no?' He bends to examine the nearest branch, which is protruding at chest level. 'This unnatural lighting requires that, no? These *tannenbaum* – How do you call them again in French?'

'*Pin.*' I like his thinking. Surely this is some sort of word game, or at least there's a clue in this weird air doggerel that's sprung up out of nowhere.

'So very similar to the English word for them — pine. Hmm.' His thoughtful rub turns into a half-irritated scratch, digging through the chin hair to get to the skin below. 'Well, French may not be my first language, but all of the imagery of the poem-of-sorts –' *That's a good disclaimer to add to the description of the verses*, I think. '– seems very much connected to the trees. Root, branch, blossom, limb...'

He trails off but only because he's mulling it over. Isaac raises his head, his eyes scanning the air-words over and over, shining brightly. Both the words and his eyes.

'It talks about the *blossoming bounty*,' he says and turns to Johannes. 'What do you call the cone that the pine tree produces in German?'

'*Tannenzapfen,*' Faust replies.

'*Gesundheit.*' I can't help myself. Isaac shakes his head and sensibly ignores me for saying, 'Bless you,' in German. 'And what about the seed inside it, the pine nut?'

'The *pinienkern?*' Faust's trying to follow along, but he's not there yet. It says something about just how sharp Isaac is that he's a step ahead of even Johannes Faust. Though Faust kicked it off. Great teamwork, really. Sets my heart aglow.

'Right. *Pinienkern* in German. Pine cone as the English call it. *Pignons des pins* as we say in French.' Isaac's pacing now, marking a narrow stretch between two trees, turning each time he reaches one.

'Yes, for us, the trees themselves are the *pinien*, the family, but for you, it is the seeds.' Faust is nodding. I'm not sure if he thinks he has the solution too or if he's just enjoying a conversation about etymology and linguistics.

'Right.' Isaac stops, then twirls on his heels. 'So now imagine these puzzles aren't just random or standard but are, in fact, designed to test each group who comes through.'

Johannes thinks about this for a moment. 'It's a leap of supposition but not impossible. Not even implausible.' His tone pitches up. I can tell he's getting excited, just trailing along, following the breadcrumbs of logic that Isaac's dropping.

'Right, so, in French, *pignon* has two meanings. The seed of the pine –'

I feel it. I feel the impossibility of it, the weight of something so other and indescribably larger compressing itself down into the grubby paltriness of our reality. Nithael's presence pushes itself into our world, and his planet-sized wings wrap themselves between the ordered illuminated forest.

'– and the outer flight feathers of a wing.'

He reaches out a hand, and Nithael's impossible neon wings perform more inexplicable gymnastics, bending around and through the glowing trunks. Shrinking and shaping until the tip brushes across Isaac's outstretched palm. Then Nith's presence dims, retreats, and is gone back, away from our level of reality, which gives a metaphysical sigh of relief. Some things are just too big, regardless of their size, to be contained in something as small as our dimension. But left in Isaac's grip, balanced across his hand's lines, his skin visible through it, is a jagged streak of blue neon that might just be, if you squinted at it while tilting your head to the side, the outline of a feather.

I'm massaging the back of my neck, squeezing and rubbing the muscles. It seems a bit of a stretch to me but worth trying. There's also the whole "Nithael manifesting a part of himself in our reality" thing to get my head around. I suppose I shouldn't be surprised though. Our reality is little more than a sandpit for him. And he's driving a JCB digger.

Isaac walks forward slowly, reverently, bearing the pinion feather like it's a holy relic, which considering an angel just plucked it from his wing for him, I guess it kind of is. He doesn't kneel before the scales – which is a shame because I had a joke ready about telling him to get a sense of balance rather than falling over – but he does lower the object gently down onto the raised pan, depositing it with great care so that it stretches across it.

And then, despite my doubts, the scales start to tip, the feather pulling the pan downwards until they're in balance. Then further down until the other empty pan is hanging in mid-air while this one touches the pedestal itself.

It worked. Well, blow me down with a feather.

CHAPTER FIFTEEN

HOME, 30 OCTOBER, PRESENT DAY

Well, I guess that makes Isaac a featherweight. Although Aicha would probably tell me that would make me bantamweight. Because of me being a cock.

All around us, the trees start winking out, the lights disappearing like we're a group of hungry and unwelcome dwarves intruding on an elven picnic in Mirkwood. Although anyone intruding on an actual elven picnic would probably find themselves providing the entertainment first –dancing till they were left with nothing but bloody stumps and still not stopping– and then probably the main course afterwards. The Fair Folk work up a mean hunger being pettily cruel.

My hand's in my etheric storage, rummaging through my invisible other-dimensional bag for my sword pommel. Lights going out when you're being judged as worthy or otherwise don't tend to be good news. It's often the equivalent of the moment before they're thrown on as everyone shouts, "Surprise!" except where they're shouting it while trying to simultaneously smash your head into a bloody pulp against the wall with a whirling morning star. Plus, it's rare I'm judged as worthy of being picked anything but last even for team sports. I'm not expecting miracles down in the dark under the home of the jentilaks.

Except, despite my fully justified and fully earned fears, nothing leaps out at us as the peculiar forest extinguishes. That doesn't stop cold sweat beading on my forehead though. I'm not exactly at a point where the lights going out in an underground cavern I can't walk out of isn't going to trigger my trauma. This is pretty much my personal idea of Hell right now, and the Good God knows it's only because I'm able to keep hold of my sword guard like it's a tight grip on my sanity that keeps me from gibbering in fear. If I have that, it means my magic's working. If my magic's working, I can blow this fucking mountain to rubble if needs be. There's a tiny part of my logical mind that starts yabbering about how doing that will also mean burying myself underneath it, but compared to going back to the eternal dark, I can live with that.

The other thing keeping me from going into full-on meltdown mode is the presence of the others. I can hear them, feel them close by. As the lights go out, we instinctively huddle up, ready for danger, and the press of their flesh against mine grounds me, cuts the red wire of my explosive terror before I blow up and take us all with me. I'm not alone. I'm not trapped. The bodies around me are alive, not foil-packed, stored, and ready for me to use up as I die over and over, jumping into them as I go, thirsty and cold in the unseeing, uncaring black.

To say I'm on high alert now is probably an understatement. My pulse is hammering away, doing a mile a minute. If I could strap it up to a generator, we could have this place lit up like an overly enthusiastic Christmas fan at a Home Depot with an unlimited budget for LED decorations.

But the anticipated attack doesn't come.

Instead, I start making out details again, the black greying. My own hand, my sword now fully drawn from storage without me having realised, comes into view. I'm proud that the tremble is almost unnoticeable. It feels like I must be waving the sword around like a small kid playing at pirates, but actually, it looks remarkably steady. Centuries of training can compensate for a lot. Then the top of Mephy's head, that sheen of his lustrous black fur comes into view. And if I can see the sheen, that means it's reflecting. Which, lo and behold, is the case.

The room's getting lighter and lighter. Proportions wise, it might be the same room, might be an entirely different one. Size-wise, it looks pretty damn similar, but the main difference is the luminescent trees are missing. The surfaces are still the same – black marble or something damnably close to it – but now they glow with that same strange warm light as the walls of Home do. I'm not going to lie. I feel my chest loosen even though we've remained enclosed in what is, in effect, a sealed cave. That's bad, but being in a sealed cave *back in the dark* was a whole 'nother level of terrible. Now I can see, I have my magic, and I have my friends. Considering two of them are from dimensions that find our reality about as convincing as a cardboard rocket ship, I'm feeling pretty confident that we can tear our way out of here if push comes to shove. Don't get me wrong; now I've been back through the dark, I'm mightily aware of those black walls, of how limited an amount of space we have. But it's big enough that I can draw breath, and I can see the walls instead of having to just grope for them. It's enough to keep me sane and to keep the panic under control. For now.

Of course, being inside a black marble box does have certain similarities to getting entombed, but I can put that out of my mind. It's a bit like trying not to think about purple elephants when someone mentions them, but I can manage it. Honestly.

'What do we think comes next?' Mephy growls, and I could fling my arms around his neck in delight at him breaking the weighted silence if I didn't think he might end up biting my nose off in surprise if I did. I quite like my nose. It helps keep my face in proportion. Plus, I already snore badly enough.

'I'm not su–' I break off as all around me, the ground rumbles. My sword arm's up, in guard before I can even think of it, and the image of King Aeëtes scattering the hydra's teeth in the old film of *Jason and the Argonauts* springs to mind. Are we about to do battle with a skeletal army? The fact that this wouldn't be the first time if so says a lot about my life.

But it's not an undead skeleton army that comes clawing its way out of the ground. No. It's something less threatening, yet somehow almost more bizarre.

Because what looks like half a mole scrabbles its way out of the ground.

I don't mean that in the sense of just the front part, sword-chopped off from the hind legs, the little digging claws dragging out a severed torso. No, it's like the creature's been split vertically down the middle, like one of those diagrams you get in science textbooks, packed full of arrows and corresponding labels, explaining all the details of the internal structure you can't normally see.

What shouldn't be packed full, however, is this half a mole. All of those organs on display – the glistening ropes of intestines, cross-sectioned so I can see the internal ridges, the open-heart chambers, the lung branches that almost seem to be waving in the breeze of the mole's movement like its sable hair – should be spilling out, collapsing into a huge big bloody pile on the outside of the body. Trust me. I've been bisected. While still alive. Watching your organs pool at your feet is a unique experience. A one-off, as well, if you're anyone but me.

This creature, however, seems entirely unbothered. It just pokes its weird half-head in a snuffling movement at the ground, like it's hunting out grubs here in the Heart of Home. It's unnerving because it only has its left-hand paws. How does it not just overbalance, flopping onto the cut-open side? It's as if it has ghost limbs keeping it upright when it should be collapsing the moment it tries to move. Well, actually that's not quite right. It shouldn't be collapsing. It should be dead. I'm an expert on death. I know these things. Meanwhile, there's another slight rumble, and over on the other side of the room, a second half-mole as bizarrely halved as the first pops up.

I'm waiting for it all to go to shit, of course. For them to suddenly grow, become as huge as houses, those razor like digging claws – capable of breaking through dirt and stone, more than capable of doing the same through flesh and bone – becoming weapons to do unto us as some sadistic fucker has apparently done unto them, slicing us in half.

I'm casting my eyes around, wary, ready, anticipating attack at any second, so I don't scream like a little girl when the sky-writing glitters into existence. Incidentally, what a stupid turn of phrase that is. The only time I've ever known a little girl to scream like that saying suggests is with sheer maniacal glee. Little girls are *fierce*. They brook no nonsense and are ready to destroy you with casually constructed logic it's impossible to argue with. This idea of them screaming and running away at the first sign of something frightening is definitely a male construction. They're far more likely to go and poke it with a stick and ask it if *it really thinks this is an acceptable way to behave and what would its mummy and daddy think about the whole affair*? Honestly, put me up against giant mutant murder-moles rather than an army of little girls any day of the week.

The writing's not enough to distract me from the clear and present danger of these tiny half-moles who I am convinced must be plotting our downfall, only waiting for our guard to drop so they can transform into terrifying death machines and pounce. I'm so convinced, I can't take my eyes off them long enough to scan what the sky words say. Luckily, Isaac clears his throat and reads it out loud, his voice ringing clearly off the four walls.

"There's a breaking mistaken for healing and a hope that is taken to wing

There's a place for those tainted by stealing and a throat that is aching to sing

When the chase is a taste of their feeling but they're groping in chaos's spin

In the gape in the face is revealing and there's growth and remaking within."

And now I do scream because suddenly the room's alive, and with it comes noise. Unexpected noise, an exploding flurry that assaults the senses with sudden overwhelming accompanying movement. That only ever means an ambush to me, so I'm spinning around, my hands flying up into the guard shapes of a hundred different martial arts, my fingers aglow with talent.

The murder moles! The murder moles are coming!

CHAPTER SIXTEEN
HOME, 30 OCTOBER, PRESENT DAY

They always told me I broke the mould. They never told me the mole'd break me.

Thankfully, I'm wrong. It's not gigantic half-moles with rippling musculature made for shredding humans and elongated keratin claws to match. What it is instead is more. More creatures. More normal-sized creatures.

More normal-sized half-creatures.

They're normal-sized, but suddenly the room is full of critters. Only critters that have been sundered. Half-foxes yip around the area, their high-pitched barks apparently not hindered by only having half a throat. What might be a large mouse or a small rat skitters across the floor behind one of them, its tail muscles bunching as it wiggles back and forth. My rodent identifying skills aren't the best, even when the creature in question is whole. Twittering birds flutter past on half a wing, yet somehow don't drop into a plunging death spiral – bluebirds, chaffinches, rooks. I even spot half a woodpecker, get to see its elongated tongue (perfectly designed for digging deep under tree bark for those tastiest of insects) is wrapped around the outside of its brain, wound around and around to keep it safe. Part of me wonders if it gets a headache each time it swallows involuntarily. Part of me is more concerned by how much of a headache the impossibility of everything we're seeing is giving me.

'Okay.' Faust makes me almost jump out of my skin with one calm word. Apparently not everyone is as highly strung as I am. Probably no bad thing. 'So what does all this mean?'

'That someone felt what *Pet Sematary* was really lacking was some early Disney-film vibes to make it perfect?' I'm still trying to get my head around the chaotic nature scene combined with a slice of 1980's body horror we seem to have found ourselves in.

'There was the mention of wings,' Isaac says thoughtfully. 'There are plenty of those around.'

'Brilliant.' I don't break into a slow hand-clap but only because I'm still basically throwing ninja hand-shapes in all directions, waving the sword around, expecting the other shoe to drop at any moment and nature to show itself in bloody tooth and claw, even if said teeth are held in only half a mouth. 'You've cracked the case, Columbo. We've spotted that, yes. Some of the creatures have wings, and the puzzle is solved. Next ridiculous trial please, Home.'

'Sarcasm is the lowest form of wit, Paul.' Ouch. Faust's tone is that of the perennially disappointed schoolteacher. The one who sees your potential and sees you squander it time after time. 'None of us have any idea as to how to start in this strange and peculiar scenario. These seemingly pointless musings may be the very key in how to resolve this particular trial.'

I can feel my chin drooping with each word, my head hanging lower and lower. So much so that I don't even point out that "strange" and "peculiar" mean the same thing. I don't feel it'd really help my case.

'Don't worry, lad.' Isaac's gentle tone only makes me feel worse, like even more of a cad. 'We're all a touch on edge. Just see if you can be less of a blithering idiot, okay?'

He's trying, the Good God bless him. Trying to take the place a certain missing Moroccan warrior occupies, in terms of keeping my tongue in place and my ego in check. I'm lucky to have such friends. I really should stop taking the piss out of them.

'So the talk about chaos's spin,' Faust speaks up, draws the conversation back to the matter at hand. 'What do you think this could mean?'

'Well, it's a pretty good summary for what we're seeing,' I start, waving my hand at the squawking, swirling, yipping madness that now occupies the same space as us.

My words are cut off, though, by the sight of Mephistopheles.

The gigantic demon dog has his paws up against what must be one wall – the sense of perspective is difficult, confusing, with the pitch nature of all the surfaces, despite them somehow being lit up, allowing us to see. Hanging from his mouth is the still fluttering wing of what was once perhaps a wood pigeon. Or half a wood pigeon, but now all that's left is half a wing, which gives half a last beat and then disappears down Mephy's gullet.

We all stare at the huge Doberman, who swings his head from one to the next of us, radiating bemusement. He opens his mouth, pauses, lifts a paw as if to ask us to pause –a pause paws if you will– to wait patiently for a moment. Then he gives an enormous burp that seems to shake the very room itself. He puts his paws down, then looks around at us once more.

'What,' he says, puzzled, 'the fuck are you manos all looking at?'

'Mephy,' I hiss, my voice lowered as if to keep Home from hearing us. 'You're eating the trial!'

'Oh. Oh!' The demon dog sounds relieved. 'Yeah, of course I am! Bloody delicious it is too.'

'No.' Johannes' tone is strict. 'Bad, Mephy. This is not acceptable, to be consuming that which we have to solve.'

'Sorry,' Mephy says and then whips his head left, seizing up a half-mouse that's scuttling past, tossing it up into the air and catching it in his mouth before swallowing it down. 'Not sorry.' The words are obscured by his mouth being full. Or half-full at least.

'Dude!' I get it. This is what Mephy is like, what all demons are like as far as we know. If he wants to do something, then he does it. Controlling his urges isn't his cup of tea-flavoured whisky. Still though. 'This isn't the time for you to be grabbing a quick snack!'

'What are you talking about, mano?' Mephy might be conversing with us, but his eyes are whipping about everywhere else, tracking the movement of the little creatures that are gambolling around their own little natural paradise despite looking like they should be swimming in formaldehyde rather than frolicking at our feet. The dog hunches back, then pounces on another half-mouse, his jaws snapping forward in a crunching motion –*snap, snap*– and the half-mouse becomes a quarter mouse, then no mouse at all.

'In my belly! Get in my belly!' Mephy shouts in a passable impression of Fat Bastard from the *Austin Powers* films and then springs onto one of the half-moles who kicked off this whole weird experience, chomping it down in about half a second flat.

'I'm talking about you ruining our chances of getting the sword because you've decided it's time for a spot of light lunch!' I shout, feeling my temper rising. It's unbelievable. This is serious stuff, incredibly important, not just on a wider scale – stopping whatever fuckery this demon arsehole is up to

– but on a personal one. Saving Isaac. To me, at least, it doesn't come more important than that.

'I'm not ruining it, mano!' The demon dog laughs, a peculiar choppiness to the sound, like when you talk into a spinning fan blade, the movement seeming to slice the sound waves. It takes me a moment to realise it's because he's talking over a mouthful of woodpecker wing. 'I'm solving the bloody puzzle, aren't I?'

I choke slightly. That movement when your anger is rising up into your throat and suddenly you realise it might not be necessary, your reaction might not be justified, and it seems to sit, bobbing up and down on your Adam's apple like a carousel horse, waiting to see if it comes screaming out of your throat or slowly transforms into embarrassment.

'You... you are?' I don't know if it's a question, a statement of disbelief, or just utter confusion verbalised on my part.

'I am! This one's my puzzle, manos! Custom-made for me!' The demon dog is practically frolicking himself, spinning in half-leaping circles, trying to snatch birds from the sky while a half-fox gets pinned by one landing paw.

'Because you like eating critters?' My confusion isn't getting any less, nor is my disbelief lifting.

'No! Well, yes, obviously. But no! That's not why.' I can't work out if Mephy's being deliberately obtuse or if he's just too busy having the time of his life to give me a proper answer.

'Then why?' That bobbing anger is ready to surge back up, just itching for the chance to be right.

'Because this is a game we used to play back home!' The half-fox disappears down Mephy's maw in a couple of quick gulps.

'Hunting?' says Isaac.

'Eating?' suggests Faust.

'Splitting innocent creatures in half for a giggle?' Is all I can come up with.

'Quite!' Mephy nods sagely.

'Which one?' I'm not screaming. Please note, I am not screaming. I've no idea how, but somehow, I am not screaming at my friend and his utterly useless answers.

'All of them! Plus sometimes being the creatures, of course.'

'Being split in two?' I can't quite get my head round this.

'Yeah, totally! Not just two though. Three or four. Ten maybe. I used to play sometimes with Beelzebub, and his party trick was turning into a swarm of flies. That'd be the game, right? Divide yourself into as many parts as you wanted and then run and hide. Then the other one would try to find you. Swallow down the bits so as to keep you safe inside their tummy. Then there'd be no arguing about demonicos cheating later on.'

'Sorry.' I think I understand what he's saying, but it's so implausible, I remain convinced I must be wrong. 'Are you saying you'd become multiple beings to play an overly complicated version of hide-and-seek?'

'Well, when you say it like that, it sounds *shit*.' Mephy shakes his head disbelievingly. 'And it was brilliant, I can tell you! Plus, as a grand finale, the demonico who got swallowed down reassembled inside your stomach and came bursting out after you ate them all. Brilliant!'

Evidence once more – if evidence were needed – that it doesn't matter how close Mephy and I are, I'll never understand demons any more than I'll ever understand angels. They just don't operate in the same way we do.

'But still, that's a bit of a stretch, Mephy!' The protest sounds weak in my ears because, honestly, it sounds like he might have worked it out after all.

'Nah, nah, nah. Think it through, mano.' Mephy's tail is wagging a million miles a minute at the joys of both winning the argument and hunting the half-animals. 'What do those glowing words say? Something about chasing and tasting them, right? About a gaping face, then them finding healing within? Within, get it? Within my fucking belly – *Get in here!*'

And with that, the demon dog is lost to us once more, gone in the thrill of the chase.

I look up at the words again. Look across at my two equally bemused human friends. I try studiously not to look at my demon one, to ignore the crunching, twittering noises and joyful barking coming from him as he frenetically tears around the room.

'What do you reckon then?' I say eventually, hoping they have an answer to it because I don't have a clue.

'It fits. Sort of.' Faust scratches at his beard, as if hoping it contains a magic thought genie who might grant him understanding if he just rubs it hard enough.

'I guess so.' Isaac nods slowly. 'Nithael says it fits with what he knows of the demons. In a slightly condescending way, I'm sad to add, but still a confirmation of sorts.'

Further discussion on that bit of information, either the tacit agreement with Mephy's assessment, or Nithael's bad attitude, is cut short. Mephy gives a yowl of victory. Turning around, we see he's trapped the last piece between his paws – another half-bird of some sort – and we watch as he makes short work of his final snack. Then the glowing words fade, and the room's lighting does too. Half a second later, we find ourselves plunged once more into total darkness.

Huh. Guess he was being a good boy after all.

CHAPTER SEVENTEEN

HOME, 30 OCTOBER, PRESENT DAY

Why, this is Hell nor am I out of it. Think'st thou that I, who saw the critters of Home and tasted the eternal joys of moles, am not tormented with ten thousand hells in being deprived of everlasting bliss?

When the light comes up, initially it's a bit of an anti-climax. To be honest, I'm not entirely sure why whoever's running this show bothered with the whole "fade-to-black" motif this time. When the lights went down, we were sitting in a large black cube of a room, the walls glowing to give us light. When they come back up, we're in exactly the same place, with the same light source.

'Apparently, this is the next scene,' Isaac murmurs, and I nod. Of course. Makes sense. They're marking that trial as done for us. It's still a bit theatrical for my taste, but whatever. I get the impression it's not every day someone comes along to have a crack at getting their hands on Joyeuse.

The magic's probably enjoying having some more participants along for the ride.

While we're still looking around, two of the pillars, like the ones that previously held the scales, push their way up out of the floor, forming rectangular columns about a metre in from each wall. As I watch, a thin streak of blue light shoots across from one to the other, then hangs, humming between them. It looks like someone extracted the fluorescence from a fluorescent strip light and connected it to the mains. They've left off the protective encasing glass but have kept the tell-tale hum. It practically screams "don't touch me".

Once again, words spring into being in the air, this time hanging above it. They read:

Pain gets carried all wrapped up, a burden for pilgrims to bear
A load that is carried by Atlas and that loops round a heart like a snare
At each twist it draws tighter and captures, in a hurt we're unable to share
If we'd live to heal here in the after, then those circling tendrils we must pare.

Oh. I have a really bad feeling about this. And thinking the bad thoughts that accompany that bad feeling, like unwanted party guests who turn up with that dude you really didn't want to invite in the first place but did so just to be polite, prompts me to realise what the sound of that bar of light really reminds me of.

It's not the hum of a fluorescent tube. It's the sound of a lightsabre at rest. I don't doubt if you could swing it somehow – perhaps by getting the Hulk to break off one of the pillars and twirl it around his head or something – that it'd go *whoomp whoomp* as it cut through the air.

And those unwelcome gate-crashing bad thoughts are pointing out what happens when lightsabres make contact with flesh. And that if these puzzles have been made specifically for each of us...

Then there's one of us here with a history of having to chop their limbs off to escape from a locked room, thanks to that fucknuts of a Nain Rouge called Cyril. I absolutely hated it the first time, and my desire to repeat the exercise, particularly now that I'm not sure of coming back in a brand spanking new body if I bleed out, is precisely zero.

'Tell me...' I say slowly, looking for the right words to say that will prompt the two Einstein-level geniuses flanking me to come up with a better answer than the one I have running through my tiny mind. 'What does that suggest to you?'

Open questions, Paul. If I keep the questions open, it increases the chances of them not just mirroring the shitty direction my thoughts have headed in, hollering and wolf-whistling as they go.

'Well, "to pare" means "to remove", "to cut away",' Isaac says thoughtfully.

'Thank you, that's just what I meant, Isaac. When I asked you what you thought, I meant can you explain the difficult words to me. In fact, you've still lost me. I think we're going to have to get into a game of charades. Two words; two syllables. Fuck you.'

Okay, it's a bit much on my part, maybe, but dread is seeping into my soul, and my soul insurance isn't going to pay out for any damages caused; there's a waiver clause that keeps the insurance company from being liable. 'Zac cocks an eyebrow at me, concern radiating from his gaze. I close my eyes, pinching the bridge of my nose and exhaling slowly.

'Right, sorry, 'Zac. All part of your deductive process. Carry on.' I roll my hand, trying to make it look like a magnanimous permission to continue talking rather than a gesture telling him to hurry the fuck up already.

'Right, well, as I was saying, lad, before being so rudely, bloody interrupted –' It's a good thing Isaac's done plenty of harrumphing already. He must be harrumphed out; otherwise, I'd be the subject of uber-harrumph-ing right now. '– but the paring suggests to cut or chop away.'

'And the poem speaks of these bands wrapped tightly. Bands of, hmmm, trauma, I would say?'

Which of course fits me to a T. Hell, my chest is constricted right now with what often gets described as "mind-numbing terror", but that's a bol-locks description. My mind isn't numb. It's absolutely aflame, screaming at me in a falsetto tone as the terror burns through it, the flames licking at my very sanity.

That probably counts as trauma, yes.

'And it says they're looped round the heart...' Isaac's back into pon-dering mode. His previous concern for me's gone as a question occupies his mind instead. It's not that he's stopped caring. Just his attention is so utterly and completely subsumed that someone could saw his kneecap off right now, and he'd only notice when they shouted timber and he toppled over.

'So the answer is to chop away all that is surrounding the heart!' Jo-hannes pumps his fist in the air, like he's just scored the winning goal at the World Cup. I feel like I'm watching down at the local betting shop, having placed all my life savings on the opposition.

I think Isaac finally switches back out of "academic wrestling with a logic problem" and back into being a human again, clocking my hangdog expression.

'What's up, lad?'

I heave a huge sigh, one filled to the brim with how much I want to fuck this all off and go back home. In fact, fuck home, I'll settle for the floor of a bar, curled up under one of the barstools with someone just pushing a glass of single malt under every twenty minutes or so. Even better, I'll drape my coat over the top of it, like a makeshift tent or a kid's fort, and I can just pretend the world outside of it doesn't exist. Nothing but me and my malt. Perfection.

But that's not going to happen. And the reason why that's not going to happen is because of the man standing in front of me, looking absolutely fraught now he's realised how miserable I am. There's precisely zero chance I'm going to abandon Isaac to get munched up by an armful of hangry demon energy. So whatever needs to be done, I'm going to get it done. Down like a clown, Charlie Brown.

'So we've worked out these puzzles are tailored to each of us, right? Playing to our strengths, our experiences?'

Nods all around. Only Mephy doesn't, but, honestly, he's still walking on cloud nine. We've just been to his own personal vision of nirvana, and he's slightly glassy-eyed, no doubt reminiscing on that particular triumph.

'Well, you and Meph have done yours. I reckon this one's mine.' Of course it is. Of shitwankingly course. Isaac gets to pluck a wee feather from his angelic buddy's delicate, downy wing. Mephistopheles visits his happy place and gets to fill his eternally rumbling stomach at the same time. And me?

I sigh and walk closer. The humming gets louder, becoming like the buzz of a thousand angry wasps whose nest has just been destroyed, and my picture is plastered all over wasp TV, with wasp news presenters naming me as public enemy number one. The light-bar-cum-lightsabre hangs suspended right in front of me. It's about as welcome a bit of interior design as a fucking "Live Laugh Love" sign.

Now, never let it be said I'm a reckless idiot. I mean, I am, but never let it be said. Otherwise, I'm likely to idiotically and recklessly punch you in the jaw. But for once, I decide caution is the better part of valour. So instead of doing what I am ninety-nine point nine percent sure I need to do, I decide to test my spectacularly idiotic theory first.

There's no good way of psyching yourself up for something like this. The best thing you can do is almost fool yourself, lie to your conscious mind until your subconscious buys it. Then you can catch it off guard before it instinctively prevents you from whatever idiotic thing you're about to do.

So I stand there in front of it, looking it up and down as though I'm still thinking about it, still considering a course of action. Like I'm not actually committed and might change my mind, and anyway even if I do it, I won't do it *now*. No, it'll be in a while. Probably an hour or two if not longer...

Then quick as a flash, I stick my pinky finger out on my left hand and bring it slicing down on the beam.

It's just like a laser or sabre or any other sort of "light based cutting equipment" you can come up with. The sensation of incredible heat giving a passionate kiss to all the nerves bundled up in my finger simultaneously almost overloads me. It certainly keeps them busy for a moment as they report back on just how ridiculously hot it is, so there's a millisecond of receiving that information alone before they suddenly realise their good buddies in the lump of flesh after the second knuckle aren't responding to radio communication anymore. In fact, the connection's been severed.

Along with my finger.

Now the pain messages ramp up, really freaking out as they realise that burning is nothing compared to actual severance. And not in the "you're fired; here's a nice final payment package and some lovely benefits, as well as a shitty mug we picked up for you to say sorry" sense. Nope. In a "finger in an industrial accident; Barry told us that blade cutter wasn't working quite right; let's wrap that up in ice and hope the paramedic's a dab hand with a needle and thread" kind of way.

Do you know what's probably the most messed up part about it? I don't even scream. Not even an enraged primal bellow of fury. No half-bitten whimpers. No screeches of agony. Just "hello, blinding pain, my old friend", a fatalistic embrace of its familiar bite.

What does take me a moment is getting up the courage to look down.

Once I do, I could cry with relief. Pain I can deal with. Permanent mutilation without the quick save option of jumping ship and picking up another body is a whole different fish kettle. But to my immense relief, my gamble has paid off. This test clearly is designed for me, particularly the me that went through the Nain Rouge's torture chamber version of an Escape Game.

Lucky me. My finger is still attached even though I saw it fall off.

Unlucky me. That means I have to do a whole load more cutting.

Chapter Eighteen
Home, 30 October, Present Day

If history is going to repeat itself, could it perhaps choose the time I got to taste the Good God's homebrew whisky, hmm? Rather than the time I had to mutilate myself repeatedly. And the Nain's whisky wasn't even that good.

I look up at the others and grin weakly. It's a smile I don't even vaguely feel like making, but it's necessary. Isaac's wincing still, biting his lip as if to keep himself from making the cries of pain I didn't. Faust is white-faced, his mouth agog. He's not as used to me having to dismember myself to solve shitty puzzles, so it's taken him off guard, from out of left field. And Mephy...

Mephy's eyes are fixed on the finger that fell off. I try to ignore the saliva that's forming at the corners of his mouth.

'As I thought...' I start, then stop because the hum of the laser blade behind me changes pitch.

'Ayy. Eee. Eye. Oh. You.' I enunciate the vowels carefully and precisely and watch the blade follow my tonal changes in pitch. Brilliant. Not only is it chopping me to pieces, but it's mocking me, imitating me like a five year old as it does so. It makes me glad I didn't scream. If it'd done that while I was in huge pain, I'd have probably fallen into a blind rage and done something stupid like tried to kick it. Wouldn't have ended well.

I walk back over to the group to have the conversation without the thing that severed my finger taking the piss out of me, even if it was decent enough to give me said finger back again afterwards.

'What the hell was that?' Faust's regained the power of speech.

I sigh, then shrug, going for nonchalant. 'It was a guess. A guess that turned out to be correct.'

'You guessed *chopping off your finger wouldn't be permanent*?' Johannes' voice climbs up in pitch and volume as he progresses.

'You've not been along for many of Paul's hijinks, have you, chap?' Isaac tries for a smile, but I can see the shadow over his eyes. Our relationship runs two ways. He's been the closest thing to a father to me these last eight hundred years, but that means I've also been like an errant son for him. It's hard to bear when I think how much that must mean he's suffered. So my solution is to try not to think about it as much as possible. Otherwise, I'd never get half the things I need to do done. The guilt and shame would be too much to bear.

Faust shakes his head. 'We mostly just did the studying he needed and the drinking and partying we both did when he stayed.'

'There was that one time with Matthias Buchinger,' Mephy pipes up, his eyes still fixed on my severed finger.

'I was very drunk!' I protest. 'And I felt bad for him being the only one without any hands or feet!' Matthias had been quite the character. Renowned throughout Europe for his musical abilities, his stagemanship as a court magician, and a ladies man, with a rumoured seventy bastard offspring left in his wake. All of which was made more remarkable by him having been only seventy-four centimetres tall and born without hands or feet. We got on like a house on fire and did some serious drinking when our paths crossed. Deciding to chop my own limbs off in a bout of extremely drunken empathy is exactly why I need someone like Aicha with me at all times, to save me from myself.

Johannes sighs. 'Ah, yes. I almost succeeded in blocking that particular misadventure from my memory. I assumed that was a one-off, an unusual blip, if you will.'

I shake my head. 'Nope. If anything, that was me being restrained and considerate of your delicate temperament, Johannes.' I give him a grin to let him know I'm joking. Kind of. For a man bound to the only demon ever to walk our plane –before the new one came along– he's fairly soft-hearted. Another thing Isaac and he have in common and another reason why I've tried to spare him from too much exposure to my habit of dying and dying badly.

Now, though, I can't spare him. I need to get all of them on board with the unbearable agony I'm about to inflict on myself. I can't risk them getting in the way, trying to stop me. Can't risk them hurting themselves the way I'm about to hurt myself.

Isaac rubs his forehead with his left hand as if he might somehow massage his brain through the skin and skull and soothe the ache I'm no doubt causing there.

'How much?' he asks.

Oh. He's clocked it. 'Most of my chest, I guess.'

Faust looks from one of us to the other. 'What? What are you talking about?'

Isaac ignores him for a moment, his eyes fixed on me. 'Have you thought about what that might do to you?'

I nod. 'It could kill me.'

'It probably will, lad.'

'No, it probably won't. We can live without our heart beating for a number of minutes at a push –'

'With accompanying brain damage.'

'... with accompanying brain damage, but if the magic of this place is going to heal my finger, surely it'll repair my brain too? At least there's not much of it to fix.' I really hope I'm right about this. Turning myself into a vegetable isn't a life goal. I'll take the risk to save Isaac though.

Faust's been watching us, his head flicking back and forth like a woman in a nineties hair shampoo advert, and now his frustration boils over. 'What are you both talking about, for goodness' sake?'

Isaac smiles apologetically, then nods, aware we've bordered on rude by excluding Johannes from the conversation. 'The little poem-slash-ditty thing says you need to cut the bonds around the heart –'

'And that nice machine there is perfect for severing body parts and repairing you straight afterwards.' I jerk my head towards the laser cutter that looks like a futuristic version of a cheese-wire. 'I've been in a similar situation before, which speaks volumes about how absolutely spectacularly rubbish my life can be at times. A Nain Rouge trapped me, and, well, the only way out involved a whole bunch of self-mutilation and instant healing. Apparently, these trials have decided to take me on a trip down memory lane.'

'You've already had to cut your own heart out?' The horror soaks through every syllable of Faust's voice, every line of his face.

'No,' I admit. 'That's a new addition. The trial's own little fucked up twist it added just to keep things fresh. I've never had to remove my heart from my chest before...' A memory pops up, waving frantically for my attention. 'Actually, not true. There was one time, but I died straight after, and it has nothing to do with the current situation.' I pause, frowning. 'I think.'

'Your life is very messed up and very messy, my friend.' I know the expression that's settling on Johannes' face. It's one I've seen many times on Isaac's. He's run through all of the seven stages of grief, seeing me go off to do something inexorably stupid, and now he's arrived at acceptance. I'm going to do what I'm going to do, and there's nothing left for him to do but wait patiently to pick up the pieces of me afterwards. Possibly literally, in this case.

'So what's the plan, lad?' Isaac's wearing the same grim set look as Faust. Brilliant. They've both come to terms with me chopping my own heart out of my chest.

Now I just need to do the same.

I give them what I hope is a light, easy grin and wave rather than the terrified rictus-like expression I fear is plastered across my face. Then I turn my back to them and let it drop. With them behind me, I don't need to keep up the charade.

There's no question. I am not looking forward to this.

What I'm working on is the literal nature of the lines. They don't say "give us your heart while we chant Kali-Ma" thankfully. They say I need to cut away the bonds imprisoning it. The same ones I've felt constricting my chest as soon as we came here. I'm going to slice away all that trauma and terror...

By cutting my chest into pieces. Repeatedly.

Deep breaths. Amazing just what a useful thing that is. Particularly for those about to do something mind-bogglingly stupid. I've become a master of them, considering how often I need their steadying hand. Honestly, learning how to breathe properly in the face of brain-numbing terror is probably the only thing that's allowed me to survive through the centuries and all their trauma. Well, allowed me to die repeatedly but also to have anything resembling a life when reality and all its assembled ensemble of horrors has been waiting just outside the door, carrying heavy-duty coshes inside their ill-fitting trench coats to beat me down with.

Next, I take a second while still calming myself with my breathing pattern to examine the laser wire. It's set at a convenient height, pretty much exactly level with my heart itself. The number of times I've had to stab myself in it means I'm aware of precisely where it is. I test, pushing up onto the balls of my feet, crouching down after, aligning the wire each time.

Good. This worked with my digit. Let's hope that little test run means I'm not about to die in terrible screaming agony. Fingers crossed and all that.

I push back up onto my toes like the world's most ungainly ballerina and shuffle forward. Let's just put it this way: the Moscow State Ballet isn't about to come offering me a job. Each half-step forward brings that beam of light, capable of dismembering without difficulty, closer and closer. I get myself to the point where I can feel the heat starting to scorch my skin, my nerves waking up and tugging at my attention with greater and greater alarm, pointing out that I'm way too close to this incredibly blazing hot thing, and wouldn't I like to back up and put some distance between us and this clear and present danger?

Instead, I take a last check, lifting myself up slightly more, a last deep steadying breath –desperately hoping it isn't my last one, full stop– and then step forward.

Have you ever been chopped clean in two? If so, please send me a letter. You're also clearly a reckless undying lunatic, and it'd be great to know there're others out there like me. Perhaps we can set up a network of immortal maniac penpals. Except I'm probably not immortal anymore, and I'm still trying the same sort of shit I did when I had that as a backup, an ace up my sleeve. The only thing that allows me to move forward is the man standing at my back. *Worth it.*

The pain is indescribable. If that sounds like a copout, then please go ahead and chop your torso in two with a giant laser cheese wire. Then come back to me with an accurate description. I'll wait.

Assuming you haven't done that, let me tell you, it's quite unlike anything else. I feel it go through my flesh and ribs like a hot knife through butter, which has never been a metaphor I've wished to apply to my own body. On the positive side, it means it happens quickly. On the negative side – and I can assure you, it's mainly all the negative side – feeling parts of your body liquifying from extreme heat is distinctly unpleasant. A moment later, it clips through both my lungs. I know this because they both deflate instantly, like two over-enthusiastically blown-up balloons seeking revenge on the kid doing said blowing by exploding and scaring him half to death. A feeling I know well because somewhere, under all the agony, that's exactly how I feel. If this doesn't work, I may have just killed myself. Not an unusual thing for me to say, but there's no knowing if I'll get the opportunity to say it ever again.

I'm too busy trying to suck in air and failing, making those inward wheezes like a stuck pig in reverse to be aware of the laser reaching my spinal column. That is, until the previous pain –on a level of intensity most masochists could only ever fantasise about, mainly because they'd die before they ever reached it– manages to kick up a notch. That and my lower body gives way, my legs buckling as paralysis hits everything below the cut point. A second later, I'm falling. I think so anyhow. To be honest, I black out for a moment, coming to on the cold marble floor. An eminently sensible decision by my overloaded nervous system, all things considered.

Oh, sure, I've felt similar levels of pain before. But normally only very briefly, one split second of high-grade agonized nerve-firings. Then I was gone, popping back up in a new body. This time, though, I don't die. Which is a good thing and precisely what I was banking on. But there's a downside.

Not dying means the nerves are mightily confused. There's been heart-stopping –literally– levels of pain, and I feel it kick back in like the big bass drop in the rave that gets all the sweat-drenched dancers back up on their feet. The healing magic of the place is obviously working; otherwise, when I push back up to my feet, I'd just slide neatly into two piles of Paul Bonhomme, whereas instead, I stay stuck together, to my tremendous relief. But those nerves are baffled, confusticated, utterly bamboozled by what has happened, and they are making that clear by continuing to broadcast the same agonised messages they were sending when they got liquified even as the magic heals them.

Is this what it's like for Aicha every time she gets dissected or atomised? Do her nerves still keep screaming at her even after she's finished reforming? By the Good God, I didn't think it was possible for my admiration for the woman to increase, but apparently it can. Which only increases my determination to get this fucking done so I can get back on the hunt for my missing friend. For that missing part of my heart.

So while I'm already in levels of pain beyond what most people could even imagine – and certainly beyond what pretty much any have ever felt and lived to tell the tale about – I give a limp attempt at a reassuring wave to my party of horrified friends, crouch, and step forward once more, back towards them.

They say you can get used to anything thanks to the resilience of the human spirit. I'm not quite sure who 'they' are, but I'd like to make them walk through a laser beam capable of slicing instantly through flesh and bone twice. See how they feel about that particular statement afterwards. Because I can assure you, it doesn't hurt any less the second time.

The sense of burning extending from shoulder to shoulder, cauterising through my oesophagus so I can't even scream, sealing each blood vessel it passes through in a riotous cacophony of agony, is quite the unique experience. And trust me when I say that. I'm a connoisseur of self-inflicted pain.

If anything, I think the nerves higher up in my chest have been listening in on the messages of pain radiating outwards to every extremity. That they heard my brain thinking, *Surely this level of agony can't ever be topped*. To which said nerves responded, *Hold my beer*. Because this is even more excruciating than the first time. Which, considering said first time involved popping both lungs and cauterising my spine, is quite the achievement.

Of course, it goes through my spinal cord again, and I flop downwards, ready to get a little more up close and personal with the floor. But I stop, suspended in mid-air. The lack of feeling in my extremities –I'm still feeling plenty of screaming complaints from other nerves, and the spinal cord itself is striking my cortex like a bunch of furious brain goblins are wielding razor-sharp miniature pickaxes– means it takes me a moment to work out what has happened. As the pain dulls down from "head-explodingly intense" to just "the sort of agony that would drive most men insane", movement starts to come back, and I look up to see Isaac holding me, that telltale glisten showing in the corners of his eyes.

'You absolute bloody lunatic.' He's struggling to hold back the tears. There's a quaver to his voice that speaks to the emotions running rampant right now. Personally, I'm just soaking in the endorphins as the pain diminishes, and I get to celebrate that totally ridiculous plan working and me not actually dying.

'Has it taken you this long to work that out, 'Zac?' My voice cracks slightly, but I manage to back it up with a grin of sorts. Granted, working out whether it's a smile or a grimace might not be easy, but, hey, it's still muscle movement. That means I'm still alive. Go me.

'Not at all, but that was something else, lad.' I can hear the urgency to his words, that moment when all the emotions spill and splash together until they're driving themselves into the syllables, trying to force them all out simultaneously. Damn. He really thought I was going to die. And he knew I was doing it for him.

'Isaac.' He looks up as I fix him with my stare. 'I made it, man. I'm still here. Still alive.' *Let go of the guilt.* I want to say it to him, but it won't help. He has to get there himself.

There's a noise behind us, as if God's bass guitar just broke a string live on stage. I try to whip around to see, but my body has other ideas and is determined to be a bit more careful, not entirely convinced it isn't going to collapse into two parts if it moves too quickly. By the time I look around...

The neon cheese wire I just chopped myself in half with –twice– is gone, and the room plunges once more into darkness. I'm too glad to see the back of my self-mutilation aid to even care about the pitch black of the cavern for a moment.

Sadly, only for a moment.

CHAPTER NINETEEN

HOME, 30 OCTOBER, PRESENT DAY

Ever since I walked through that laser cheese wire? I'm only half the man I used to be.

It's easier to breathe, both in the sense of having my lungs intact and once the lights come back on. It's funny how I can dissect myself without hesitation, chop myself in half like a slab of meat on the butcher's table, but I can't cut away this lumpen fear that sits like a gnarled tumour in the base of my soul. Still, those are thoughts for later on, when I've the luxury of sufficient time to self-psychoanalyse. Preferably surrounded by a selection of fine spirits and a bucket of ice to assist with the process.

Right now, we need to deal with the trials at hand rather than those of the mind already deeply ingrained. And as the glow from the walls grows, it's a particular and peculiar scene that stands before us.

A river is now running through the middle of the room, a strong current pulling it as it races from where it appears at one wall and disappears into the other. It's deep, dark, and wide, the depth impossible to measure in the strange half-light of the chamber. There's a rowboat with oars tied up to a docking pole made of the same black material as the walls and floor, that's grown out of the ground, on the same side of the waters as we are.

Also, we're not alone.

Three figures stand on the bank. They're hazy, translucent, so as I can see the cresting foam forming on the water behind them. I risk opening up my *sight* a tiny bit, which confirms it for me. These are part of the test, not actually what they seem to be. I know this because I don't start weeping blood.

Because one of them appears to be an angel. And one of them appears to be a demon. And standing between them is a human.

'Looks like we were right,' Isaac mutters, and there's a vaguely triumphant tone to his voice. By the Good God, there's no one as satisfied as an academic who's had a preposition confirmed. 'This has all been designed for us.'

I can't disagree with that. Although, I'd have thought the whole "chopping myself in half, twice, and not dying" probably counted in the "designed for us" column too.

The three figures aren't real. They're a part of the test's magic. As such, they look correct, but they're less daunting proportions-wise. The angel glows like bottled neon but isn't the height of the expansive chamber; rather it's standing only just taller than the man himself. The demon is squat, with bulbous musculature stretching under red skin, which is raised with blister-like bumps. Horns in the corkscrew shape of a goat's protrude from the flat forehead, and the eyes are black on black.

'That's bollocks.' The huffing from my feet tells me Mephy is less than impressed. 'The angelico gets all glowing fanciness, and the demonico looks like someone smashed them with the ugly stick for half a century. Stereotypes, that's what that is. Bloody prejudices.'

So the magic's managed to offend Mephy's sensibilities. It's interesting, though, that the angel looks about right, while the demon, according to Mephistopheles at least, isn't correct at all. I make a mental note of it, wondering if it's part of the solution.

The man in the middle is diaphanous, gossamer-like. I don't even know how I know he is a he, but somehow, it's clear despite the lack of defining features. All I can see is a grey human shape, like a mid-evening shadow cut out and given depth. It makes me think of the Greek myths, of tales of shades in the Underworld.

Unless I'm wrong, this "man" is supposed to be dead or else to represent his soul. And he has a demon standing on one side and an angel on the other.

'Is it a guidance job, do you think?' I ask, thinking of the whole "devil on my shoulder" image. Perhaps we have to help this spirit make a choice between the two supernatural forces flanking him?

'Maybe...' Faust starts, but trails off as silver filigreed lettering sparks in midair.

Three forms: one mortal, one evil, one pure
The angel would seek for the demon with war
The devil would consume the human for sure
And all three must enter into Hades' maw

'Racism!' Mephy barks, his voice rumbling in the back of his throat. 'Blatant racism! Just because he's a demon, he's evil? And he wants to *fucking eat* the human? Why? There's no fucking meat on half of you, and those that have it are packed full of preservatives and saturated fats. Basically processed meat. Might as well go to Burger King. Why would a demon eat a human in a world with free-ranging *fucking cows*?'

It's hard not to snigger at this outraged indignance, the volume increasing as his tirade continues. The only thing keeping me from doing so is not wanting him to sink his teeth into my arse to check which taste camp I fall into.

'And as for the poetry,' he carries on, 'they're not even trying anymore. That was practically a fucking limerick. "There was a mano from Occitan, wanted to hide his sword without a plan; he was racist as fuck, so the image he took, was a demon who ate meno from a can." Bloody Nora, mano. That was better than the bullshit this cave came up with.'

'I'll help you write a letter of complaint to the management,' I say wryly, fighting the urge to pat him reassuringly as I don't want to lose a finger. Again. 'But can we concentrate first on getting out of here?'

'Well, it is most intriguing.' Faust scratches his beard thoughtfully. 'Apparently, this is my test, no? So far, everything has played to our strengths. The ethereality of Nithael and his connection to Isaac. Mephy's...' He waves his hand to encompass all the traumatising things words can't. 'Physicality. Your experience of pain and self mutilation.' Yay, go me. 'So this time, it's got to be my turn.'

He steps forward and examines the three figures. 'Quite a conundrum. The demon wants to eat the human. The angel wants to kill the demon –'

'Racist!'

'Because, yes, he is racist; thank you for that addendum, Mephy. And we need to find a way to bring peace between them so they all can progress to their eternal rewards.'

'Just give him a fucking pitchfork, why don't you? Talk about stereotyping bullshit.'

I get the feeling Mephy really isn't happy about this whole setup.

Johannes steps closer, studying the three characters, then takes a hasty step backwards as they lift their heads to look at him.

'I am the guardian of man –' the angel starts, but Mephy interrupts.

'See? The guardian of "man" – not "human". This is some prejudicial bullshit!'

The last word echoes around the cavern. Johannes sighs, pinching his forehead between thumb and forefinger with his eyes closed. Then he opens them with a forced smile and bends down to speak to the demon dog.

'Mephistopheles, my dearest friend,' he starts. 'I think we all understand that you find the regressive nature of this particular puzzle, created by an ancient Frankish warlord and buried under a mountain for well over a thousand years, offensive. Now do you think you could be kind enough as to shut up and allow me to concentrate so we can eventually get the hell out of here?'

Meph lifts his huge canine head and huffs, sending a cloud of doggy breath into Johannes' face. 'Fine.' The grumbling tone is clear. 'I didn't realise there was an expiration date on bigotry, but fine. I'll shut up then. Shutting up now. No more words from this *actual demon rather than that offensive stereotype*. Humph.'

With the grumpy canine quieted, if not mollified, Faust returns to his study of the three figures. 'So,' he says to the proud-looking angel, 'you were saying before you were so rudely interrupted –'

'I'll give you rude. 'S rude to portray people or species according to untrue or hurtful generalisations; that's what's rude. Bloody manos and their bloody puzzles...'

Faust beams at the angel, and you can hardly even notice his eye muscle twitching.

The angel lifts its face and swivels to look at him. 'I am the guardian of man –'

'*Humanity.*'

Johannes shoots Meph a warning glance as the angel continues.

'– here to keep all the children of the Lord Almighty safe. I am his sword and shield, smiter of evil and cleanser of the path to the Heavenly Gates.'

The angel puts his head back down, and the man lifts his.

'I am man,' he starts, and it's only because of all the interruptions from Mephy so far that I manage to avoid adding, 'Hear me roar,' by biting my tongue. 'First among God's creations. Full of promise and first to fall.'

His head goes back down, and the demon raises his, an expression that can only be described as devilish flickering into life on his face.

'I am the tempter of man,' he says, his voice sibilant and low, 'the worm that turns the apple to rot, the blight that blemishes all it touches.'

To give Meph his credit, he doesn't actually get into a full-blown argument about this, no matter how much he's undoubtedly itching to. The huff he huffs though would have the Big Bad Wolf taking notes.

'But I have my part to play.' The demon doesn't seem to notice the interruption from his real-life counterpart. 'Leave me with man, though, and I will indulge in my wicked appetites.'

'The only wicked appetites I have is for their sexy legs. And I don't eat those. Not often anyway.'

We all ignore the low, growly voice. Johannes hasn't moved, drinking in all they've been saying. He looks at the demon, who is still waiting, staring back.

'Can you respond and answer my questions?' he asks it.

It hisses the answer back at him. 'Of course. Though my words are slippery and liable to be full of twists and mistruths.'

Faust nods thoughtfully. 'Of course, of course. Add in the "lying devil and the truthful angel" aspect. Yes, I see.' He turns back to us. 'It seems to me that if this puzzle is built around our strengths but also our reputations, that perhaps I am best known for the bargains I struck, eh? The truth of the matter is more complicated, of course, but that seems the most logical way to resolve this particular conundrum, as you say.'

The theologian is in full swing. This is theory, his favourite playground outside of disco bars. He marches back and forth, stroking and coaxing at his wild beard, striding as though aiming to translate the momentum into electrical energy, to spark his thought process.

'So,' he muses, turning on the angel, 'you are actively seeking the destruction of the demonic companion who stands beside you, am I correct?'

'Yes.' The angel nods. 'His presence is an abomination, an insult to the face of God.'

'And yet,' Faust continues, 'did you not say to me that you were here to protect all the children of God?'

'Of course.' For the first time, a reaction forms on the angel's face. A small furrowing of the brow.

'Then is not your former comrade also one of God's children? Are you not also sworn to his aid?'

'What?' Now the angel's looking really confused. 'No! God threw him down, cast him into the pit for his wicked pride and arrogance.'

'Ah!' Faust raises a finger. 'But didn't God do the same to man? Wasn't he also cast from the Garden of Eden for his disobedience? And what is disobedience but a prideful arrogance, a belief that we know better?'

'But, but...' The angel bugs, almost glitching. 'But man is the offspring of Adam –'

'And the original sin is passed along to each generation!' Faust sounds triumphant. 'So if this is the case, and based upon your appearances, we are definitely following the established traditionalist doctrine as the foundation pieces for this particular puzzle, then Man still carries the weight of that initial sin and remains banished from Eden. If the banishment is still in place, how can one argue that God has forgiven him and considers him one of his children?'

'Be...becau... because God s...se...sent his son –' the angel starts, but Johannes is on a roll now.

'To forgive all sinners. To bring all who repent unto God!' My goodness, it says something of Faust's abilities as both a debater and a logician that what should be dry theology has been turned into the equivalent of a gripping court drama. I could do with some popcorn.

'So,' Faust continues, ignoring the angel, who is struggling to control himself, his image flickering and crackling. 'If you are here to protect all of the children of God, even those who have not repented, who are not saved, then you must, by definition, be here also to protect your fallen comrade, giving him the space to demand absolution and seek a path back to salvation. Unless you are arguing that he does not have free will?' An eyebrow arches up. 'That God made him decide to fall? That his evil doing is God's work?'

The angel shakes and stutters like an automaton who's just been overloaded by a logic puzzle based around the Three Laws of Robotics.

Faust holds up a hand. 'Think about that for a moment, will you? Now let's talk about you.' He turns his attention to the demon on the other side of the man shade.

'You.' He points a finger like a rod of justice. *J'accuse.* 'You say that you want to eat this man, yes?'

'That's right.' The demon uncurls again, a hungry wickedness evident in a tooth-filled grin. 'I'll munch upon his bones and soul.'

'Okay, why?'

The demon blinks, the smile faltering. 'What do you mean, why?'

'Why do you want to eat him?'

'Well, to... to... consume his flesh and soul.'

'Okay.' Faust twirls on his heels and resumes his high-powered lawyer pacing. 'So let us deal with the first part first, hmmm? You present a physical hunger for the flesh of man. Is it just because you are hungry? A specific preference for man meat, so to speak?'

'I... Yes.' The demon doesn't have steam pouring out of his ears, but otherwise, he's also doing a malfunctioning *Westworld* robot impression, much like the angel.

'Yes? Yes to both? Okay, well, then if it is mere hunger, there are much easier options that do not require you to battle the heavenly host. And if it is the specific taste, then I can recommend a little roast pork with the crackling, yes? I am assured there is a remarkable similarity between that and human; although, of course, I cannot vouch for it personally.'

Oh, good. Johannes hasn't experimented with cannibalism. Not that I was really worried about that, but it's always nice to have the confirmation.

He carries on, 'Now, regarding your second point. You say that you wish to consume his soul. Am I correct?'

The demon calms, straightens. Obviously, it feels we're back on more solid ground here. 'Yes! I will devour his very being!'

'So he's damned, is he?' Johannes asks mildly.

The demon freezes. 'What?'

'This man here.' He waves a hand at the faceless shade. 'He, in particular, is damned, is he?'

'I... I do... I don't know,' the devil answers, his face shuddering and shaking.

'Well, because it seems to me that if he is not damned, if he is saved, then you will not be able to consume his soul, mmm? That belongs to God himself, protected and purified and out of your reach, am I right? Unless you are claiming to be stronger than the Almighty himself?'

'No... Y...yes?' The demon is totally confused now, his face clicking back and forth between the shade next to him and the academic torturing him with words.

'Right! So you only have the right to devour his soul if he is damned. Except, it seems to me that that is a rather merciful escape for a damned soul, eh? To cease to exist, to be devoured by you? And that seems a form of release. Almost a help rather than a punishment. What would your boss have to say about that, eh? I know there are a lot of damned souls out there, but if all you naughty devils' –he wags a finger at the baffled red figure like a schoolboy caught mid-lark by a secretly amused teacher– 'start munching your way through them every time you have a little rumbling of the stomach, then they will be a finite resource and gone before you know it! Do you have the permission of Lucifer himself to start consuming *his* lost souls?'

'I d...don...don't know.' The demon is flickering now, in and out of existence.

'Well then.' Johannes treats him to a full-watt, kindly smile. 'It seems to me that it is not a risk worth taking until you have confirmed with the chief devil himself that you may man's soul and have also ensured that he is actually damned and you aren't poaching the property of the other team. And the only way to manage that,' he continues brightly, 'is by getting to the other side and either accompanying him down to Hell or wave bye-bye as he heads up on the upward escalator. Perhaps stopping for a roast pork sandwich on the way.

'So.' Faust turns and spreads his hands wide, launching into his closing argument. 'We have established several truths during the course of our enlightening discussion, yes? You –' He points a finger at the angel. 'Are duty bound to protect your fallen brother, as well as the man himself, seeing them both safely to wherever their eternal paths may take them.

And you –' The digit this time is for the devil. 'Cannot, by any stretch of the imagination, consume this man, not without specific permission and only after establishing in which direction' –he points up, then down– 'he's actually going to go. As such, my friends, you are both required to accompany this fellow across the river without any of this silly squabbling you are talking about and see where exactly he ends up. So into the boat with you and off you go, and don't let me hear any more of this disagreement nonsense, okay?'

As he spoke, the angel and the devil stared at him, aghast, their grip on reality having slipped more and more, with them glitching, folding, and half-disappearing like computer game characters mid-crash. Now each opens their mouth...

'Noooeeeeeeeeeee....' The angel's noise gets slowly higher and higher pitched.

'Yeeeeeeeeeeaaaaaaaaa....' The devil's voice rumbles, stretches, a grating cacophony of sounds like gears grating, grinding against each other in all the wrong ways.

And then, with a noise that sounds like thunder being played by a celestial through a super-powered distortion pedal, the two of them tear into pieces, collapsing inwards. I half expect them to leave black holes when they're gone, but instead, the river winks out of existence, the man-shade too, and the lights of the walls start to fade.

'Bloody hell, you made them explode, mano!' Mephy's voice is full of admiration. 'Take that, you stereotypical wankers! *Boom*! *Kapow*! Faust for the win!'

It might have made Mephistopheles happy, but as the room fades to black, I can't help feeling like Faust just broke the ancient riddle of Charlemagne.

And I reckon it's probably out of its warranty period by now.

Chapter Twenty
Home, 30 October, Present Day

I told you that academics are dangerous. Against their might, even angels and devils reach their nephi-limits.

J ust because the cavern's not been particularly malicious to us so far – if you don't count making me chop myself in half twice – it doesn't mean we're full of trust towards what it might have in store. As soon as the lights go down, we back up, positioning ourselves instinctively in such a way as to guard each side, to protect each other if shit goes down.

As the walls start to glow again, building up, we find ourselves still in the same cavern. But now we're not alone.

Not in an "army of the undead ready to overrun us and eat our pineal glands" sort of way, though. Nope. We've been joined by someone who looks like a knight, judging by the armour, the metal glimmering on his helmet as the light increases, and the clink of chainmail audible as he moves, but who also looks like...

Well, like an accountant. If Methusaleh had got into the numerical arts.

He's sitting behind a modern-looking desk, complete with a computer screen, an in- and out-box for piles of paper that look pretty evenly stacked, and one of those little swinging ball clacking toys. The ones that are supposed to represent perpetual motion or be relaxing but which make me want to insert them one by one into a specific cavity of the person who invented them. There's a photo frame, such as one might use to display loved ones or a proud personal moment but instead, holds one of those memes using wide-eyed adorable teddy bears with a border note saying, 'You don't have to be cute to work here, but it helps'.

The man himself has somehow, against all the odds, managed to put a tie on, which, I'm going to tell you, clashes rather badly with his whole armoured get up. It would even if it wasn't bright pink and blue, with more teddy bears all over it, but that certainly makes the effect even worse. He's obviously immensely proud of it. We shouldn't be able to see it because his white beard reaches down below the edge of the desk and disappears out of sight, but he's parted it, making sure it falls in two bunches down to each side, allowing the tie to shine through in all of its naff glory. His face is so lined by wrinkles that, for a moment, I wonder if he's the anthropomorphic embodiment of origami, but that seems like a weird choice for a riddle or guardian even by the standards of these peculiar trials. He has twinkly eyes and a broad smile, although I suspect he might wear the same expression whether he was giving you a pay rise or firing you. Possibly out of a cannon.

'Well, now, bless my soul!' The old fellow smiles even wider as he clasps his hands together in delight. 'I cannot believe it. After all these years, all these centuries, finally someone has passed the Trials. I never thought I'd see the day! And yet, here you are, on the other side, no tattoos, ready to take Joyeuse into righteous battle once more!'

I can't believe it. We've made it. It's over. We're going to get Joyeuse, Isaac can expel this demonic bullshit out of his arm, and then we can go demonstrate exactly what I went through for us to get this sword on the demonic scumsucking knobjockey. Repeatedly. With explanatory labels. Then we might finally be able to get back on the hunt for a way to get Aicha and Jakob back.

'So let me just review your progress in getting here, shall we? Well done again, my fine fellows! One moment. I'll just pull that back up *here* and...' He hammers away at the keyboard, waggles the mouse around with some determined clicking, then sits back, his fingers steepled to his lips, and watches the screen.

There's some sound, though it's tinny and low, but I catch snatches of what we've just been through. Conversations, arguments, Mephy's outrage, my stifled screams. The old knight just sits there, watching it all, the same expression on his face. We hear the moment when the angel and demon fuzzed out of existence and then silence falls. Still the man sits there for a minute, his fingers pressed to his lips, staring at the blank screen.

Finally, he turns, taking his hands away, and looks at each of us carefully, one by one.

'Well –' he starts in the same measured tone, but then stops, breaking off.

He takes a moment to think, looking at us all in turn still. Finally, he speaks again.

'What in the name of all that's holy is wrong with you people?' His tone is indignant, outraged, like he's just watched footage of us robbing his granny's house on her home security cameras rather than beating the Four Trials of Charlemagne.

I think I speak for all of us when I say, 'I'm sorry, what?' Looking around, I see similarly blank, confused, slightly offended expressions on each of my companions' faces. I don't get what he's talking about. We've completed the Trials. He told us so himself. Why is he so upset?

'Have you any idea what you've done?' The querulous tone is underlined with shock. It's the sound of a headmaster looking through the notes of why a group of unruly schoolboys has been sent to his office, only to find out it's for first-degree murder while burning down the school. And I still don't even know why we've been sent to the office instead of being feted like the heroes I thought we were. Nonetheless, we all shake our heads guiltily in answer to the question.

'Twelve hundred years. Twelve *hundred years*!' The knight's voice rises, and he slams his gauntleted hands down on the desk, making us jump. Looking at them launches my mind into a whole question about how he can speed type while wearing heavy metal mittens, but I don't think now is the time to ask him that. He doesn't look very receptive to deviations from the point he's trying to discuss.

He pauses, shakes his head, obviously fighting to regain his composure. 'Twelve hundred years ago, Charlemagne left me here, having set up this Trial with the help of the Heart of Home. Magic and royalty coming together to create a perfect test, to ensure that only one noble of spirit, strong of heart, sharp of mind, and holy of purpose could come and claim Joyeuse. Twelve hundred years I have waited patiently, sitting in attendance for a mighty hero to arrive and claim that legacy. And *you* –' He points a quavering finger at us, his voice rising again. '*You broke the tests*!'

Ah. Apparently we didn't pass the tests. We just snapped them in two. Oops.

Isaac is far from happy. 'What do you mean, we broke the tests?' The indignance in his voice is now matching that of the old knight. 'We worked them out. Understood they'd been tailored for each of us. And then solved the puzzles.'

'They were *not* tailored to each of you!' You can sense that were this man less of a bureaucrat, he'd be screaming at us right now, showering us with flecks of furious spit. As it is, he's gripping the desk tightly, clearly trying to keep his rage under control. 'They are the same tests that they've always been! For the whole of the time I've been here!'

'Ah.' Isaac's expression falters momentarily, then brightens again. 'Ah, but wait! Maybe that's because the puzzles were designed for us all that time ago. Perhaps someone with a touch of the *sight* put it all in place, ready for our arrival. Did you think of that, eh?'

'No. They. Didn't.' The old man grinds out the words without snapping any teeth, which is a pretty impressive feat of magic all of its own considering how tightly he's clenching his jaw. 'Because I designed these tests, and I can assure you it wasn't done with you and your ridiculous solutions in mind.'

Oops. So not only did we break the Four Trials, but we're now talking to the person who created them. Someone who's dedicated an extended existence beyond the ken of most mortals to wait for someone to solve them. Only for us to blunder in and take a sledgehammer to them, like a demolition squad wandering into the wrong house and starting to knock out supporting walls while whistling a merry tune.

I can't shake the feeling that we're probably not his favourite people right now.

CHAPTER TWENTY-ONE

HOME, 30 OCTOBER, PRESENT DAY

I guess the tests he devised never survived the Trial period. Defective product if you ask me.

I smile my most charming smile, the one I use for getting a free upgrade on my cup size in an exorbitantly priced coffee shop. 'But it still counts, right?'

'Counts? *Counts?*' Again the utter furious disbelief is spelled out in every syllable. 'I wait for an eternity – or so it's felt to have someone worthy come through my Trials, and you ask if breaking them *counts?*'

I'm tempted to point out that they're not really his trials but Charlemagne's, except I don't think that'll help our cause. Johannes is still looking baffled, alongside Isaac, and I can see how much it's distressing their intellect, this accusation of inconsiderate destructiveness.

'I really don't understand, sir.' You can hear Faust's upset by that. Not understanding is like a cardinal sin for him. 'We did what was required for each test to progress to the next one. You said yourself we do not have the tattoos that mark us as having failed.'

'You progressed, oh yes, you progressed all right,' the knight mutters, shaking his head. 'But you didn't progress *correctly*. Not once, not once! Four chances, and every time, you messed it up completely.'

I can see even Faust's legendary politeness and patience is starting to wear thin. 'Would you be so kind as to explain precisely how, sir?' The words are measured but weighted. He's getting pretty fed up with this desk-jockey, antiquated knight being pissy with us without taking the time to explain why.

'Fine,' he grumbles. 'Let's go through them one by one. The first trial. Partially a test of the brain, partially of the purification of the spirit.'

He sees the blank looks on all of our faces and tuts, exasperated. 'Really? You got some of it. The pines, okay?'

'That's right,' Isaac says proudly. 'And the *pignon de pin*. The pine nuts. The play on words and the pinion feather of Nith's wing.'

'No!' the knight shouts, then stops, closes his eyes, and takes a deep breath. 'It is a linguistic puzzle, yes, but the word was based on the English for the trees. Pine. Do you know...' He breaks off, rubbing his eyes with the back of his hand. I can't help feeling he's close to tears.

He takes a moment, then starts again. 'Do you know how often language changes? A lot more regularly than we imagined when we set these puzzles up. The original one, in ninth century Frankish, made no sense whatsoever to the modern visitor, and that wasn't fair. Do you know how difficult it's been to keep abreast? Borrowing texts off the Heart, learning every modern linguistical variation, searching for something that makes sense to all and sundry so as to give each person taking the Trials a fair chance? I have dedicated endless weeks at a time to tweaking that particular challenge, keeping it relevant. I... I can't.'

He stands up and paces back and forth, clanking like someone searching through a crowded kitchenware drawer in a stranger's house. Eventually, he regains his composure. 'The whole point of that test was to lay down some of your burdens. To be able to give up some of your losses and to be at peace. Yes, it was also a first examination of your knowledge, to make sure you were sufficiently travelled and learned as to recognize the connection to the double meaning of the modern English word. Pine – the tree. To pine – to miss, to suffer from a fruitless longing. The idea was you would see that and then speak to the scales. To lay down some of those things that you miss, that hold you back and cause you hurt. The weight on your soul, you see?'

'Okay.' Isaac rubs his chin doubtfully. 'Sounds a bit convoluted, in all honesty.'

'A bit convoluted. *A bit convoluted*?' Again, I have to salute the old man's self-control. He manages to catch himself, keeping the volume just below a screech. 'I have spent literal lifetimes perfecting and modernising that particular riddle, and you tell me it's *a bit convoluted*?'

Isaac flushes, turning slightly pink, clearly abashed. 'Well, yes, but I mean, it was very clever too. Very, very clever.' He keeps his tone reassuring, obviously feeling bad for having upset the old fellow.

I'm still confused though. 'So how come what we offered worked then?'

The old knight's head swivels slowly to look at me, blank disbelief written large. 'Are you serious?' He waits, studying me, then shakes his head. 'You are. You're actually serious. That was the *feather of an angel, a literal angel*. In what world do you think that isn't going to break the scales? That is a sacrifice of incomparable value. Even the weight of loss can't compare to the load that carries. Honestly!' He goes and sits back down, looks us over. 'It's cheating, is what it is. Plain and simple cheating.'

Ouch. 'Well, I'm sorry that we had the foresight for one of us to soul-bond with an angel nearly a thousand years ago just to allow us to cheat at this moment and upset you.' Okay, I know we're supposed to be winning this guy over, but, honestly, he's just being rude now.

'Yes, yes.' He waves his hand dismissively, although I'm not sure if he's acknowledging I'm right or just because he wishes we'd all fuck off. 'Anyway, that's hardly the worst of it, is it?'

The knight sighs, massaging his temples –I can't imagine that is particularly comfortable with scratchy steel, but I guess maybe he's used to it– and gathers himself again. 'Then we had the next test.' He sighs, shaking his head as though trying to dislodge the mental images. Considering what happened on the next test, I'm not surprised.

I wince. 'So you're saying the idea wasn't for Mephistopheles to tear apart those, well, already torn apart animals?'

'Yes, you got it spot on. Bang on the money.' Ooh, look at him. Able to perfectly match my sarcasm tone for tone. 'I set that whole puzzle up because, actually, Joyeuse can only be wielded safely by a gluttonous monster. Those are the sort of qualifying criteria one looks for in a hero of the land.'

'I'm not a glutton!' Mephy's tone is furious. 'You released lots of tiny, hoppity-skipping critters into the room. And I'm a dog! At least physically. That comes with the territory. Or are you being discriminatory once again?' I can hear the realisation strike with that last question. 'Hang on, if you designed all this, we need to have some serious words about how you present demon folk. Downright offensive that was, mano.'

The ancient knight doesn't look very worried by Mephy's outburst. 'Yes, we'll get to that after.' He peers over the desk at the demon dog. He doesn't have spectacles to lower accusingly, but he manages to get the same effect into his staring even without them. 'You really thought we created some sort of hunting ground for you to "get your freak on", as they say these days, hmm?'

If I thought this whole setup was bizarre before, what with an ancient knight from Charlemagne's era discussing a demonic Doberman running on a rampant murder-feast through a magical trial inside the Pyrenees... Him then quoting Missy Elliott pushes it into the realms of totally fucking out there.

'Well, I did think it was mighty considerate of you all, mano.' Mephy sounds a little embarrassed. Guess he doesn't like being wrong any more than the rest of us. 'How about we call that even for your tactless speciesism and say no more about it?'

'So what was the answer for that puzzle?' I ask. To be honest, Meph got chomping down so quickly, and the animals started dying so fast, I didn't give it any further thought.

'Did you read any of my verse? Did you pay it any mind whatsoever?' The old fellow doesn't just look indignant now. He looks genuinely hurt, blinking back rheumy tears.

I smile sheepishly. 'Sorry, Mephy got busy so quickly, I was more concentrating on distracting myself from what he was up to than contemplating the air poetry.'

'Well, yes,' the old man harrumphs, but nods, 'I can understand that, I suppose. Well, the whole idea was that any worthy agent able to wield Joyeuse would be a healer as well as a fighter. Able to find the magical strands of life inside them. Weave them back together. Make them whole once more. *"There's a breaking mistaken for healing... growth and remaking within."* Don't you see?'

I smile and nod assuringly, although in my heart, I'm thinking just how long that would have taken. Catching each half-animal and then threading their life-force back into a whole? Knitting their essence back into a single being? I'm kind of glad Mephy went full-on Fat Bastard mode instead.

'But that's what I did anyhow!' Mephy's indignance levels are rising again. 'Demons reform when –'

'Er, I think he meant for us to do it without devouring them whole though, Mephy.' I add helpfully. At least I think it's helpful. The look on the guardian knight's face says different.

Of course I've brought myself to his attention, and now he peers at me, a stare weighted with utter disbelief. 'And as for *you*. As for you...'

He breaks off, shaking his head. 'What is your malfunction, eh? What is so wrong in how you are wired up that you think the answer to a problem is to *slice yourself in half? Twice?*'

I stutter and stumble over my words, 'Ah. Well, um, you see, this isn't, sort of, the first time or not quite anyhow, if you will, that I've had to do something like, well, sort of like that, sort of.'

'That wasn't the first time you've had to mutilate yourself to solve a puzzle?' He quirks an eyebrow at me. 'How many times have you had to?'

'Recently?' I count in my head. *There's the Nain Rouge's escape room (one), when the shit wizard had me trapped (two), biting off my own tongue in Ben's laboratory (three), getting Isaac to kill me after I possessed Jack of Plate (four), the cave under the Wilds of Faerie (five), Aicha killing me with a knife so I could take Maeve's body (six), and then, of course, my sacrifice on Bugarach itself.* 'Seven?' I'm sure I've missed a couple, but that's not far off.

'And how recent is recent?'

'The last year or so?'

'And you've been alive...'

'For about eight hundred years. A bit over, actually.'

The knight stares at me in disbelief, then shakes his head again sadly. 'You are completely and entirely messed up in the head, and your life is a living nightmare. I am terribly sorry for you. As, incidentally, was the puzzle itself.'

He straightens up, clearly going into explanation mode. 'The whole idea of that one was to confess the pain that you carried. To ease it from your heart. To pare away the vines it wraps around us, constricting our ability to love freely, to live at ease. And your interpretation of that was that *you needed to chop your still-beating heart out of your chest with a laser beam.*'

'Well, to be fair, I thought it meant I needed to chop around my heart with a laser beam. Cut the ties constricting around it. I must admit I was relieved by only having to do it twice.'

'Only,' the knight mutters. He's like a negative nodding dog, his head constantly shaking. Hearing his reasoning, seeing it from his point of view, I'm not really surprised though. 'You *only* had to chop yourself in half twice. These puzzles' –he raises a trembling hand, though I'm not sure whether with age or emotion– 'were designed to help a holy spirit purify itself prior to receiving Joyeuse, and you used it for self-mutilation? I designed that wire out of unfiltered *talent* so that it'd change in harmony with your truths until it sang as your soul reached a perfect state. Instead, you chopped yourself in half with it. Of course you bloody overloaded it.'

'Oh, I've been Perfect before.' I wave a careless hand. 'Didn't stick.'

'You do surprise me.' The wry tone to the old man's voice is better than shocked–slash–horrified indignation, I guess. Maybe.

'And finally, we come to you.' The knight shakes his head as if trying to make sure my idiocy doesn't stick to his brain and infect it as he turns his attention to Johannes. 'A simple final test, a little logic to ensure a certain level of smarts for a man who will wield a sword made for fae nobility.'

'But I got that right! I destroyed them with logic!'

'Yes! Bloody yes! You *bloody destroyed them!*' This time he can't help it. The old man screeches with rage, his face reddening. 'Do you know how difficult it is to make independent magical beings capable of speech and reasoned discussion? How much *talent* it takes to refine them, to keep them working? To be able to operate with something simulating free will itself?'

Wow. Now that I think about it, that's an incredibly difficult thing to pull off. Next to impossible. And to keep something like that running for over a thousand years?

'They were my magnum opus, my great life's work. My pride and joy. And you –*you!*– you come along and play your little word games with them until they break...break into a thousand pieces...'

The man can't help himself now. He's sobbing, great heaving cries as tears roll down his cheeks. Johannes stands, his mouth open, completely flabbergasted. A look of horror creeps its way into his face as he realises he's the reason this ancient knight is bawling like a baby.

'Oh. Umm.' He starts, then stops. Starts again. 'I'm terribly sorry. I thought that was the test. Umm. There, there?'

He reaches out to pat the knight's shoulder, but the man pulls back, a look like thunder on his face. 'No. No, that just isn't good enough. All you had to do was think it through, and instead, it's all blah, blah, blah, talk them to death. To actual death!'

For a moment, I think he's going to cry again, but he maintains his self-control. 'What on earth made you think it was a problem to resolve with words, man?'

Faust is still looking utterly flustered. 'Well, there was the whole thing with them presenting themselves and their propensities. I assumed it meant we needed to persuade them otherwise –'

'You assumed wrong! And what about the boat? The river? Did you just think it was there for background effect?'

The sheepish nod he gets back only adds to his put-upon expression. 'Good God, man, the amount of work I put into all of that, and this is the thanks I get?'

'So what were we supposed to do?' Johannes is close to whining. He desperately wants to understand what he's done wrong.

'It was a logic problem! Took me decades to come up with. And seconds for you to destroy.' He glares at Faust, who wilts under his gaze. 'The idea is that you cannot leave the angel and the devil together nor the devil and the man. And there's only room in the boat for you and two of the three. A fiendishly difficult conundrum that no one would eve –'

'The fox, the chicken, and the grain!' Isaac shouts triumphantly because, apparently, we've not yet broken this poor old knight's spirit entirely. There's still room for him to grind it into dust, along with the simulacrums Faust broke linguistically.

The ancient chevalier stares for several long seconds, his mouth working up and down with no sounds coming out, at Isaac. 'What?' he says eventually.

Isaac's clocked the atmospheric change now, and you can see that he wants to back-pedal, but sadly, there's nowhere for him to reverse except straight into a brick wall. 'Um, well, yes, the, err, the fox, the chicken, and the grain riddle?' Every syllable is dragged out of him against his will.

I am delighted to not have said anything, to have sat back and stayed schtum while the two academics fumbled over their words. The knight's expression has gone past frosty to so cold I'm surprised he's not causing snow to condense out of the air between him and Isaac.

'Would you care to tell me this riddle, sir?' The syllables are just as elongated as Isaac's but for entirely different reasons. His stretching of them seems to be a representation of what's going on with his temper.

'Ah, um, yes,' Isaac stutters under the spotlight of his stare. 'Well, you see, it's a, umm, a childhood riddle –'

'A riddle. For. Children. I see.' The knight's expression dips closer to absolute zero at this point. 'Do go on.'

'Umm, a *fiendishly difficult* puzzle that almost no child can solve, of course!' Isaac's attempt to calm the emotional bull that's stomping its hoof and breathing steam from its ringed nostrils is to wave a red hankie at it. 'Well, basically, um, there's a man who has a fox, a chicken, and a sack of grain –'

'How does the mano have a fox?' Mephy lifts his head off the floor, cocking an ear.

'What?' Isaac blinks.

'How does he have a fox?' The demon dog lifts his back leg to scratch behind his ear, a blissed-out expression on his face as he does so. 'Ahh! That's better. Anyhow, yeah, how does the mano have a fox? Foxes are wild animals. Good way to get your nose bitten off, that is, having a fox. Is it in a cage?'

'No, um. It's a tame fox.'

'Fuck off! There's no such thing!'

'There is!' Now it's Isaac's turn to glare at Mephy, although it doesn't have quite the same impact as the old knight's version.

'Right, okay, whatever. So your mano, he has an impossible fox, a chicken, and a bag of grain. Carry on.'

'Okay.' Isaac's levels of fluster are approaching max. He pulls out a hankie –sadly, not red– and mops at his forehead. He's definitely feeling the pressure. 'Anyhow, so the man has to get the three of them across, but he only has space in his boat to carry one of them. If he leaves the fox with the chicken, it'll eat it. If he leaves the chicken with the grain, it'll eat it –'

'Magic chicken, is it?'

Again Isaac breaks off at Mephistopheles' interruption. 'What? What are you talking about?'

'Simple. Is the chicken magic? Does it have some sort of telekinesis power? Or is it like a chicken centaur? The body of a chicken with the torso of a really tiny mano? It'd have to be tiny because otherwise, well, that'd be totally ineffective. It'd overbalance instantly. Or get crushed under the weight...'

Isaac stares at the huge dog with utter incomprehension. 'Mephistopheles, I say this with all due respect, but what in all of creation are you blathering on about?'

'Does he have arms, this chicken? Opposable thumbs? Or some equivalent power to help him out?'

'No?' The bafflement scribbled across Isaac's face is a wonder. Normally he's doing this to me whenever we have a theoretical debate, and now he's completely lost as to where Mephy is taking the conversation.

'So what's the problem with leaving the chicken with the bag of grain? Just make sure you've tied it up properly. Is that it? Is that the answer? Tie up the bag of grain properly instead of being a lazy shithead of a mano and let the poor fox go because it's cruel to restrain wild animals?'

'No, Mephy, that's not the answer!' Now Isaac's getting annoyed, wound up by the dog's logic. Mainly, I suspect, because he can't argue with it. 'The...the fox is domesticated. We've already said that, and the chicken...the chicken has a razor sharp beak or something...'

'They do have those sharp spurs. Nasty little fuckers. Tasty though. This domesticated fox. Well trained, is it?'

'Brilliantly! Trained to absolute perfection!' Isaac's really struggling now.

'Well, there you go then!' Mephy sounds triumphant. 'If you've trained it so bloody well, then it won't eat the chicken, will it? Plus, if the chicken's

got this razor beak thing, surely it'll be able to look after itself? First time
the fox tries to grab it, it'll be all like, "*bwaaaarrkkkk hi-ya!*" and after it
catches a few face lacerations or loses an eye, old Reynard is going to take
the hint and leave it be! So take the bag over, then come back for the fox
and the chicken.' Mephy pauses, thinking. 'Along with a pack of bandages
to stop the bleeding.' He nods, clearly content with his solution.

'That's not it! That is not the answer! First you take the chicken over,
leaving the fox and the grain. Then you take the fox over but bring the
chicken back so the fox can't eat it –'

'Why not just take the fox first then if you're just rowing the chicken
back and forth?' Mephy clearly thinks Isaac's answer is stupid, and I am
enjoying the hell out of being on the other side of this equation for once,
not being the one having their idiocy pointed out in great detail.

Isaac flusters, turning a charming shade of red over his mistake in this
simple puzzle.

'Ah ha!' the knight cuts in. 'So it is a fiendishly difficult conundrum –'

'No. No! I just – You!' Isaac points at Mephy. 'Shush!'

I might be confused as hell, but I am really wanting some popcorn right
now.

'He *can't* just take the fox first,' Isaac says triumphantly, 'because then
the chicken would be left with the grain –'

'The chicken with the magical powers.'

'– and the boat isn't big enough to take the fox and the chicken at once.
So yes, it seems like he's just rowing the chicken back and forth to some,
but he *isn't.* Because then you take the grain across, leaving the chicken on
one side. Then go back and get the chicken last, and you've got all three
across.'

'Couldn't you have made the chicken sit on top of the bag of grain? Maybe tucked the fox under your arm or got it to sit on your lap if it's so domesticated?'

'No!' Now Isaac's really getting pissed off. He yells the word at the demon dog, his frustration boiling over. 'I didn't make the bloody riddle up, did I?'

'No,' the elderly knight says. 'I did. Except not with animals and grain. With the balance of the holy order, of the spiritual war between good and evil that hangs over our existence and our soul every day that we exist.' His voice is low, calm, but the sort of calm that's like the first winter ice over a pond that can crack and splinter at any second, swallowing the unwary whole. 'I created that puzzle. Spent decades on it. Figuring it out. Creating the characters. Building it magically.'

All of us are looking at him now, sucked in by the intensity of what he's saying. He's not stopped staring at Isaac, and all I can say about that is rather him than me, assuming he doesn't actually attack him. 'Years and years, I spent making this perfect question to solve about the state of grace, the risk that hangs over all who must endure this life of imperfection. And you're telling me that it's *been turned into a child's riddle*?'

We all stare at him. I'm biting my lip, but none of us know what to say. The ancient knight walks back to his desk, seats himself, folds his arms on the surface, and then buries his head in them.

Considering how well he reacted to Johannes' attempt to console him, I decide to leave him be for the time being and instead wave the others in to huddle up.

'Right, so –' I start, but Mephy cuts me off.

'So the devil was the fox in this version, right?' He's not prepared to let this go. He's like a dog with a bone – or a demon-dog with a logical puzzle he's decided is illogical.

'Nope.' I'm going to disillusion him so we can hopefully just crack on with getting the sword and getting out of here. 'The angel's the fox. The devil's the chicken. The man's the sack of grain.'

Mephy pauses, looks at me wide-eyed, then turns and trots over to the desk. He pushes himself up so he's propped up on it and stares over the top at the Trials' designer, who seems to be sobbing quietly into his exorbitant beard. 'Excuse me, mano.'

It takes a moment, but eventually, the knight looks up. Probably taking a moment to get himself under control. 'Yes? What?'

'Your puzzle is bollocks. Borderline racist. Also, obviously the devil is the fox. Sort it out, will you?' Mephy gives an annoyed chuff, blowing hot dog-breath on the poor old man and then pushes himself back down before strutting over to us.

My intention was to discuss how to get the knight's attention again without dealing him any more psychological scars. Mephy's made the first part happen, albeit probably not the last. Now that he's focused on us instead of the offence the world has woven to his artistic temperament, I may as well take advantage of it.

'Sorry, Sir Knight, can you just clarify, did we pass the Trials or not?' I give him my most winning smile, pushing as much of my natural charisma as I can into my expression.

'I mean, did you "pass"? No, you didn't pass. Only in the sense that you "pass" a wall if you knock it over with a catapult and then stroll over the rubble.' He sighs, melancholic. 'All of that work for nothing, for you to have just demolished it like that. But it counts, I suppose.'

'You suppose?' I don't want disclaimers like that on it. I want definites to deal in. 'Does it count or not?'

'Look, if I give you Joyeuse, will you all just go away?' There's a pleading tone to the old knight's voice. I can't avoid the feeling that we've somehow ruined the poor chap. It takes a certain *je ne sais quoi* to break another human being by accident.

'As long as you'll allow us to leave with it, aye, absolutely.' Good work, Isaac. That's an important disclaimer to have thrown in. Just because the knight's only about one cutting insult away from collapsing into a blubbering mess doesn't mean he might not try to trick us. Especially considering we've just ruined his life's work in a few minutes flat.

'Allow you to leave? *Allow you to leave?*' he shrieks, his voice cracking with emotion. 'In what world would I not allow you to leave? That would mean being trapped here with you forever. I'd ask you if you were mad, but you've all demonstrated that you quite categorically are. Here...'

He lifts his hands morosely to the keyboard and presses three keys with one metal-covered finger. Then, with a sigh, he hits the enter key.

As he does so, the floor in front of the desk splits open, and another of the marble-like columns grows out of the dark floor. Only this one has a sword wedged straight into the top of it.

I can't help myself. 'Do I get to be King of Albion if I can pull it from the stone?'

'No, you get to fuck off. Now take it. Begone. Never darken my doorstep again.'

The old knight slumps back down, burying his head in his arms once more. I think he's been pretty categorically clear anyhow. Looks like we've not gained ourselves a fan here. I do vaguely consider offering him the chance to come adventuring with us. Partially because it'd probably do him good to get outside after being stuck inside a trans-dimensional trial arena for, apparently, over a thousand years. But mainly because I'm a terrible fucker for poking a bear to see at what point it'll rip both your arms off and beat you to death with them.

Except. Except the sword is there. And Isaac still has that demon energy in his arm. So I tell that little voice in the back of my head that's encouraging me to wreak mayhem –I won't call it a devil on my shoulder; don't want to upset Mephistopheles any further with such stereotypes– to shut up as I step forward, wrapping my hand around the hilt of Joyeuse.

It is beautiful. Wrought metal polished till it looks like silver... I blink. Oh. It is silver. Of course. Sword for high fae. It's overlaid in fine golden filigree, with a crown design on the pommel. The guard is similarly bedecked, fine detailing wrought into it all over. But the blade...

The blade is a delight. Silver swords sound awesome – and when they're magical, they can be very awesome indeed – but as a general rule of thumb, if you make a weapon out of silver, all you end up with is something very pretty but very brittle that'll snap off inside the first person you stab with it. This has been wrought to a degree where it is as solid as the finest steel. When you've fought with enough weapons, varying from one-off legendary weapons like this to a handy nearby ballpoint pen to shove up a lamia's nostril directly into their brain stem, then you learn to recognise that quality instantly. I have centuries of expertise with weaponry, and this is something quite exquisite and perfectly designed for killing anything you want to be dead already. By the Good God, I wish Aicha was here. She'd adore this weapon. Cherish its perfect curves, the way it's been forged as a love-letter to what can be made of a slicing edge. I can't wait to show it to her. Hell, when I get her back, when she comes home? She can have it as a welcome back present. I'll even wrap it in a pretty bow.

It slides clean out of the pedestal, and I can't help raising it above my head and striking a pose. For the sake of the knight's last remaining strands of sanity, I resist roaring out, 'Kneel before me!' as I do so. Never let it be said that I am entirely inconsiderate. Just mostly.

My moment of posturing done, I'm about to hand it over to Isaac when the lights start to dim. Looks like we're finished with the Trials.

Although based on a yelled, 'Don't ever come back!' and a muttered, 'Good riddance,' from the knight, it might be that the Trials are finished with us.

CHAPTER TWENTY-TWO
HOME, 30 OCTOBER, PRESENT DAY

Considering his whole "purification of the soul" schtick, I guess the Trials' Guardian is going through his own "dark Knight of the soul" moment now we've left him.

The darkness lifts from our eyes, and we find ourselves back in the Heart of Home, sitting on the cold floor. A grating noise behind me draws my attention, and I crane over my shoulder to see the pit containing the actual Heart close up and seal shut. I'm guessing Hell itself would need to freeze over before the knight residing inside ever lets it open to allow us access again.

In front of us stands Dunixi, his features creased with worry. I can see him surreptitiously inspecting us, looking over any exposed skin, no doubt searching for tattoos. Then he catches sight of Joyeuse.

He gasps and claps his hands. 'You obtained it. My felicitations, fine fellows. Well done! Were the Trials torturous? Implausibly fiendish?'

I look around. 'Um...yes. Yes. Very much so. We really had to work very hard – '

'And we definitely found all the right answers and certainly didn't break the Trials themselves!' Isaac finishes brightly, utterly unconvincingly.

Dunixi looks at him, then me, then the others, obviously trying to work out why we have such stretched, pained smiles painted onto our faces. 'It didn't run entirely smoothly?' Our expressions don't change, which is an answer in and of itself. 'Well, no matter. You have the sword!'

Oh, shit, yes! That reminds me. I push myself up to standing and then kneel once more, presenting the sword on the flats of my hands, tilting it towards Isaac. 'You have my sword, my liege.'

'If I thought you'd pop back up afterwards, I'd take it and your head, lad. Now stop messing about, will you?' For all his words, there's a softness to Isaac's voice. He wraps his left hand around the sword handle and steps back.

I lift my head, my eyes fixed on the aforementioned hand. As I watch, the sword starts to glow, the silver shining from the inside like bladed moonlight. It builds and then flows outwards, through Isaac's grip, up his arm. The blackness marking it disintegrates, his flesh regaining its normal colour. Isaac pushes up his sleeve with his right hand eagerly, bunching the material together so we can watch as every last strand of the darkness that has marked his body, threatening to consume it, along with his life spark and maybe his very soul...

Vanishes. Wiped away by the glow of Joyeuse's power flooding up his arm.

My next breath feels incredible. It's like it's the first time I've breathed properly in weeks. The trial might have talked about cutting away some of those constrictions wrapping themselves around my heart, but the reward for passing them – or breaking them, potato, potahtoe – has done just that. Some of those terrible worries that have been crushing in on me are alleviated, lifted away.

Allowing me space to draw in a real, relieved breath. And it feels marvellous.

Of course, it's not like all my worries have just dissipated and I'm about to break into a Disney musical number about how wonderful life is while woodland critters frolic around my feet in a synchronised dance routine. Aicha's still missing in a different dimension, and we still have a demon incarnate on our plane to deal with before I can get back to the essential task of searching for her.

But for right now, for this moment right here, I have a win more important than most I could ever want.

Isaac is safe. He's not going to die.

I'll take that now, tomorrow, and every day until I close my eyes for the very last time as a victory worth celebrating. Having the old bugger here with me gives me a rock to anchor to, a moral compass to navigate life's rapids by.

A reason to stay tethered to humanity and the here and now.

He tentatively hands me the sword back, and I stop the easy breathing. Now my breath is bated, as is everyone else's, all eyes fixed on his arm.

If the demon essence comes back, he'll have no choice but to keep hold of the sword until we can find the bastard who infected him and extricate the antidote from him, along with his major organs while we use his intestines to play skipping rope.

The seconds tick by as we all stare, hoping, praying in some cases, even myself who doesn't believe in anyone worth praying to, other than perhaps that strange being outside of life I met who sent me back. But I get the feeling the Good God has already done more meddling than they'd have liked and as much as they're prepared to do for the time being.

After a few minutes, when no blemishes reform on his arm, Isaac looks up at me, and his face splits wide open with a delighted smile.

'It bloody worked, lad! It actually bloody worked!'

He laughs. I laugh. Then I drop the sword and throw my arms around him as we bounce with excitement on the spot. Faust issues his full bellied roar of happiness and joins us, so we're spinning round like a trio of prima donna footballers celebrating a World Cup winning goal. Then Mephy chuffs with glee and...

'No! No, Mephy! Bad demon! Get the fuck off my leg, dude!'

'But I thought we were celebrating?' His injured tone doesn't mean he's stopped dry humping my calf muscle. I shake my leg as hard as I can until he finally dislodges.

'We are!'

'Celebrating without leg-fucking? What sort of celebrating is that?' The confusion and outrage in his voice is real.

The time has come to have a little tete-a-tete with Mephy over his habits. 'You can't just do that to anyone's leg when you want to blow off a little steam!'

'Well, you're not just anyone, are you? You're my pal, mano. And this is how I say hello to my pals.'

I'm struggling to get my head around this one. 'By shagging their legs?'

'Well, I would in this form!' Mephy's tongue lolls out. 'Definitely taking this one with me when I go. But, no, by making myself vulnerable. Presenting my private parts front and centre for you to do as you will with. Could you, or could you not, make my jiggly bits go kaboom if you really wanted to?'

There's a distinct feeling creeping over me that I'm losing the thread of this conversation. 'I suppose so. But that would seem like a good way for me to lose a hand.'

'Oh and the rest, mano!' Mephy grins, brightly. 'I'd bite your fucking arm off at the shoulder. And then keep chomping. Wouldn't do my family jewels much good though, would it?'

'I guess not?' Again, I can't help feeling this is supposed to be my role in a conversation. Confusing the hell out of people, rather than people from Hell confusing me.

'Right! So, still counts as putting myself at your mercy. I wouldn't just do it to any old Tom, Dick or Harry. Crying out loud, what do you take me for, mano? It's just the demonic hel-lo-you're-cool-we're-friends-you-sexy-legged-bastard-dance basically!'

'Right.' I think this over. 'Well, I'm glad you don't just do it to any random stranger, but let's go for explicit consent instead of just "he's powerful enough to make my ballsack explode if he really objects" as a rule of thumb from hereon in, okay? Call it dimensional differences.'

'Fine.' He sighs. 'May I fuck your sexy leg, Paul?'

'No, Mephy. No, you may not.'

The hound whines and grumbles something that might be, 'Spoilsport' or might be some heinous demon incantation to give me endlessly itchy haemorrhoids, but he doesn't try to jump back up and rub his red rocket against my calf again. We'll count that one as a win.

Speaking of wins, I look at Isaac and clasp him on the arm, unable to stop myself from grinning. 'That's the first part done, my man. We're making progress!'

'We are, lad. We really are. Now we're back at full strength. Well, we will be once we've had a chance to recharge back home.'

Yep. Of course. Getting Isaac back behind the wards is the priority now. Back on home turf, where he can draw on the energy contained therein to replenish his supplies. Normally, with Nithael on board, being out wouldn't be much of a concern. But they've both been pouring themselves into combatting the demonic infection, attempting to battle it to a stand-still for months, and they must be running on empty by now.

From here on in, I'm angling to get us gone. Dunixi has some questions he wants to ask about the Trials, which we do our best to *umm* and *ahh* our way around. It's only now that we've got back and are over the embarrassment of destroying the life work of an ancient warrior – and arguably, the forerunner to computer programmers the world over – that I realise he has only given us Joyeuse, not Roland's sword. The huge jentilak shrugs and tells us we're welcome to go through the Trials again and ask for it. Considering it is, by all accounts, a lovely fae sword but not one we desperately need right now, I'm happy to leave it where it is. It allows the old knight, who I also now realise we were too busy feeling terrible around to ask for his name, a purpose to his continued existence inside the Heart of Home. Part of me wonders if he gets lonely, isolated in a meta-dimension made of magic. But he seemed happy enough with his internet connection and even more delighted to see the back of us, so I assume he's managing okay. He certainly wasn't begging to sign up to the Bonhomme Gang. Plus, until we get Aicha back, there're no open spaces. She gets a veto on any new members.

We leave through the same magically distorting stone gateway, the en-trance distending, then shrinking back behind us as we breach back into the surface world. When I turn around, it's once more just a low-level henge, little more than a cairn. The farmer's carelessly left supplies are still leaning up in it. I wonder if they really are the farmer's or an additional form of camouflage by the jentilaks. Regardless, I can't see the way in. The doorway's closed to us. That's okay. We got what we came for.

I've strapped Joyeuse to my belt with a nifty scabbard that Dunixi gave me as a parting gift, like a shaggy mountain man version of Elrond in the last Homely House. It's little more than a metal sheath, but it's super lightweight, and there's something reassuring about having it clank against my thigh for the first time in a couple of hundred years. I've got so used to storing blades in my etheric storage rather than having them serve as a fashion accessory as well as a lethal stabby thing that I forgot that sense of weight it adds to the world.

I cast a *don't look here* spell on it so as not to scare the bejeesus out of any other mountain hikers we should cross paths with. Running into sword-wielding maniacs in the wilds of the Pyrenees sounds like the setup for a horror film – especially considering the huge black dog *actually possessed by a demon* that we have with us. The likelihood of us having to perform CPR on some poor old sod having a heart attack is considerable.

We make our way back down the sloping path, and it's all very pleasant. The sky is blue, that sort of deep cerulean colour where clouds have been banished to the tops of the mountains so they can hang out, looking like the most picturesque cotton candy imaginable without spoiling the rest of the vista. The air is crisp, but even that is invigorating, that sharp bite inside the lungs that helps remind you that you are warm, that your blood runs hot, that life pumps through your veins and you are still here, no matter how immeasurably unlikely that is, all things considered. The trees hold green, refusing to buckle under the cooling skies. I've a mythical sword strapped to my belt, and we've descended a good part of the hill without me banging my knee on it. All-in-all, I'm feeling like things are going fairly swimmingly.

Which, of course, is a spectacularly stupid thing to even dare to contemplate thinking and one that makes Murphy pull out his rulebook, consult it with due care and attention, and come to the conclusion that, by the letter of the law, he has no choice but to fuck us up right royally.

Chapter Twenty-Three
THE PYRENEES, 30 OCTOBER, PRESENT DAY

Let it be noted here and now, Murphy and I are not friends. He's not getting an invite to my next birthday party. And he's off my Christmas card list.

We're only about five minutes away from the car park when my instincts start screaming blue murder. You must have felt this feeling before. That sensation when the world somehow subtly changes, when the subconscious part of your brain has clocked something threatening or terrifying but has decided that the only way it can now communicate with you is via charades. With both hands tied behind its back. So you know something is wrong – awfully, horribly wrong – but you don't know what.

Trust me. You don't survive as long as I have – even if you've also died as often as I have – by ignoring those feelings. When I hiss, a kettle-whistle of warning, the others all screech instantly to a stop, their heads swinging left and right, so they must have the same alert klaxon going off inside their brains.

Except for Isaac, of course, who bumbles straight into my back. Thankfully I've taken a strong stance, half-crouched, scanning the horizon, so it doesn't knock me over. Faust shoots a hand out to steady my mentor, and the alert state of the rest of us is enough to bring him to a halt, recognising the way we're scanning the horizon even if he doesn't have the same survival instincts going bonkers. I cannot tell you how often I am glad he has an indestructible angel to keep him alive. There's no way I'd let him cross the road on his own otherwise.

For a second, I see nothing. The breeze stirs through the burnished leaves, picking some of the last stragglers as it travels through to tumble downwards. Each one falling pushes me up another notch of alertness, my vision snapping to it, tracking everything in our surroundings. The mountain air carries that pastoral mix of alpine freshness with the abundant remnants of passing sheep flocks that would sting the nose anywhere else, but seems somehow right in the context of this place. There's nothing in that sense's realm that's causing me to be on my guard.

Then I see it. What's caught my eye, even if the absolute dickhead of a seeing apparatus decided to send it to the silent, unconscious part of my brain rather than doing the sensible thing and labelling it as 'URGENT' before delivering it directly to my cerebral cortex.

Shadows. In between the tree line below us.

I go full *Apocalypse Now*, finger gesturing from my eyes to the foliage, which is picked up by the others, although I take no chances with Isaac. I grab him, point deliberately, and mouth, 'Baddies,' at him because I wouldn't put it past him to assume I was just waving to some nearby hikers before going blundering down blithely, whistling a merry tune.

We break off from the main path. There's a gap, in the bushes, large enough we can pass through without creating a disturbance. I don't know for sure that whoever's lurking farther down the path is a baddie, of course

–it could be the aforementioned hikers or a couple enjoying a bit of out-door fun and games– but it's rare my internal warning system goes into overdrive without reason. Not unheard of but unlikely. And there's no harm in playing it safe. Worse case is we traumatise some young lovers mid-hammer and tongs. Mind you, if they've decided to engage in their private business so close to a public footpath, they'll probably enjoy being intruded upon anyway.

I crouch behind the hawthorn bush and wave the others down. 'Isaac, Johannes, you wait here. Keep an eye out. If we engage, make sure no one else sneaks up on us.' Having someone watching our six for a potential ambush is never a bad plan. 'Mephy, you're with me.'

The hound nods –*it aint nothin' but a hound nod*– while the other two look less content about the whole situation but acquiesce nonetheless. Which suits me down to the ground. Honestly, I'm feeling ready for a rumble. We've done so much running around, chasing our tails. Cutting ourselves in half on etheric cheese wire. Unnecessarily. Part of me hopes it's the demonic wankgibbon waiting down below. Mephy seemed pretty confident he could give most visitors from down there a spanking, and with me backing him up, the odds have got to be in our favour.

We close the distance carefully, easing forward, our feet gliding as silently as possible, searching out the clear spots in the grass where autumn's fallen debris wouldn't crunch or crackle underneath them as they come down.

For once in my life, stealth pays off. We close the distance without the fucker being aware.

Because, believe you me, fucker he is. He's a youngish man, seemingly of a similar age to my own body, somewhere in his thirties, possibly early forties if he has a natural baby face. He's wearing a suit that screams money, apparently both individually tailored and inordinately expensive. His shoes are Italian, also handmade if I'm the judge, and I'd laugh about how ill-equipped he looks for a walk through the mountains if it wasn't for the fact that all my survival instincts are hollering as loud as they can to kill him or run away. His hair is neat, parted along a central line, a dark black mass that's been coiffed to within an inch of its life, not a single hair out of place, although his goatee beard, which has been equally neatly tended to, is a lighter colour, with strands of red that make me wonder if he's dyed his hair. All in all, he strikes me as the kind of guy one might find at the head of the table in a high-powered boardroom, the chief exec of an oil company working out how many irreplaceable natural habitats they can destroy this week before heading home to sleep like a baby. The sort of fellow who'd take *American Psycho* as a how-to guide, who'd happily stab tramps for kicks on a Friday night. That's only added to by the fact he's wearing a sword scabbard, presumably ready to go tramp-stabbing.

And that's before I *look* at him.

Because that's when I start to feel that first full twinge of fear.

The fact that he's swarming with demonic energy is always going to have that kind of effect on me.

He's not the demon, not the knobsocket manifest in flesh. That wouldn't cause me quite this sort of worry. We'd know who we were up against. He has that same demon essence covering him. It almost seems to be soaked into his skin, to be drenching him below his clothes, staining his very aura.

And that isn't all. Because there's an actual demonic aura too. He's not the demon manifest. But he's definitely a very close personal friend of the bastard.

He's also obviously no friend of ours. Which is made even more clear when I realise who the second person is, as the bastard drops them down off his shoulder and props them against a silver bough.

An actual friend of ours. Gil.

The young man's wrapped in dark tendrils of demonic magic, bonds that are tying him, restraining his arms, wrapped tight to his body and thighs, though his lower legs are still free. Not that he looks capable of walking as he looks like he's out cold. A stickier working, tar-like, covers his mouth, keeping him from making a noise. Judging by the rapid heaving of his chest, it's making breathing almost impossible as well, although at least he is still breathing. The only good news is, seen with the *sight*, it doesn't look like he's been repossessed, even if the guy holding him prisoner looks like even more of an arsehole than your standard repo man. But that does little to make me feel better.

They got him. Again.

I mean the demon, obviously, but also *anyone*. The Family, the lower dimensional cuntspawn who possessed him, the walking, talking advert for executive disfunction now holding him prisoner. Someone of ill intent got their hands on the young man *again* and I promised him. I promised him I'd keep him safe.

Promised him I'd do better.

What I should do here is continue with the plan in hand. Sneak up on the scumball. Shank him in the heart. Fuck him up nice and silent and permanent-like.

But I'm not very good at that approach at the best of times. And seeing what's happening to Gil, seeing him tied, helpless, his eyes rolled back into his head so as I'd think he were dead if I couldn't see those hitching chest movements? Brings out the worst in me.

People talk about seeing red. I understand that. It's a pretty image. Because, for me at least, I don't see *red*, per se.

I see rage.

Fury colours my very vision, tunnelling my attention to the arsewipe who's dared to put his hands on that brave young man whose shoes he's not worthy of licking, like he no doubt does his demonic master's. Deepthroating the whole boot. All I can see is his complacent stance as he wipes at his forehead daintily with a crisp white hankie from his breast pocket, unbothered by the suffering of his captive.

So I can't help myself. Elemental magic has never been my forte, but right now, I want to see that bastard *burn*. Fire leaps to life in the palm of my hand, builds into a crackling, condensed inferno, and I throw it, a targeted strike, threading through the undergrowth, aiming straight for where the bastard's heart would be if it hadn't withered away a long time ago.

It's not subtle. And it's too loud, too much light and movement to catch him unaware. Maybe if he'd had his back to us, but he doesn't. He's facing towards the path, his eyes straining, a hand across his forehead to shade them, no doubt looking for us. Probably waiting to negotiate an exchange. Joyeuse for Gil. Of course, that'd match up with past behaviour. Team Demon has seen what we'll go through to save him. Seems logical we'd give up the sword to get him back.

So because he's looking, if not exactly at us, then at least in the same general direction, the movement grabs his attention, snatches at his peripheral vision. Perhaps his version of the early warning system that tipped us off farther up the path about him. Either way, I see him clock my actions just as I release the working from my hands. His eyes go wide, and for a moment, I think the shock will paralyse him, keep him from acting until I burn him up from the inside out.

Sadly not. His hand whips out as though to slap Gil, but instead it passes just short, grazing across his jaw. As it comes away, it's dripping with the black essence that was covering the boy's mouth. The bastard's other hand grabs the substance, and he stretches it between his palms, a viscous mess that somehow hangs in the air, suspended when it looks like it should gloop down to cover his shoes. Throwing it up in front of him, like a gothic matador taunting a fiery bull, he catches the burning ball in the material and enrobes it with the essence, slowing it, sticking it to the *talent*. The impact twirls him around, pirouetting, but he's not out of control. His hands spin like a kid doing cat's cradle, faster and faster and then the black sticky matter dissipates, disintegrating away. When it's gone, so is my fireball.

And the enemy knows we're here. So much for the element of surprise. Aicha would definitely be delivering a slap to the back of my head right about now if she were with us.

But she isn't. So it's on me to get this one done. To save our friend. This time without anyone else paying the price for my mistakes.

Now that the goo's gone from Gil's mouth, he seems to stir. His eyelids flutter, crack open, and he's propped in such a way he can see me first. Even from this distance – a few metres away – I see the relief hit, a smile flitting across his face. But then he sees where he is. Who's closer to him. The smile's gone, and sheer panic has taken its place.

'Paul!' He screams the words at me. 'He's the demon's tether! He's De Montfort's son!'

Then his eyes travel downwards as though he becomes aware that he can't move, that something's tying him up.

When he sees the demonic working, black snaking trails wrapped around his lithe form, he doesn't scream words anymore.

No.

Now he just screams.

CHAPTER TWENTY-FOUR

THE PYRENEES, 30 OCTOBER, PRESENT DAY

De Montfort's son and in league with the demon? I'll be delighted to nail him tether wall.

Trauma – true, soul-scarring trauma – is a terrible thing. It's a beast we carry with us every time we walk into the dark. It digs its claws into our brain and seizes control, riding us, making us into a loa's *chwal*, their horse. Turning us into beasts. Adrift from all that makes us evolved, that marks us as civilised beings. Drags us back, lost, into our primal selves. Locked down in terror's eternal night, unable to function, unable to even think, let alone dream of escaping. When we're taken by trauma, when it's turned on, triggered, there's nothing else. I've said before that as human beings, we can't really understand the concept of the infinite, that we're limited to a finite existence where everything begins and ends. Being trapped in trauma's embrace might be the exception for that because surely nothing feels more endless, more eternal, more inescapable than when we're drowning down in its depths.

I've made that same sound. Not that long back either. Locked away in the dark to die over and over again, to be driven mad by the endless misery.

By this shitheel's father. The same chucklefuck doing it now to a young man who deserves anything but to suffer further.

And still Gil is screaming, that terrible wordless noise that carries so much meaning, that packs so much anguish into an undulating wail. I want it to stop. Want him to be okay. Want him not to be suffering because of me, once again.

'Mephy, can you do anything? For Gil?' It's worth specifying where I want him to concentrate his efforts.

My eyes are locked on the scene in front, but I can hear the doubt in Mephy's voice when he answers, 'I can, sure. It's a working. Undoable, mano. But don't you need my help with him first?'

'No. Save Gil.' That's first priority for me. Get him out of the personal hell he's been plunged back into. 'I can deal with the shithead.' That's priority number two. To be applied with great prejudice.

Joyeuse leaps to my hand. It seems appropriate. If this is the weapon the bastard wants, let's give it to him. Point first, straight through the midriff.

I charge forward, my feet leaping over bracken and branches, picking up speed. Closing the gap as the fucker's still turning back. Hoping to at least take advantage of the distraction caused by dealing with my magic. Ideally gutting him before he even notices.

Sadly, not. The fucker – De Montfort's son, apparently – turns back, his eyes widening as he sees how close I am, and draws his own sword. A cutlass, of course. Daddy's boy through and through.

The weapon is up in guard as I close the last distance, already committed to a hammering overhead blow, though I've kept to the ground. Leaping strikes are beautiful to see but easy to punish if the opponent sees you coming. The villain whips up his own blade and catches the edge on his cross-guard, then drags it down and sidewards. I sort of hoped Joyeuse might just slice the weapon in half, but either his own sword is magically imbued or that isn't where Joyeuse's magic lies. Either way, he drags my blade sideways, steps back, and raises his own into a standing poise.

'Stop!' he shouts, his hand outstretched. Towards Gil. My panic level spikes. The bastard's trying to do something to his hostage, our friend. Stop his heart? His breathing? I act. Unleash a flurry of blows, breaking his concentration, forcing him to wrap both hands around his pommel, to twist and shape it to match my furious onslaught.

'Mephy?' *C'mon, you amazing demonic bastard. Step up here.*

'I'm working on it.' The hound's tones are muffled, strained. 'He's safe though.'

That's enough for me to breathe again. Mephy's protecting him. Whether because of that or my harrying, whatever Demon Fart Junior was hoping to do didn't work.

Which makes a thought occur to me. Even if I consider he's had a military education provided by his father, this Wankshaft Mark 2 is holding up remarkably well under my onslaught.

My eyes narrow. 'Simon, you pox-ridden whoreson, is that you?' I stare at him, suspiciously, analysing every inch of his face, looking for any sign, any betraying lip quirk or crinkle of his eyes to show me that the original bastard wasn't actually consumed by his master on the top of Bugarach, that he somehow survived that whole shitheap of a showdown.

We break apart, and for a moment, the man stands facing me, agog, his mouth doing an impression of one of those singing trout wall placards from the eighties, only with its annoying voice box removed. It gives me a breather, a moment to check over my shoulder. Mephy's biting through the black smoke-like working wreathing Gil, breaking it bit by bit with each chomp. *Perfect.* Now to keep him focused on me.

'So is that you, Simon, you scumsucking knobgoblin? Do I really have to kill you all over again?' I act bored, but my brain is racing. There're so many questions. How did he manage to survive and come back again? And how did he get his hands on Gil? He should have been safe, stored away behind the wards. Even if they wavered, like when I came back to Toulouse, around the farmhouse itself, they should have been impenetrable.

The bastard finds his voice at last. 'Why?' There's a plaintive tone to it, a demand for answers.

It stumps me. 'Why, what? Why would I kill you again? Because you're a plague on the face of the planet. Because we've only still got a planet at all thanks to me killing you?' A bit dramatic perhaps. It wasn't really me who killed De Montfort. It was his ally Papa Nicetas, when he ate the bit of the Grail energy in his soul that kept De Montfort reincarnating. But De Montfort was the agent for all that mayhem; he engineered the whole fucking debacle over the centuries. He brought me endless misery and suffering to both further his plans and just for the shits and giggles. If he's come back all over again, killing him permanently might become my over-riding mission now that Isaac's free. Even stopping the demon can take a back seat. I fear De Montfort's machinations far more than I do even that other-dimensional dickweed.

The man turns white. Looks like I've just slapped him across the face. Like that was a terrible shock.

Good. Fuck him. Time for some action.

While he's reeling from that apparent bombshell, which makes me suspect he isn't actually De Montfort returned because nothing I just said would have been even the slightest shock for that shithead, I take advantage. Swing my sword. And as I do so, a thought hits me. I push my *talent* out into Joyeuse, set the silvered blade crackling with my own green power, run it up and down the edges, interlacing across the face into a growing power storm.

And the blade responds. Sings in response to my magic. I can feel it, the way my *talent* dances down the length of the blade. It's like the sword comes to life, in harmony with my needs. So this time when I swing it, an over the shoulder looping movement, round and down as Demon Fart The Second overcomes whatever it was about what I said that knocked him off balance and brings his swaggering pirate sword up to meet mine...

This time it does shear through the blade. Nice and clean.

The sharp, curved end of his cutlass falls with a clatter to his feet. Not on his feet, sadly. Severing his own toes would've been poetic, but it doesn't actually happen.

He doesn't look worried either. Not by that. Not as much as he should. Instead, he just looks at me, his face wan, the skin drawn around the eyes. 'Please. Stop. Don't make me do this.'

Shit. I don't know what could be so bad that even this villainous fuck-knuckle doesn't want to do it. But whatever it is? It can't be good news for me.

CHAPTER TWENTY-FIVE
THE PYRENEES, 30 OCTOBER, PRESENT DAY

Fuck fighting to the pain; I'm
ready to fight to the death.
Ideally his death if it's all the
same to you, Universe.

Now isn't the time to let him get his breath back, to allow him to do whatever Hail Mary manoeuvre he's working up the courage to perform. Pressing the attack is the only sensible option.

My sword is a blur. Sweeping spins that slam down against his defences. And I may be convinced –almost– that this isn't Simon come back to piss in my cornflakes one last time, but you can see he's been trained by that military arsewipe. Because somehow, despite only having half a sword, despite it becoming less than half, shortened each time he blocks my blade, shearing off another length, he does manage it. He does block me. The remnant is always just in the right place, frustrating each killing blow.

'Stop!' he shouts again. 'I don't want to fight you! Please! Why would you think I'm my father?'

'If you didn't want to fight, you shouldn't have kidnapped my friend!' Typical villain. Now that he's losing, he doesn't want to play anymore. I've fought enough whining fuckwits to know giving them an inch of space will result in a knife in your guts. I grunt with the exertion, feeling the ringing impact of my edge on his as it severs another length. He has little more than a long knife's worth left now. 'As for why I thought you were your father? I guess Daddy didn't tell you your actual role in his plans.'

He backs up, dances away from my swinging blade, his eyes staring madly. 'Wait! What do you mean?'

'You weren't his heir apparent, arsehole.' I grin savagely. This bastard may not be as bad as his father, but he still put his hands on me and mine. I'm quite happy to disillusion him as to where he stood in his dad's parental goals. 'You were his spare body. Daddy came back in his progeny's form each time he died. You were his standby if the shit hit the fan. Luckily for you, he was destroyed instead of the world, which was what he was trying to destroy. Unluckily for you, I'm here to finish the job this time.'

'Please! I'm not against you! Please believe me!' His hands are held up, pleading, outstretched, and for a moment, my resolve wavers, my blade tip dipping. 'I don't want to do this!'

Then Gil screams again, another of those souls-in-torment howls that breaks my battered heart to hear, and it is enough. It's more than enough. It's far too much, and I'll not stand for him to suffer another second. Time to finish this bastard off and free my friend.

Demon Fart Junior sees it. The change in my face. The hardening of my resolve. 'I'm sorry,' he whispers. Then he stretches his hand out and from it, a blade forms.

But not a blade of steel or silver or hell even some sort of meteorite, a fallen star straight out of legend like I have. No, this one is made from a fallen angel if the stories carry any sort of truth. Which I doubt they do, but damn, it's impressive nonetheless.

Because it's pure demonic energy that hardens out of his hand. It's not black in the sense of a colour. It's the full absence of light, a miniature black hole thrown up into our reality. It's like Hotblack Desiato's spaceship from *The Restaurant at the End of the Universe*, so black it seems to consume anything that touches it in the visible spectrum. And it is absolutely awash with *talent*, way beyond what humans can normally have hidden away up their sleeve.

Still, it's only a sword, right? Only a manifestation of another dimension, infinitely more powerful than our own, packed with creatures who have mastered all aspects of the physical, embraced them, and become lords of the reality they can reshape around them.

My only hope is that Joyeuse is more than a match for it. A legendary magical weapon against demonic energy made manifest.

Let's find out.

The dickhead's not trying to plead with me anymore, not begging for his life. I think he can tell no words will make any difference, not when Gil's suffering so much. His cheeks droop, but his sword doesn't. I wonder what manifesting this blade is costing him, to make him look so desperately sad. Some terrible impact on him, obviously. Perhaps it's feeding off his life force, eating up a year of his life every time he swings it against me.

Aw, diddums. I'll be happy to help out by ending his life right now.

We circle for a second, stepping cautiously around, looking for an opening. It serves me a double purpose too. I can see what's going on with Gil. The panic's bitten in hard, and he's trying to drag his hands free from the restraining wisp-bonds. Looks like all his yanking is hurting though as the restraints seem to be fighting back. Now Mephy sets his teeth through them, clamping his jaws together, separating that part into two strands. Gil slumps in relief, his cry cutting off. He's not free; there's still more of the stuff wound around his torso and upper legs, but Mephy sets to work on that too, gnawing away at the sticky material, and it looks like having his arms back, having some freedom of movement, has taken the edge off of Gil's sheer terror.

'Don't do this. Just listen to me!' Looks like the scumsucker's not done trying to wheedle his way out of this. Or perhaps he's just trying to manufacture an opening. The Good God knows there has been plenty of times I've spun a line to an opponent, caught them off guard with a non-sequitur or blinded them with rage through a carefully crafted insult.

I don't want to listen. Don't want to give him space to weave some more shit that'll hurt me or, worse still, hurt Gil. I've not forgotten that outstretched hand earlier. How he pulled that demonic working off Gil to deflect my magic. Perhaps he's just stalling, building up another attack.

No time for talking. Time to end this.

I feint, stabbing for his midriff. As he brings his own blade into a defensive position, swung low to intercept, I bring my left hand up and grab the blade in a double grip, changing the momentum by forcing it upwards. I twist my wrists and drag Joyeuse back sidewards, aiming for his neck, looking to separate his head from his shoulders in one simple move. He sees it and stumbles backwards, tripping over his own feet. It's probably the only thing that saves him, the momentum instinctively flinging his arms upwards to bring the flailing blade up into contact with my own.

Then I'm taken into a whole world of pain.

As my sword-blade touches his, I feel it *conduct*. The silver carries the demonic energy whistling along it like a knife in a plug socket –trust me, as someone who's had to do that not long back in Paris, I know what it feels like– and out. Through every nerve in my body.

Look, I'm going to assume you've never felt what it feels like to burn violently while still alive, your whole body crisping up under a heat that has every sensory organ screaming simultaneously, giving the lie to the idea that we are one individual being rather than a collective group of organs that get along relatively well most of the time. It's an indescribable feeling, one I highly recommend avoiding.

There's perhaps more chance – although, again, I hope not or that I'm only speaking to a minority who got pulled out seconds before the end – that you've felt what it is to go through the ice on a previously-believed frozen solid lake in a bitter mid-winter. To plummet into the lightless depths, the cold so sharp it slaps that desperately precious breath out of your lungs to bubble upwards, outwards, away, swallowed by the frozen silence. This feels similar but different. The burn is there, the complaining, but it steals your senses, numbs you into an agonised ending, dragging you down like the nameless ones are claiming your being to feast on in the silent depths of Ry'Leh.

Some few of you can claim electrocution on some scale or other. Perhaps it's just the static shock, built up from too much polyester versus too much atmospheric charge. Perhaps it's a drunken piss on a fence you didn't realise was electric. Maybe you thought you flicked the correct circuit breaker, but it was *that* one, not *this* one, and next thing you know, you're halfway across the room, every hair raised up as though it got frozen in place after the velocity dragged you backwards. Real full-on electrocution is that, only turned up to eleven on the Spinal Tap amp dial and not ending until it burns out your neural pathways, your nervous system, your heart itself.

I've experienced all three at various times and to varying degrees. What I've never felt before is all of them together at the same time.

Every inch of my skin, every centimetre of flesh, every speck of matter that makes up my body that can react to sensation, good or bad, gets hit with an overload of information. There's a proximity between extreme freezing and the bite of the flame's tongue, of the running race of electricity's current as it carries from head to toe. But this message is all of them at maximum impact simultaneously. It's an intensity that the human form isn't made to experience. Each of them individually is only something normally felt at this level just prior to agonising death. All of them happening together is an entirely new level of pain I didn't realise was possible.

It wasn't on my list of life's aims to discover it.

My knees buckle, giving way underneath me, my own dead weight driving me downwards, slamming hard into the ground, so as I'm amazed my kneecaps don't shatter. Although, considering how overloaded I am with the rest of the pain, perhaps they do. Broken bones and shattered articulation would be nothing compared to what I'm feeling right now. I'm aware of my body but separate from it, floating in an ocean of agony, everything soaked in the white-out of excruciating sensations flooding every inch of my being.

The fucker could kill me now. I'm defenceless. But he's a villain. And if there's one thing villains love to do, it's gloat.

He leans forward, no doubt to deliver some zinger of a putdown before he does just that – puts me down. There's a ringing in my ears, like a concussion grenade has just exploded. Possibly inside my head. I can't help feeling that would still hurt less than this does.

My sword clatters to the ground, released by numbed fingers, unable to remember the need to clench. I've no weapon now. But what I do have is a hard head.

I snap my head forward, smashing my forehead clean into the bridge of this new Darth Shithead's nose, spreading it across his face.

The bastard might be trained in martial warfare –and top-style marks for how well he's fought even while hindered by a formal business suit– but he's still mainly human. Feeling the cartilage in his nose shatter staggers him and sends him reeling backwards, his free hand pressed to his face as blood gushes from his ruined nostrils. It'd be a brilliant moment for me to apply my own finishing move.

Sadly, I've used up all my reserves pulling off that one single act. I'm still flooded with pain; just doing that one instinctive manoeuvre has drained me dry. Springing to my feet is a long way from possible. The best I can manage is to stretch out my left hand slowly, painfully and fumble around until I wrap my hand around Joyeuse's pommel. I start dragging it out of the formidable grip of the long grass.

My opponent shakes his head, spraying blood everywhere, throwing off the stunning effect of my Glasgow kiss. He's wounded but not enough to put him down. And he still has his terrible demonic blade, the one that makes Joyeuse conduct the other-dimensional *talent* directly into every fibre of my physical form.

He looks at me. 'Yield!' There's an edge to his voice. Like he's begging. Of course, that might just be the gargling caused by the blood dribbling down the back of his throat.

Mephy's not seen what's happened, not yet. I guess I must not have cried out when our blades clashed. I'm not surprised. My jaws feel clamped shut, the control only just starting to come back into them. My agony was probably silenced by my body being completely overwhelmed.

But Gil has.

The initial relief over the bit of freedom he got has passed, and his eyes are fixed on me, sorrow clear on his face. Looks like I didn't need to make a sound for him to realise how much suffering I'm going through, even if it's slowly fading. Our eyes meet, and his flick down to the blade on the ground. Silently, carefully, he stretches out a hand, his palm open and gives me a nod.

Oh, fuck me. The brave lad. He never stops. The meaning's clear enough. Mephy's snapping away at the last strands holding him back, and he's only a few seconds from being free. He wants me to throw him the sword. He's ready to come riding to the rescue just like he did with Melusine, a simple Talentless human slaying a mythical beast through cold steel and a will of iron.

It's not a bad plan. In fact it's a great one. So as the fuckwad I'm fighting takes a step forward and shouts 'Yield!' again, I switch my grip on Joyeuse surreptitiously, readying myself to pick it up and hurl it, javelin like. I'm confident enough that I can drop it just short of Gil's feet, where he can sweep it up and enter the fray.

Meantime, I need to buy him a little time. So I step one foot over Joyeuse, obscuring my movements. Reaching into my etheric storage with my other hand, I pull out a fresh blade. It's simple metal, but it springs to crackling life with my *talent*. I push myself to standing, my left hand still hidden behind my back, Joyeuse coming up with me.

Screaming, 'Never!' at the bastard, I wave my other sword, keeping him focused on that.

It works. Just not how I expect it.

The man looks at me, his eyes full of sorrow. 'You're right. You won't. There's no choice and no time.' He spins his demonic energy sword around and stabs it straight through his stomach.

I feel my eyes popping, like they're trying to leap out of my head. Apparently "never" was the safe word, and it's persuaded him to commit seppuku. A far easier end to the fight than I expected.

Except, of course, I don't get that lucky. Because the blade doesn't cut through his abdominal wall, spilling blood and guts everywhere. It's absorbed into him. And from his back, a crackling pair of pitch-black wings, not bat-like but more like a giant eagle's were they soaked in pitch-tar spring out. The now winged man bends his knees, leans down, and launches himself forward. As he comes rocketing towards me, his hands spread wide, that same black energy strings between his palms, held aloft, the material growing upwards and downwards until it covers his body like a scutum, a Roman shield, large enough so as to not leave a single gap where I can strike, a battering ram of the same demonic energy that overloaded me with pain just by touching my blade.

Behind him, Gil screams, 'No!' and breaks into a stumbling run, the last strands parting around his legs. Mephy, his job done concerning Gil, swings his head round and whines as he sees what's happening. He twists, bunching and springing, his teeth bared, hurling himself towards the flying man. But the momentum is with my opponent. The two of them may be entering the battle, but it's too late, far too late.

Demon Fart Mark 2, now with real demon energy and movable demon wings, is going to crash into me long before they get anywhere near him. Considering what the touch of that energy did to me when it transferred through my blade, I am utterly convinced that the touch of his demon shield is going to kill me instantly.

Or at the very least, make me wish it had before it actually finally does.

CHAPTER TWENTY-SIX

THE PYRENEES, 30 OCTOBER, PRESENT DAY

My odds of surviving this aren't just slim; they'd have to turn sideways in the shower to get wet.

My doom hangs in the air, this black viscous oblong obscuring the man, blotting out the sun, oil-feathered wingtips poking out from the corners, like the obelisk from *2001: A Space Odyssey* has decided to fuck off messing with humanity and just evolve itself. My brain's going haywire, trying desperately to think of a way out, but there's none. Nothing. I don't have the force to move myself aside, not much anyhow. And the wings mean he's guided. I'm not stupid enough to believe that just because I can't see through his demonic magic barrier, he can't peer through to his heart's content.

The only thing I can come up with is to thrust my sword at him, driving upwards with my right hand. My hope is that, for some miraculous reason, my normal weapon will work where Joyeuse didn't. That perhaps it being made of steel might save me from the hellish conduction that came when I connected with the silver blade.

It works, and it doesn't. It works in that when the black barrier hammers down towards me, straight down on top of the sword, it doesn't send the same debilitating shock through me. Whether it is because of the different metal or –more likely– that this is a different working, that the pain overdrive stimulation is something integral to the demon sword he manifested, I don't suffer that same feeling of all my nerves getting triggered simultaneously.

It doesn't work because the barrier just eats my sword.

Now that it's so close and descending rapidly, there's an transluscency to the material. I can make out the vague blur of the features of the man on the other side, a shadow puppet show made by the sun shining from behind. So I see the shade of the blade running into the material. It doesn't come out again.

The substance just chews it down, chomps it up. A parody of what Joyeuse did to the fucker's cutlass, swallowing it whole.

This is it. I can't do anything, can hardly think, can't even breathe. The whole of the sword-blade's gone now. In a second – half a second – it'll reach the cross-guard and then it'll start on my fingers. I try to release the handle, to pull back, but it's going to be too late. This is the moment where I'll find out if I get one more 1 UP or whether it's Game Over, cue tinny 8 bit wah-wah-wah-waaaah music.

But that's not what happens. As the sword blade is eroded away to nothing, as my hand flies open but can't possibly pull away...

The shield shimmers, pulls back. Then is gone.

I find myself with my open hand resting around the throat of Simon De Montfort's son, Joyeuse in my left hand. And he doesn't look shocked. No.

He looks resigned. This is a choice.

There's a split second with me there, my fingers wrapped around his neck, the legendary weapon ready, where I want to. I really want to. Just squeeze tighter. Swing up and stab him straight through the temple. Finish it. Finish him. He's De Montfort's son. The demon-bearer. If I kill him here and now, that might be it. The demon might have to flee back to his own dimension. We'll be safe from whatever this fucked up situation is, and I can get back to trying to find Aicha.

It's so tempting. Until I think of her.

Because she'd recognise the truth here. Same as I do deep down. This is a surrender. The real Hail Mary by the man in front of me. Putting his life in my hands to say *please*. Please hear me out.

And I feel it too at the same instant. He may not have intrinsic *talent*, but he's been trained by an expert in the Talented world. His mind's been wrapped in mental barriers, the sort anyone can make to keep out the uninvited, with no need for magic of your own as long as you have enough discipline. They come tumbling down. It's the equivalent of dropping the drawbridge, inviting in the invading hordes on your doorstep. As they fall, he mouths that one word, the one single thing I know he's been trying to say if I'm honest with myself.

'Please.'

Seeing that, this huge gesture, this thing that is more than a displaying of the throat –because I could go in there and wreak terrible havoc – tear his memories from him one by one, wipe out his personality for my own personal amusement– I know there's no choice. Not when I think of her too. Of what Aicha would want me to do.

I dive in through the open door. Into the young man's mind.

The next moment, I'm not on the verdant Pyrenean pastures anymore. I'm in a corridor, a plain thing. Wooden floorboards and cream plasterboard walls, with two doors that lead off it.

It is still eminently impressive because it took me lifetimes to build the like. We're in his mind palace. And I say "we" because he's here with me.

He looks much the same. Still wearing a tailored suit that probably costs the same as my house in Toulouse. Still perfectly crisp, whereas I hope our fight outside has left the real one at least slightly rumpled. It's not good for my ego, the thought he might have got through the battle without breaking a sweat. But even if he did, that isn't the case now.

He's sweating profusely. In fact, he looks distinctly unwell.

'Thank you.' The words are almost a gasp. I'd think he was about to keel over if we weren't inside his own mind. Though if that is the case, then our time here might be limited. As might his time on the planet.

'It's fine. What the hell is going on? Who even are you?' This is beyond weird. One moment I'm fighting this dude for my life – for the life of Gil – and the next, when he has me at his mercy, he throws himself open, defenceless, and invites me into his brain for a quiet chat and a cup of tea. Although I can't help noticing that he hasn't offered me a cup of tea. Which would be rude if he didn't look like the effort of making one might kill him.

'I'm trying... trying to keep *him* at bay. Time is limited.' I don't need to ask who the "he" is. It's obviously the demon. The whole place shakes, plasterboard dust drifting down from the ceiling as miniscule cracks appear. 'It's a breach of the compact. I've slowed... slowed time as much as I can... compared to outside... but still...'

Still, we don't have long. The building shakes again, the cracks growing, and I understand why. What he's attempting – slowing our pace of time compared to the outside world – requires *talent*. Talent he doesn't inherently have if, as I assume, he's half-Cagot, and hasn't died yet. Meaning he's borrowing from the demon, while, apparently, also trying to keep him away.

That, at least, I can help him with. It seems strange to be aiding him when a moment ago I was aiming to filet him, but, well, in for a penny, in for a pound. I step forward and press my hand to his cheek, pushing my *talent* in and taking the strain for the time-slip. It's a gesture, really. We're inside his mind. I could have just pressed against the nearest wall and destroyed him, but I want to show him I'm listening. That I'm giving him a proper chance.

His expression eases, and the tremors stop. The man's breathing becomes less laboured, more natural. 'Thank you.' He nods in appreciation, then sinks backwards. A simple wooden chair is there an eye-blink before he makes contact with it, and he rests for a moment.

But not for long. Time is still of the essence. 'Phillip De Monteguard.' He sticks out a hand, and I shake it, still thoroughly bemused as to what's going on.

'Paul Bonhomme, but I'm guessing you probably know that. Now what the ever-loving fuck is happening?' I think it's best to get straight to the point.

'Your friend. Gil. He was right. I am De Montfort's son. I'm demon-bound.' He bows his head, then lifts it back up to look at me. Tears sparkle in his eyes. 'I thought I was doing the right thing. Thought I was the hero. Then, well...' He breaks off as he stares past me.

He starts again. 'I realised something was wrong. Badly wrong. That I must have made a mistake. So while he was distracted, while I had a moment where he was too absorbed in his undertaking to realise what I was up to, I rescued the boy. Brought him to you.'

Oh. So when we saw him dragging Gil along, it wasn't some attempt to ransom him for the sword. He was delivering our friend back to our loving arms.

Which I tried to kill him for.

Whoopsie.

CHAPTER TWENTY-SEVEN

INSIDE DE MONTEGUARD'S BRAIN, 30 OCTOBER, PRESENT DAY

Need to make this quick. His mind palace is going to be a mind pile of rubble in not very long at all.

'I'm sor...' I start, but he waves it down, shushing me with his hands.

'It's fine,' he says wearily. 'I'd have done the same in your place.' He hunches over, dejected.

As sorry as I feel for him, there's also a shit ton of questions I need answers to. Starting with the simplest. 'How did you know where to find us?'

'He knew.' He shrugs. 'Some of what he knows, I do. What he wants me to know. Or doesn't care that I do. It didn't used to be like that. It used to be a true partnership. But since Papa died, he's changed. Been completely different. Secretive. Controlling.'

Wow. There's a whole lot to unpack in that sentence, but one sticks out more than the others. 'Papa?'

The man looks up at me, and those tears are back but running freely, streaming down his face. 'Yes. Papa. He was the only family I ever had. Well, until I was bonded, of course. But that was more like a marriage in many respects. But, yes,' he says, a touch of defiance in his tone. 'Papa.'

I never thought I'd see anyone cry for the death of Simon De Montfort – except for tears of joy, of course. But this young man, this Phillip, has made himself open and vulnerable. I'll show him a modicum of respect, at least. 'You said he raised you to believe you were on the side of good. What happened?'

'He was never...' De Monteguard stops, then starts again. 'Never a *loving* father. Strict discipline was the watchword.'

He waves a hand, and a screen pops out of the wall. One of those foldaway flatscreen TVs that positions itself, angled so we can both see. It springs to life and images fill it. A boy, preteen, training. In sword and stave. Studying endlessly. Pushing his body and mind to the limit and beyond. And a man I'd have been happy to never see, ever again, not even like this, knowing he's dead. Simon De Montfort. He's silent, cold. Serpent-like, poised and watching. A baton, held like he's a sergeant major, tucked up under his left arm. His right hand is quick to seize it, to deliver out corrective raps. To knuckles. To knees. To shoulders. To the skull. I see the boy's tears stream, see him catch another whipping baton across the cheek that spins him to the floor for having dared cry. The boy rubs at his face, wiping away the mixed moisture, the combined blood and tears. I see the determination fix in his gaze.

'I never cried again.' De Monteguard's words are almost a murmur, yet they carry to me perfectly clearly. 'Not once. Not until he died.'

By the Good God, what an existence. A terrible way for any child to be raised. Just another stroke of callous evil by Simon De Montfort. 'Did you not have anyone else? Any friends?'

De Monteguard shakes his head. 'No. Not until later. I was home schooled. Raised by him or else by tutors brought in. Carefully selected. Cold fish, the sort who wouldn't get concerned by the idea of an isolated child.' I bet that didn't keep them alive. Bet De Montfort still bought their final silence with a blade to the ribs. He was never the type to leave any loose ends lying around. I'll keep that thought to myself though. The man whose mind I'm in is already suffering enough.

'There was one time.' The screen flickers to life again, and a country lane appears, tall poplar trees stretching overhead towards each other like poised dancers, thin and bare, the ground swathed in a blanket of crisp snow. There, coddled in a drift, is a splash of red all the more vivid against the blank canvas it's painted on. And inside it is a dog. Little more than a pup. Some sort of bastard, a lean mix of setter and border collie at a guess. The left rear leg is a mess, shattered, perhaps by a trap, perhaps by a vicious creature such as the one who shakes his head at the boy, dismissive and uncaring.

'He told me to leave it.' Simon De Montfort has already turned from the scene and is walking on. 'Told me to put it out of its misery, even. Said that was the only kindness anyone could offer.'

Instead, the boy, pulls off his thin jacket, a blazer that must already be offering little protection against the bite of the wintery air, and swaddles the animal. He lifts it gently, cradling it in his arms. Then he carries it along. Simon turns and sees what's happening. His lip curls in disgust, but there's something else. Something the boy will have missed. A glee in his eyes that makes my heart plummet. Whatever he has planned can't be good.

'Two days.' De Monteguard's voice cracks as though parched, though I suspect it's from too much moisture, the tears pushing from behind his eyes rather than too little. 'For two days, I nursed it.' He shakes his head. 'I never even knew if it was a boy or a girl. It seemed rude. Impolite to check. Probably meant it was a girl, but... Well I never knew. I never knew.'

I see the boy in his room. It's more like a cell, a monk's austere place of meditation, stripped bare of any frivolities. A bed, a bench, a small table, and a glass of water. It's hard to believe the child ever thought this could be what love looked like. Although, of course he never knew anything else to compare it to. And we will long for our parent's love, hang on their every word, even as they beat us black and blue. I bet that coldness became a driving fire in the young lad's heart. To prove himself. To earn that love.

But he's gathered a cardboard box from somewhere. Packed it with his own blanket, which is little more than a rag. If the place is as cold as it looks, as quick to pick up the outside chill as I suspect, the boy must already have spent each night shivering, but still he's given up what little covers he has to make the animal comfortable. The puppy lifts its head, and the boy starts when a tongue shoots out, its rough surface startling him as it licks his hand. Then he realises what's happened, and I get to see something I reckon must have happened ever so rarely.

The boy laughs. A genuine, warm sound that carries with it all the freedom that joy can give us, even in the darkest of places.

It would be a balm to my soul if I'd not seen that look on De Montfort's face when he saw that De Monteguard had picked up the animal.

Then there it is. The boy is running down the corridor, his feet flying under him, almost tripping, his excitement painted across his face. The door is flung open and there...

There it is. The empty box. The blood-stained blanket, vacant. The room once more entirely empty and void of life.

'He passed judgement.' Phillip's words are a whisper, the weight of what he's saying pressing down on them, smothering them. 'I ran through the house, searching. I found Father with Dog. With my friend. He said that Dog was lamed. Broken. Useless.'

His voice drops even further, almost inaudible. 'I told him. Told him he wasn't useless. Not to me.'

Silence for a moment. Just as I'm about to reach out to him, he shakes it off and looks up at me. 'He said I was right. Said he'd let me into a secret.' There's a lip curl at that idea, a grimace, that I know comes from a little boy who desperately wanted to believe his father, even in the face of yet more trauma. 'He said he'd tied Dog to me. Made him a protection charm. That somehow you'd got wind of us, of me. Attacked us. Used dark magic to attempt to murder me, to kill me before I could become a threat to you.'

The tears are falling now. 'He said the attack had failed because Dog had protected me. But that the hurt had fallen on Dog instead. That Dog was going to die because of you.' He shakes his head. 'But I knew he also meant Dog was going to die because of me. That it was my fault, too. He said the only thing we could do now, the only mercy, was to end Dog's suffering.'

'He made me watch. I... I thought he was going to make me do it. Force me to kill Dog. "Put him out of his misery," as he put it. But, no. He did it. And do you know what's the worst thing?'

I shake my head, my own mouth dry at witnessing yet one more example of the horrors De Montfort was capable of.

'I was grateful.' De Monteguard looks at me and all that guilt, that self-loathing is burning in his regard. 'I was so grateful that he did it instead of me. Grateful that Dog died in my place. Do you know I even thanked him for it? Thanked him for killing the only friend I ever had. The only friend until he bonded me to my demon. And yet I never saw through it, never doubted him. Not really. Not until he died.'

The screen flicks off, and I look at him, watching as he dries his eyes again, see that same resolve light up. 'He raised me with you as my bogey-man. Told me tales of the terrible nightmarish powers of Paul Bonhomme. The unkillable force for evil. Rapacious. Murderous. Destructive. Told me he'd thwarted your evil doings time and again, but he was never able to defeat you permanently. That he was raising me to carry on his endeavours, to fight the good fight when he was gone.'

He laughs bitterly. 'Except it wasn't going to be him who was gone, was it? That's what you were telling me. It wasn't only you who wouldn't stay dead.'

I shake my head, stay mum. There's no need to say it again, to hurt him further. He's heard the details. And there's more I need to know. 'When did you start to suspect?'

'That he was lying to me?' He looks away, his cheeks pulled up, wincing, as though the thought causes him physical pain. 'Never. Not really. Not while he was alive.' He stops, considers. 'Perhaps, a little. When he wouldn't let me help. At Bugarach. He just left me behind. Under lock and key near as damn it. Said it was to keep me safe, but it didn't feel like that. For a moment...' He breaks off, taking a deep breath. 'For a moment I convinced myself it was... that it was because he loved me. But it didn't *feel* like that. Not really. Not deep inside.'

He sighs, a hurricane of a sound, twisted by bitter regret. 'I always wanted him to. Always wished he did. Clung onto the idea he might deep down. So when he died, when my demon told me he was dead by your hand, that he could get revenge, I threw myself into the mission.'

'So what changed it?'

De Monteguard shakes his head, and his distress is clear. 'We were so close for so long. It was the first time I ever had a friend. Ever had someone who cared about me. Who understood me, who soothed my soul when I held the tears inside. But after Bugarach, it all became different. *He* became different. Driven. Motivated by other things, things he wouldn't share with me.'

The demon. I realise he's talking about the demon himself.

'Our shared truths became silences, and his requests became demands. Plus, the longer things have gone on, the more... *distant* he has become. We were partners before, bound together, but he's kept me more and more in the dark, cared less and less about what I think or feel. Just used me. A tether to this world. A thing. Not a friend. But part of that, part of him not really caring has meant things have got through. I felt what happened on that plane in Germany. He waved me off, saying there was no real danger, but there was. Especially if you, Paul, were the monster you'd been made out to be.

'You could have just killed them all, those possessed passengers, slaughtered your way to safety. Instead, you saved them all at great risk and cost to those you loved. Hardly the actions of a murderer. And those actions there? Risking innocent people? Using them like a tool? That isn't how the good guys act.' The pain on his face is awful to see, like that of a parent seeing their child's face plastered over the news for terrible wrongdoings, faced with what those they've loved unconditionally have become. 'I couldn't allow it. Couldn't just stand by while he did whatever awful thing he had planned next, with your friend Gil. I couldn't be an accomplice to his evil actions, be any more complicit than he has already made me.'

Suddenly, a tremor strikes. The walls rumble. Plasterboard dust clouds rain down on us. 'He's coming!' De Monteguard looks terrified but not surprised. He's been expecting this. 'He's nearly here. I've broken the terms. He'll seize control. When he broke into Toulouse, when he captured your other friend, he left me guarding him. When I felt his concentration gone from us, I raced here, knowing I'd have a little time but not much.

Hours maximum. But using his power, forming the sword to keep me alive, pulled his attention back my way. The moment I used the wings and took the risk to let you in, he knew my plan and headed straight here. He can travel to me almost as swift as thought. Our time's nearly up.'

'What do you mean?' Now the questions are pouring into my brain, and I'm trying to get them out, quick enough to get answers. 'How did he get past the wards to get Gil?'

'The wards were useless.' De Monteguard's speaking just as rapidly, trying to get the words out fast enough as the whole place trembles, the tremors building, the walls vibrating wildly. 'They were attuned to Isaac. Once he became infected with the demon energy...'

Shit. It becomes clear as day. 'The wards became attuned to demons too. He could just waltz in through them anytime.'

I'm furious with myself, enraged almost. That I didn't realise it. Didn't see the risk. Didn't spot this massive fucking flaw in our plans and then left Gil in the path of danger all over again. I want to go and slap myself upside the head repeatedly for such utter blind stupidity.

Right now, though, beating myself up isn't the priority, however tempting. I need to save the brave man in front of me, who's risked death at my hands to bring me back Gil. 'Phillip.' He's earned me calling him by his first name. 'You need to let this go now. I'll do what I can. Thank you for saving Gil from the demon again.'

De Monteguard frowns even as the place starts to waver, becoming translucent as it starts to disappear. 'What do you mean "again"?'

Ah. Perhaps the bastard kept that one from him. I'm not surprised. 'He grabbed him before. Possessed him over in Auch. Horrible shit. Like he was dead, with worms and grubs burrowing around inside him.'

The man goes chalk-white, the horror clear on his face. Poor bastard. What a thing to find out about what your soulmate has been up to. But whatever he was going to say is torn away from him as pain lances across his visage. He bends over, doubled up, his face contorted in agony. 'He's... heeeeeeere... Aaaaaahhhhhhhhhhhh....'

A terrible rumbling, like being inside the heart of a storm cloud, fills the air, a buzzing as everything falls apart, the plasterboard dust spraying in all directions.

And then the corridor is gone. And we are too.

CHAPTER TWENTY-EIGHT
THE PYRENEES, 30 OCTOBER, PRESENT DAY

There's always a price to pay.
And it seems that De Montfort's
son is still paying for the sins of
his shithead of a father.

My eyes snap open back on the hillside to see De Monteguard. For a brief moment, our gazes meet. Then he explodes backwards as though we are repelling magnets before bouncing sidewards as a black arrow dart smashes into him at several times the speed of sound.

Mephy lands a moment later, right where Phillip was. He turns, snarling, and aims to lunge again. I grab his shoulder, pulling him back. 'Wait, Mephy! Not the man, okay? Save him. He's on our side!'

Mephy shakes me off with a snarl. For a moment, I think I've gone too far, dared too much, laying hands on him like that, but he doesn't snap my hand off at the wrist. Instead, he growls, 'What the fuck are you talking about, mano?'

'He's on our side! He was bringing us Gil back. He's betrayed the demon!'

And by the Good God, he's paying the price for it.

De Monteguard looks like he's doing some form of interpretative dance, spinning around, rolling across the grass, leaping and pirouetting. But he's not. He's fighting with himself. Or rather, what he's been carrying inside himself.

Because the black demon essence is creeping across his body, like Venom grabbing hold of Spidey, taking him over. That's what it looks like, actually. An alien parasite covering up De Monteguard's body. It's horrible, genuinely horrific, too much to just stand by and watch.

So I don't. 'Come on!' I lunge forward, hurling myself at the man, unsure of what I can do but determined to do something, anything.

The "anything" I do is I break my nose on a crackling barrier of demonic energy surrounding De Monteguard and his once-demon.

'Mephy! Nith!' I'm screaming at them. 'Help me! Help *him*!'

Mephy bounds up, sniffing at the air. He lowers his nose and whines. 'We can't, mano. Not now. Not yet.'

'What do you mean, not yet?' I want to shake the Doberman, except even in this state of panic, I'm not that much of a lunatic. 'It's now we need to save De Monteguard!'

'We can't,' Mephy repeats. Isaac and Faust come tearing up. They must have closed the distance during the battle, though they followed my instruction and held back, looking for other forms of attack. Isaac inspects the working, then looks at me and shakes his head. He might not know what's going on yet, not properly, but he trusts me. He knows I want to get in there, to get involved. Apparently, Nithael can't help De Monteguard.

'Why not? Why can't you do something?' I'm close to tears now, thinking of that brave man, raised in such miserable hate, force-fed a constant stream of lies. He was bonded to a demon, not to help him, but to give De Montfort access to demonic power, no doubt to make sure he still had a body with *talent* at his disposal if things went wrong while he fucked with us. And now, apparently, we just have to stand by and watch him pay the price for saving Gil when we failed to keep him safe yet again. Innocents getting punished for the families they had the misfortune to be born into. 'You can't ask me to just stand by and watch!'

'There's no choice,' Mephy growls at me but softly, sadly. 'That's a deal he's made there, a compact he's broken. This is the result. Until it's done, we're stuck on the outside, watching from the sidelines. All we can do is cheer him on, hope he can win.'

His tone says how likely that is but also how little other choice we have. So I stand there with my friends, all of us safe and whole thanks to the actions of De Monteguard, and urge him on silently with all my strength to make it, to beat his demon in this tussle of wills. To keep control. To win. I hold on to that one thing that keeps us going in the face of life's miseries more than half the time.

Hope.

All that separates us from getting lost in the void, consumed by the savagery lurking just below the polished surface we present as a species.

Sadly, it's not enough to stop this though. To stop De Monteguard from being swallowed up by the demon essence, taken whole by compacts and an unstoppable consumption.

Then he, too, is lost.

The essence has solidified around him. Before, it looked like churning sludge, like some sort of industrial spillage given sentience, straight out of an eighties horror film. But now that it's covered him, having swallowed him whole, it changes. The material swells, bulging out into impressive musculature. The body is forced down onto all fours. Then the black goo hardens like concrete as it settles into the creature's preferred form.

Have you ever seen the original *Ghostbusters* film? The Terror Dogs from that scarred a whole generation of kids as much as the film thrilled them.

Hell, I'm an eight-hundred-year-old man, and those creatures gave me the shivers.

What stands in front of us now looks like one of those dogs but on steroids. It's like the offspring of a rhino and a bull mastiff, with two rows of teeth that'd have a shark feeling distinctly inadequate. I can't help noticing that the dark stone-like covering that's formed its hide is reminiscent of that weird marble-like material inside the Heart of Home. The creature has to be at least twice as long as me, and it looks like it could swallow me down in one bite. Oh, and it has wings.

Huge black feathered wings that stretch out at least four metres across, with sable, downy feathers as long as my forearm that ruffle in the mountain breeze as it spreads them wide. I'm not going to lie. They are impressive as all hell. No pun intended.

Crackling neon springs to life in the air around us, separating us from the creature as Nithael throws up a barrier.

Mephy goes nuts. He starts barking and yapping, bouncing round, snarling and woofing and running towards the barrier before breaking back, twirling furiously, still snapping and yowling.

'What? What is it, boy?' Faust rushes over to him, and I manage to resist asking if there's a child stuck in a well, Lassie, but only just.

'Lemme... lemme out.' Mephy's still snarling. 'Out, out, out!'

'Drop the barrier!' Johannes yells to Isaac, and a second later, the power separating us from the outside world is gone, and Mephy is through in an instant, his teeth snapping down...

On thin air. The demon wasn't just spreading his wings to show off. No. He's sailing upwards, wheeling back around like an eagle riding the thermals and then with two more downbeats, he's gone over the nearest crest, vanishing from sight.

'Damn it, no. No!' Mephy's furious, leaping and spinning in the air. 'Come back here! You blasted coward!' His furious growling is in vain. No one reappears.

The demon is gone, and Mephistopheles' snarls and howls are hurled out into an empty sky that holds no replies. The mountains swallow each echoing syllable up like hungry giants.

He's gone. Not just the demon, but the brave young man who came here. Not to ask for our help but simply to bring us our friend back. To do the right thing and save Gil. Who's paid the price for that courage, for acting correctly because he broke his deal with the demon.

It's so unfair. So fucking unfair. That someone, for once, tried to do us a good turn. Not because of what they'd get out of it. Not in some twisted Talented game where they'd extract a favour from us in exchange, no. Just because they realised they'd fucked up, ended up on the wrong side, caused us a hurt, and wanted to make it right. And the poor bastard's now been seized, hijacked by his supposed companion, his body stolen because of daring to do good. It's fucked up. It hurts, in my heart. Not least because yet again someone's paid the price for De Montfort's messed up scheming. Paid the price for helping me. And it isn't me footing the bill, when it should be. It always should have been. Somehow it never is.

But I can deal with my guilt and shame about that later. After we rescue De Monteguard. After I get back Aicha, even, after we put this shitshow right and get reality back on an even keel, or even just a not horribly odd keel for once. Right now there's a question I want the answer to, one De Monteguard couldn't give me, one Mephy clearly knows the answer to.

'Who was that?' It's no mystery that he obviously knows the fucker, based on his reaction.

Mephistopheles' whole-body fury has calmed to occasional jowl-shakes, sending sea-foam-like drool splashing out each time he does. 'Fucking Caacrinolaas.' The disgust in his voice is ladened.

The name rings a bell. I glance at Isaac, who's basically my own personal magical version of Google. However, it's Faust who answers.

'President of Hell,' he says. 'Big on bloodshed. Supposed to have some form of foresight. Very good at getting people to murder each other.'

'Bah!' Meph spits, which is a real weird gesture to watch a dog do. Not the kind of spluttering they normally do to clear their mouth, but a proper sour-lemon pucker up before hawking phlegm. 'He's a fucking idiot. Always itching for a fight. Too fucking stupid to know when he's beat.' His eyes narrow. 'Normally. Apparently, now he's fucking yellow as well. He's as bad as a *mano*.' He spits again, then trots to the nearby tree and cocks his leg. Presumably just to underline his utter disgust.

Being human – the worst insult a demon can think of, apparently. Guess they really hold us in high esteem.

I'm about to ask him for more details, to find out the backstory of why he hates Caacrinolaas so much when we hear the tinny earworm of a phone ringtone.

My heart goes hell for leather, over-speeding, revving up. The timing of this phone call feels distinctly ominous.

I pull my phone out of my pocket, but it is blank, lifeless.

'It's mine.' Isaac's voice sounds worried. 'Unknown number. Video call.'

We all gather closer together, staring at the screen, the numbers glowing, the red and green options highlighted – take the call or send them to Loserville by hitting reject, your choice. Isaac looks around at us for confirmation, for some assurance. But there's nothing else we can do for the moment but take it and be ready for the punches.

I look each of the others in the eye, noting similar states of alertness, of readiness in each of them and then give the nod.

Isaac presses the green accept button. The image flashes up, and my heart almost freezes. My hand lashes out, sending the phone skittering out of his, across the stones.

'Look away; close your eyes!' I scream at them desperately while I watch the phone roll, over and over, ready to press my own closed. To my relief, it finishes screen down, a few metres away.

I can only hope I wasn't too slow in acting. Wasn't too slow in telling them not to look.

Wasn't too slow to save my friends.

CHAPTER TWENTY-NINE
THE PYRENEES, 30 OCTOBER, PRESENT DAY

I'd like to tie his fucking trunk into a Karna-bow. After I strangle him to death with it.

The sound that comes from the phone is like someone gargling concrete through a trumpet and finding the whole thing infinitely amusing. Much as I'd love to do just that to him and see if he'd still be laughing afterwards, I couldn't give a fuck for the moment. There's a more pressing concern.

'Is everyone okay?' I'm reasonably confident that Isaac and Mephy will be fine anyhow, even Johannes with his magic and link to Meph. My main worry is Gil. To have rescued him twice only to lose him to a long-distance bushwhack would be frankly ridiculous. Glancing over, I see he looks fine. Well, as fine as he can be after getting kidnapped by a demon yet again, but relatively unharmed. Not petrified turned to stone, at least.

I make my way over and scoop up the phone, making sure the screen is facing downwards so no one can accidentally make eye contact with the still chuckling cock-faced pachyderp on the other end.

The Karnabo.

Now he speaks. 'Can I kill at distance through a camera? No. Would I kill you all if I could?' There's a pause, the answer like the cross between a goose honk and a snake hiss. 'Yessss.'

'Well, the feeling's mutual, dickwad.' Now that the initial panic is receding, anger is swirling in to replace it. 'What the fuck do you want?'

'Does he remember? No. Does he need to? Yes.'

'Remember what? It's been a long couple of days...' I say and then break off. Ah. That's what the fuck he wants. 'Are you talking about the time limit to give you Isaac? Well, I can tell you it's too late. He's not marked by your master's bullshit energy anymore. Plus, we just sent your boss running for the hills. Well, flying for the hills – neat wings, by the way – but you get the point.'

'Does that change anything? No. Is he arrogant enough to believe so? Yes.' The voice is full of contempt, of cocky disdain that makes me want to slap him so hard his trunk swings round through his ear and pierces his brain. Could I stab him with his own proboscis? I'd certainly give it a good go.

'Look, Nellie the Elephfuck, what do you actually want? Our time's not up, but we're not giving up Isaac. We're coming for you and Caacrinolaas both.'

'Does he think to bring war against us? Yes. Will he like the results when we stir up war among the humans, bring up all their anger and hate, all their petty grievances against one another for their differences, for their even more strong similarities that they despise in themselves, when the blood runs through all the land to wash away any and all before it?' A smug, pregnant pause. 'No.'

Isaac takes the phone from me and jabs furiously at the underneath of it before risking a peek to make sure he's turned off the video. The Karnabo might have said he can't strike us with his gaze at a distance, but none of us are foolish enough to take his word for it. Then he hits the mute button and looks at Mephy.

'Could he do that, the demon? The Karnabo's not powerful enough on his own to pull off something like that.'

Mephy draws back his jowls, his face grim. 'It's possible. Not easy, not to affect the whole world. But France? Maybe...' I can see him calculating in his head. 'Well, maybe a good section of Europe? If he really tried perhaps.'

Isaac looks straight at me. 'We can't allow that, lad. Not under any circumstance.'

Fuck. I know what that means. He's ready to sacrifice himself, push comes to shove. Guess we better find out when the shoving starts.

I wave at him to take the phone off mute. 'We've still got time, Karna-dumbo.' Just because we have to negotiate with him doesn't mean I have to be nice with him. Aicha would never forgive me for missing that opportunity. 'Our three days isn't up. We've got two more nights, plus a whole day left.'

'Does he think to stall? Yes. Will it work? No. When the time allotted is up, will he bring us the angel-bearer and the sword? Yes. And will their trickery allow them to escape, to concoct some cunning plan to save the day? No. Oh no.'

We'll see about that, you cock-faced wank-bugle. 'So where do we meet then when the time is up?'

'Will he be happy with the location? No. But does it belong to us now? Yes.'

And just like that, dread comes back to roost, setting up residency in my central nervous system like it had never left, like this is its forever home.

'Enough of the riddles.' Isaac speaks for me. I reckon he can see my mouth's seizing up along with my brain, the fear grabbing hold. 'Where are we to meet?'

'Will they come to the Capitole building with Joyeuse wrapped up neatly for us, or else the humans will all fall and die in their own hate? Yes. Will they leave again?' The bubbling gargle-trumpet laugh breaks out again, and by the Good God, I'll choke that sound out of him, wrapping his trunk around his throat when I get my hands on the fucknugget. 'No.'

The line goes dead, and we look at each other, ashen-faced.

We might have won a battle. Healed Isaac. Gained Joyeuse. Saved Gil. Discovered Caacrinolaas.

But that's all it was. A battle.

Because apparently, while the demons were attuned to Toulouse's wards, they did more than just breach them.

They've taken over Toulouse.

EPILOGUE - THE PYRENEES, 30 OCTOBER, PRESENT DAY

I look around at my gathered companions. Isaac – worn down from months of battling the demon essence trying to possess him, with even Nithael out of energy now, running on empty; Faust – far from home, from his centre of power and his own duties and cares, only here because of me; Mephy – furious, full of anger, hungry for blood; and Gil – beaten, more than half broken but still standing, still watching me with eyes that seem to urge me on, to say he believes in me.

The Good God knows why.

I look around at them and wish there was a sixth in our group of five. If *she* was here, I'd favour our chances so much more. She'd saunter up to The Karnabo and feed him his own magically murderous eyeballs. Up his arse. But she isn't, and I can't get back to searching for her till we save the world once again. So I take a deep breath and hold it for a moment, feeling my pulse beating down my body, letting me know I'm here, that I'm alive. And while there's life, there's hope.

Then I scan around at their faces again and see the same resolute determinedness that I hope is also on mine, that I force myself to feel in my soul.

'They took my city.' Those words bring the fire burning back, the anger that speaks in words of flame, igniting my soul, so I say them again. '*They took my city!*'

My companions stand by, readied, willing, and even without Aicha with us, those fuckers don't know what's coming. Don't know the storm they've unleashed, the fucking maelstrom that's about to rain down on their heads for messing with us.

'They took my city.' My lip curls, a half-grin, half-snarl. Anger still, sure. But also resolute certainty. In myself. In those by my side. In the steady thrum in my veins that sings of the vengeance I'll bring on those who've dared to besmirch that which I hold dear. I look around, catch each of their eyes as I stride over to pick up Joyeuse. Then I nod to them all, a nod that contains a promise. A promise of what we're about to bring to bear upon those who would do us wrong.

'They took my city,' I say again, and it's like Joyeuse harmonises with me, a crystal ring emanating back from its silvered edge that speaks of the blade's readiness to fight, to kill, to bathe in the blood of all our foes, however mighty they might be.

'They took my city. Let's take them to war.'

AUTHOR'S NOTES

S o, the penultimate chapter of the imPerfect Cathar series. Paul's back in a position of strength. He's got his team back – Isaac's well, Gil rescued, Joyeuse in hand. But what a price to pay. De Monteguard taken and Toulouse has fallen. Surely the stakes couldn't be higher, unless the whole world was at risk! Oh, wait. Hang on a second...

As always, I've done my best to incorporate real locations and real history and mythology into these stories. The "real" Joyeuse (although the jentilaks might have something to say about that) can be seen at the Louvre and is supposed to be the original sword of Charlemagne. The jentilaks themselves are a genuine part of Basque legend, where the stories say that they did indeed teach mankind all sorts of things like farming and metallurgy. Improving our lot... until we drove them off into hiding. The similarities between them and the and Yeti stories is a fascinating coincidence, don't you think?

The dolmens of the Pyrenees are true as well. They're scattered through-out the mountains. Sadly, I don't know how to open them to go visiting Home. Sounds like just the kind of peace and quiet I could do with to get some writing done.

My thanks as ever go to my editor Miranda Grant who beat me elec-tronically until I did what was necessary to get this book into the readable state it is now. My critique partner Becca Wood and my other beta reader

Becky Puff for their invaluable work. The imPs for their endless support (although the Arts & Crafts department remain banned of course) and Mel-Mel, Rachel and Jimmy for their helping to manage the organised chaos. All my ARC readers for their wonderful feedback, and the new audio proofreading team – Mel-Mel, Mardie & Darin – for their amazing contributions. Perri for her translation work, Jess for the French editing and JL Henry for the French beta-reading and proofing. My family and friends each and every time for their love, patience and support. The Semper Eadem squad. Craig Verbs, always. Everyone I should have mentioned – and probably should have since book one – but who, if they know me, will know I am a Bear of Little Brain and even Lesser Memory, but that doesn't diminish the love I hold for them in my heart.

We're so close to the end of Paul's adventures, and everything rides on a knife's edge. If you want to find out how it all finishes – for good or ill – then join me for imPerfect Demons. Book 9. The final part of the imPerfect Cathar series...

REMEMBER

Do please consider leaving a review, or clicking a star rating on Amazon. If you can click follow too, that'd be fantabulous. It keeps the terrible hungry demon Sozeb from clawing chunks from my very soul.

Just remember. Never say his name backwards. Especially when you're still in your Prime.

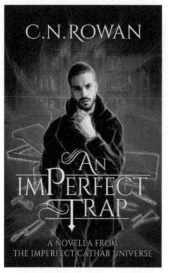

Reincarnating every time I get killed doesn't help when the trap won't let me die.

Getting trapped in a psychotic fae's twisted game isn't my idea of a fun Friday afternoon. When one of them shows up in my territory of Toulouse uninvited, I was never going to just let it slide.

Now I'm stuck, in a locked room mystery in another dimension.

What does the faeling want? And what price am I going to pay to find my way home again? There's never a pair of red, ruby slippers around when you need them.

GO HERE TO GET THE FREE PREQUEL TODAY BY SIGNING UP TO MY NEWSLETTER!

https://freebook.cnrowan.com/imtrap

ABOUT THE AUTHOR

It's been a strange, unbelievable journey to arrive at the point where these books are going to be released into the wild, like rare, near-extinct animals being returned to their natural habitat, already wondering where they're going to nick cigarettes from on the plains of Africa, the way they used to from the zookeeper's overalls. C.N. Rowan ("Call me C.N., Mr. Rowan was my father") came originally from Leicester, England. Somehow escaping its terrible, terrible clutches (only joking, he's a proud Midlander really), he has wound up living in the South-West of France for his sins. Only, not for his sins. Otherwise, he'd have ended up living somewhere really dreadful. Like Leicester. (Again – joking, he really does love Leicester. He knows Leicester can take a joke. Unlike some of those other cities. Looking at you, Slough.) With multiple weird strings to his bow, all of which are made of tooth-floss and liable to snap if you tried to use them to do anything as adventurous as shooting an arrow, he's done all sorts of odd things, from running a hiphop record label (including featuring himself as rapper) to hustling disability living aids on the mean streets of Syston. He's particularly proud of the work he's done managing and recording several French hiphop acts, and is currently awaiting confirmation of wild rumours he might get a Gold Disc for a song he recorded and mixed.

He'd always love to hear from you so please drop him an email here - chris@cnrowan.com

f facebook.com/cnrowan

a amazon.com/author/cnrowan

g goodreads.com/author/show/23093361.C_N_Rowan

⊙ instagram.com/cnrowanauthor

ALSO BY C.N. ROWAN

The imPerfect Cathar Series

imPerfect Magic

imPerfect Curse

imPerfect Fae

imPerfect Bones

imPerfect Hunt

imPerfect Gods

imPerfect Blood

imPerfect Blades

imPerfect Demons (Release date – 1st July 24)

Standalone Adventures

An imPerfect Trap (prequel novella to imPerfect Magic)

An imPerfect Samhain

An imPerfect Fable

Omnibuses

imPerfect Beginnings

imPerfect Villains

Milton Keynes UK
Ingram Content Group UK Ltd.
UKHW012254110624
443988UK00006B/424